The Time Walkers

Behroz Behnejad

Copyright © 2023 Behroz Behnejad

All rights reserved.

The right of Behroz Behnejad to be identified as the Author of this Work has been asserted by them.

No part of this publication may be reproduced, stored in a retrieval system, or transmitted in any form or by any means without the prior written permission of the publisher, nor be otherwise circulated in any form of binding or cover other than that in which it is published and without a similar condition being imposed on the subsequent purchaser. Names, characters, places, and incidents are either a product of the author's imagination or are used fictitiously. Any resemblance to people living or dead, events or locales is entirely coincidental.

For my children!

Acknowledgements

My writing life would not be possible without the support of many people, whom I'd like to acknowledge and thank.

First, I'd like to thank my children for their unwavering belief in me: "Dad, we all love your stories; everyone will want to read your book. You always told us such great bedtime stories!"

I thank my extended family in many different countries, and scattered friends for their heartfelt support, advice, perspectives, and friendship.

Thank you from the bottom of my heart.

Prologue

The old Victorian sits high up on a hill behind a locked gate. The faded grandeur of the place has a certain allure, even though the paint is peeling, and ivy creeps up its walls. As the couple step inside what could be their forever home, the atmosphere seems to transport them to another time.

As their footsteps echo through the entryway, the pair notice a photograph in a gilded frame sitting on an old wooden table beneath a chandelier covered in dust. The black-and-white photo is faded from age, but clearly shows a woman in a plain-looking dress, seated in a chair. A black dog sits by her side, following her gaze as she seems to peer directly into the camera in front of her, as if she is looking through the very fabric of space and time itself. A hand-scrawled caption beneath the photograph reads: *April 1940, Alice Walker*.

"Who is she?" The man stops, arrested by the photograph.

"Oh – you've met Alice," the realtor replies. "She was the daughter who vanished. Engaged at the time. Authorities found no explanation for it when she and her dog disappeared without a trace. I think the family just decided she was a runaway. They keep a room for her here, just up that stairway. Probably why the house has been marked down so much, in all honesty!"

The man pauses, his fingers playing at the edge of the photograph's frame as if he could reach back through it.

"Vanished," the woman beside him murmurs.

"Come now – on to the rest of the house!" The realtor says, breaking the man from his reverie.

Together, the trio venture deeper into the house, aware that they've stumbled upon a place where the past and present intertwine in mysterious ways.

April 1939

In her dimly lit bedroom, Alice sits by the window, the quiet of the late afternoon enveloping her in deep reflection. She gazes out at the street, where the world is on the brink of change, but in her heart, it's the past that occupies her thoughts.

Her engagement ring, a simple yet elegant band, glistens in the soft afternoon light streaming through the curtains. She takes a deep breath, feeling the weight of the decision she made not long ago. Her engagement to Jay Murphy was a joyous occasion, and the memory of his earnest proposal fills her with warmth.

Alice's fingers trace the contours of the ring, recalling the way Jay's eyes had sparkled with excitement as he slipped it onto her finger. Their dreams had intertwined that day, two souls committing to a future together, even as the world outside seemed uncertain and on the brink of war.

As she sits there in the solitude of her bedroom, Alice can't help but wonder about the challenges that lie ahead. Impending war looms in the distance, casting a shadow over their plans. She ponders the sacrifices they may have to make, the separations, and the uncertainty of it all. Yet, in this quiet moment, she's also filled with hope and determination, ready to face whatever the future may bring alongside the man she loves.

Alice's reverie is interrupted by a sudden, mysterious sound. It's a soft, eerie creak, like the whisper of secrets long kept hidden. Her heart quickens as she turns her attention away from the ring and toward the source of the disturbance.

The otherworldly creak sounds again, and this time she realizes it is emanating from her closet.

With trepidation, Alice stands and approaches the closet door. She reaches for the knob, her hand trembling slightly, the polished wood cool to the touch. The room around her feels as though it's holding its breath, as if even the walls are waiting in anticipation.

As she slowly swings the closet door wide, a strange sensation washes over her. The room seems to ripple, the colors around her shifting and distorting.

The closet door, once ajar, swings wide open on its own accord, revealing a dazzling, light emanating from within. Alice's heart races as she takes an involuntary step backward, the dairy she had clutched in her hands slipping from her fingers and floating weightlessly in the air. She watches in astonishment as the diary disappears into the brilliance.

Before she can fully comprehend what was happening, Alice feels a strange pull, as though an invisible force is drawing her toward the now-illuminated closet. Panic surges through her, and she tries to resist, but it was futile. Her vision blurs, and the room around her dissolves into a whirl of light and shadow.

As the world around her continued to shift and blur, Alice's voice catches in her throat, her cries for help going unheard. She is now a mere echo of her former self, lost in the currents of time, disappearing into that swift current.

And even as the world tilts around her, even as the light becomes too brilliant and blinding, even as her body fades, Alice smiles.

CHAPTER 1

Seventy years later, the tenth of June 2009, a Wednesday, was an unusually dry summer day. The ground beneath David's feet was parched, and the air around him was eerily still. David Hamilton wasn't happy that he had to leave his publisher's office and didn't have any new material to give to his agent.

After cutting his conversation short with his agent, David rushed into a nearby shop in the distance, desperate to escape the oppressive heat. Beads of sweat shone on his forehead, making the slow journey into his eyes. His throat dried, and he politely asked the shopkeeper if he could use the phone. His cellphone was out of battery. He wiped the salty droplets from his forehead with the sleeve of his already-soaked shirt.

The shop assistant passed him the phone and David took it, aware that two dark sweat stains marked his underarms.

He quickly dialed his girlfriend.

"Where are you?" she chirped on the other end. "You're half an hour late! I've been calling your phone."

"I'm sorry. My meeting with the publisher ran long because we were discussing the possible topics for my next book. But I'm on my way now. Tell Harry I'm sorry. I'll see you soon!"

He returned the phone with a quick thanks and cast a look around the shop, making a beeline for a refrigerator. Without a glance at the contents, he grabbed a can, pressing the cool metal to his forehead with a sigh of relief.

"I don't think it's ever been this hot before – it's almost forty-five degrees," he remarked, setting the can on the counter. He mopped his brow with a napkin from the counter, adding, "But it's nice and cool here in the shop. Almost makes me want to stay!"

The shop assistant gave him a curious look, tilting her head slightly, her voice rising excitedly, "I recognize you. You're David Hamilton. Oh, my God, I love your books! I'm reading *Dancing with Death* right now. I love the way you have built the old man's character, dealing with untreatable medical condition and dealing with the idea that he will be passing soon."

"Do you have your copy here?" David said, feeling somewhat flattered.

"Hold on," she dashed into a room behind the shop. "Here it is! Here you go!" She extended the book, and David opened it to sign on the first page.

She beamed at him.

David's eyes flicked to a wall clock, and he cut off the

conversation abruptly. "Oh, I have to go now, or I'll be in trouble." He strode toward the exit, turning to wave goodbye on his way out.

Outside, David hailed a taxi and climbed in. Despite the blasting air conditioning, David was still visibly sweaty, glued to his seat by the oppressive heat. The radio was on, broadcasting the weather: "Yesterday was the warmest day of the summer so far, but today we've beaten the heat record with a temperature of forty-eight degrees..."

The driver turned off the radio with a sigh and said, "I can't believe this. Poor people! But good about the rain, both here and in that place."

David nodded in agreement.

Five minutes later, he arrived at his destination, swiftly paid the fare, and exited the taxi. He sprinted across the street and into the building directly opposite. He considered taking the elevator but dismissed the idea.

"It will take longer," he muttered, opting for the stairs to the second floor instead. Out of breath and stressed, he opened the door and rushed in.

His girlfriend Lisa was in Harry's office, waiting impatiently, her hands clasped. David closed the door and began to apologize, "Sorry, I'm late. Can I catch my breath a bit before we go? And I wouldn't mind something cold to drink, if possible."

Lisa, was still annoyed that he was late.

"Of course!" Harry replied, quickly turning to fetch David a soda.

David positioned himself before the air conditioner, basking in its coolness as he complained about the relentless heat.

"I swear, it's never been this hot," he said, gazing out the window. Outside, three pigeons squabbled over a bush, each vying for the sparse shade the puny, scraggly plant provided.

Harry handed David a fridge-cold soda, and David drained the entire can in one long gulp. He took a deep breath and said, "Okay, I'm ready to go now!"

Harry gestured towards the door.

"On the way there, I have to fill you in on the details about the mansion and explain a few important things," Harry said, darting into another room to grab his bag and car keys.

Inside in his mind, David was kicking himself for nearly missing this meeting. Yes, his publisher was important, but a new house after months of searching was even more important than a book, he didn't have the faintest first idea for.

Harry's car was parked outside on the street, baking under the harsh sun with the windows barely cracked open. Despite the intense heat inside the vehicle, they climbed in.

As they left the city behind and escaped the thick traffic, Harry discussed the mansion. "The house was built in 1913 and renovated in 1923, 1957, and 1978. The property spans over four acers, and it's just a five-minute walk down to the water. The building rights are generous, providing opportunities for additional constructions or expansion of the existing house. There is a history with this house."

"That does sound promising.

"Are there any neighbors nearby?" Lisa asked.

"Yes, the nearest neighbor is only a five-minute walk away, but there are only twenty-five families living in this area," Harry replied.

"The pictures I saw of the mansion and the grounds were very enticing, straight out of a brochure. I hope reality lives up to them," David said.

"I promise you, it will. I've known you for many years. Both you and Lisa will love this house," Harry reassured them confidently.

Twenty minutes later, they arrived at the estate. Harry hopped out of the car to open the gate.

Harry struggled with the gate. The lock was old and rusty, which seemed to be causing him a good deal of frustration. After much effort and a few more beads of sweat, Harry managed to get it open.

As they resumed their drive towards the mansion, David asked, "Has the house been uninhabited for long?"

"No. The family moved to the city, to a smaller house, as they couldn't manage the upkeep of the house and the land," Harry replied matter-of-factly.

David noticed the road to the house was lined with grass, dried and browned under the relentless sun. The trees looked weary, their leaves fluttering gently like parched pieces of paper. Everything seemed lifeless. A weak gust picked up some of the brown and yellow leaves, causing them to twirl on the dirt road. They arrived at the house after a few minutes of silent observation through the car windows.

"Ah, here we are," Harry announced, prompting everyone to leave the car.

"The house looks good. And the view – so wonderful," there were so many different colors flowers planted all over around the house in a harmonious way. Lisa observed, looking out over the area, her arms swaying gracefully as she turned.

"Yes, indeed," David echoed, nodding in agreement before turning his gaze back to the house. He followed Harry up the stairs but paused halfway to look at the yard. A trampoline stood a little off, cloaked in dust and decaying leaves.

Ahead, Harry reached the door and began rummaging through several keys.

"Apologies, there are so many locked doors in this house, and I can't remember which key fits this one, so I have to try them all," he grumbled, sweat trickling down his forehead to stain his shirt. Then, suddenly, there was a click, and the door opened.

A musty, stale scent greeted them as they stepped inside, causing David to question how long the house had sat empty. Leaving the door open, Harry hurried to open a window to let in some fresh air. The house was filled with old furniture, each piece seemingly carrying the same old-world fragrance.

"They wanted to preserve the original style of the house," Harry commented, a hint of formality in his tone as if he were hosting a tour of some famous historical location.

In the guest room, David spotted three stuffed animals that appeared alarmingly lifelike, as though they were standing guard over anyone who entered. An antique clock on the wall drew David's attention, and on pulling the cord, it started ticking loudly as its pendulum swung back and forth.

Upon entering the bathroom, the smell of fresh paint hit them. Harry explained, "Due to mold and a water leak, this was renovated, and they've finished it recently. So, that's taken care of."

Back in the living room, a staircase led down to a room boasting large windows with a beautiful lake view.

"From here, you two could watch the sunrise every morning! Look at that view! The sun rises right over there," Harry said enthusiastically, pointing. "This room is used as a guest room, and every morning, the guests wake up to a beautiful dawn. It's like a host's gift to them. When I saw this house by myself, I didn't notice a lot of details about the rooms and the views from windows."

To the left of the window, David noticed a bookcase with a small desk beside it. He moved closer, his curiosity piqued as he scanned the titles. David read the titles loud, "Mystery of the Green Cat, the Catcher in the Rye, and Fellowship of the ring. There are so many books here." He passed the books, then said, "This could be my study," he mused excitedly before falling silent when he noticed a door hidden behind the shelf. He inspected it for a moment, then turned to Harry. "What's this door here?"

"Ah, yes. That has remained locked for seventy years. Whatever lies behind that door is to be left undisturbed. Lisa asked, "How do you know this?" I was planning to explain this to you," Harry began, sinking into an armchair before continuing his story. "When I got the listing for this house, the owner gave me some information. Back in 1930s, a family lived in this mansion, and this room belonged to their daughter. One day, she vanished without a trace. The family chose to leave her room untouched, clinging to the hope that she might one day return." Harry let out a sigh, appearing more troubled than before. "The police were unable to find her and eventually abandoned the search. Yet, the family held on to the hope that she might come home someday."

David watched as Lisa reacted with a sigh of her own, echoing the heavy sadness. "What a tragic story."

"Despite their unyielding hope, the girl never returned, and the family eventually conceded to despair. After three years, they sold the house. However, before the sale, they established a contract with the new owners. It stated that no one was allowed to enter her room, believing that if their daughter had passed, her spirit could find peace in her own space. Over the years, all the successive residents have respected this stipulation," Harry explained, his confidence evident as he laid out this peculiar term of the house sale."

David nodded slowly; his gaze fixed on the mysterious door. "It's an intriguing story. We will certainly respect that condition if we decide to purchase the house."

Lisa sounded slightly worried as she said, "It's certainly fascinating, but it's also a bit eerie."

Harry shrugged at Lisa's remark, "People adjust. That's what the previous residents said. It doesn't weigh on your mind every day."

Lisa sighed again, "I certainly hope not."

The tour continued through the house, leading them up the stairs and towards the second bedroom. David's attention was drawn to a black-and-white photo in the hallway. It portrayed a woman in a dress seated in a chair with a black dog by her side. Beneath the picture was a caption, "April 1939, Alice Walker."

David stopped. "Who is she?"

"That's Alice, the daughter who vanished. She was engaged at the time, but tragically, her fiancé was found dead on the other side of the lake. He drowned, according to the police. Alice was said to be devastated. Her world crumbled, and soon after, she and her dog disappeared. The authorities couldn't find any explanation aside from the theory that she had run away. They ruled out foul play," Harry revealed. "Most said she just couldn't accept his death." He shook his head.

"Why is her photograph still here? Did the recent residents know her?"

"No, they didn't know her. They found the photo in the basement, and the wife was drawn to it enough to hang it up here."

Intrigued, David asked, "How did you come by all this information about the girl?"

"When I inspected the house, I saw the picture too and had the same questions as you," Harry said. The owner had previously told him about the untouched room and showed him the contract that every owner had signed. Harry reiterated that it was an inviolable agreement: any new proprietor must sign and respect it.

David walking around the room excited, intrigue, and somewhat melancholy, pacing towards the window and back again.

reaction was a mix of emotions: intrigue, excitement, and melancholy. The house was shrouded in mystery, and knowing its backstory only amplified its charm. Yet, the girl's fate remained unknown, further piquing David's curiosity. He wondered if there was anyone who knew more about her story.

Harry had no idea where David could obtain more information, except perhaps from the current sellers. This potential meeting, of course, depended on whether they bought the house. Shifting the conversation back to the matter, Harry probed the couple for their feelings about the place, attempting to discern their interest through their reactions and exchanges.

David then walked around the property, his phone clicking as he captured the house's distinctive features. He found himself drawn back to Alice's photo. David said to himself, "I wonder there are more to this picture, what if I dig in, it could be my next book." He stood there, pondering over the portrait of the lost daughter who once inhabited the forbidden room. His curiosity was piqued, and he finally moved outside to join Harry and Lisa in the unbearable heat.

Harry showed them the additional buildings on the estate, pointing out the dock by the lake that could accommodate two boats. There stood an old chestnut tree near the dock. Upon closer inspection, David discovered a heart carved into the tree with "Alice+James" inscribed within.

Lisa asked David "Is it possible that this girl form the photo be Alice, then who is James?" David after a few long seconds said, "James might have been her fiancé." David found himself increasingly absorbed in Alice's story. He saw the potential for a book in the mystery surrounding Alice's disappearance.

After revisiting their interest in the house, David and Lisa agreed to contact Harry the following morning. Lisa besides that she liked the house, in her mind, she kept asking herself "why can't we go to that room." They seemed satisfied with their visit, at least from what David could perceive.

The ride back to the city allowed David to review the photos he had taken. He shared his intent to unravel Alice's mystery with Lisa, explaining how her story had gripped him. Although Lisa expressed discomfort with the untouched room, she said "as long as there isn't skeleton in that room." Agreed to support David.

Back home, David initiated another discussion about the house over dinner. Despite her apprehension about the locked room, Lisa agreed with David's view of using it as a study. As they decided to express their interest in the house to Harry, David felt a sense of partnership in their decision. Lisa said, "I am excited that we will start our family in this new house." And with a tender kiss, they sealed their decision.

Chapter 2

The following day, David called Harry to tell him that he and Lisa had decided to take the house.

Harry's relief was palpable even through the phone, "That's great news! Shall we set a date for signing the contracts then? Have you sorted everything out with the bank?"

"Yes, and yes. Could we perhaps arrange a meeting with the current owners as well?" David asked, eager to push forward this new chapter of their lives.

"I can get onto that straight away. I'll get back to you soon."

"Hold on, we don't even know their names," David interjected, his brows knitting together in realization.

"Philip and Caroline," Harry supplied without missing a beat. "We'll talk later."

David hung up the phone as Lisa wrapped her arms around him from behind. She pressed her cheek to his back, her warmth seeping into him.

"What's on your mind, love?" she asked, her breath fanning

against his skin.

David found his thoughts wandering back to André, the police officer he'd met. "I was considering paying André a visit." Lisa asked, "Who?" David replied, "you know my high school friend who is a police officer."

"What for?" she asked, kissing softly against his neck.

"There might be some information about Alice at the police station. Her case might still be open," he said.

"But you might not be allowed to see those documents, you know," she pointed out, caution lacing her words.

David shrugged. "The case is seventy years old. I doubt they'd mind. Fancy coming along?"

Soon they found themselves at the police station. André was buried in paperwork, his office was a mess, his face brightened at their arrival. When an overeager police dog in training appeared, Lisa was more than happy to play and keep it distracted. As David listened to Lisa's infectious laughter fill the room, he couldn't help but feel a surge of warmth. His decision to dig into Alice's past was already leading them down unexpected paths, and he was eager to see where it would take them next.

André called to Johan, "Johan! Collect your dog." Johan dashed in, breathless and apologetic, scooping up the eager puppy. His words, though playful, carried a note of sternness. David watched the scene, amused, and somewhat relieved as the puppy's energy was redirected.

With a chuckle, André assured them the puppy was a beloved, albeit mischievous, member of the station. His escapades were usually tolerated with fond smiles. Gesturing them to sit, André settled back into his chair, casting an inquisitive gaze at the pair. "It has been so long that we have seen or talked to each other, love to catch up and refresh our mind about our high school events. What brings you here?"

David took a moment to collect his thoughts before sharing his peculiar interest, "Sorry that I was missing all these years, I was trying to publish my books and time flew so fast, yes we need to see each other more often. Let me tell you what we're here, it might seem a bit strange, but we're interested in a case that dates back seventy years."

André blinked at him, clearly taken aback. "Seventy years?"

David nodded, his gaze steady, "Yes. I'm assuming the station archives old cases, solved and unsolved?"

André hesitated, his brows knitting in thought, before confirming, "I can't give you the documents that we have, but can you tell me more about this case?"

David said, "The real estate agent has provided what little information he had - the year, the name of the woman who had vanished, the mysterious circumstances surrounding her disappearance, and her fiancé's death. André noted down the details, promising to look into it and get back to them.

As they said their goodbyes, André's curiosity got the better of him, "Are you planning to write a book about it?"

David gave a non-committal shrug, a smirk tugging at his lips. "Who knows? If it's interesting enough, I might."

They thanked André for his help. As they passed through the station, they caught sight of the frantic scene unfolding. Paramedics and officers attempted to subdue the woman from earlier. Lisa looked with intensity to see what is happening to the woman, her nursing training kicked in to observe the situation. She saw that others were helping the woman. So, A harrowing sight unsettled them, and they were relieved to escape the chaos.

Once they were back in their car, David revealed his next step - visiting the local library. He explained his theory about the possibility of finding newspaper articles from 1939 that might provide more information about Alice and her fiancé.

Lisa seemed puzzled, but said, "Let's go home." but David's conviction was infectious. He was drawn to the mystery, a story that was begging to be unearthed and shared. The possibility that they might uncover evidence of a crime, a scandal hidden in the past, was too compelling to resist.

"Just imagine it," he said, his eyes bright with anticipation, "This could be an incredible story. A bestselling book, even."

His gaze was challenging, daring her to deny the allure of their quest. Lisa could only stare back, the wheels in her mind beginning to turn.

"But how do we solve a seventy-year-old mystery that even the police couldn't crack?"

"Once we've acquired the house, we'll have access to the keys. There could be something in her room, a diary perhaps, something that might offer a clue. There has to be something in there that can shed light on her disappearance."

Lisa was taken aback. "You're suggesting we break the contract and go into the room?" She stared at David, her breathing quickening.

"To uncover the truth, rules may need bending," David admitted, adding reassuringly, "no one would know we were there." He produced his phone, showing her the photo of Alice once more. "I feel like she's trying to tell us something. Just look at her eyes. I see sadness, a hidden mystery. Something happened to her, and I intend to find out what. Will you accompany me to the library?"

Lisa, however, was not on board. "No, David!" she snapped. "I'm feeling overheated and exhausted. I need a cold shower."

David, taken aback, asked, "Are you upset with me?" Lisa looked at him for a moment, then flashed a cautious smile.

"Perhaps this is strange, but I don't like you speaking about other women like that."

David was surprised, then broke into hearty laughter. "Sweetheart! She doesn't exist anymore. She passed away seventy years ago. There's no reason for jealousy."

Lisa joined in the laughter, blaming her outburst on the sweltering heat. They dropped the topic, and David drove her home.

En route to the library, they parked outside their current house to drop Lisa off, and Lisa turned to David. "Once we've bought the house, I'll help you with the research," she offered, pecking him on the cheek.

David held her hand, looking deeply into her eyes. "Lisa, this means everything to me. A dark shadow has loomed over their lives for seventy years, and now I intend to bring their story to light. There's something mysterious about Alice and her fiancé's lives. She couldn't have just disappeared. I'm going to find her, and I'll bring her back to life through my writing. It's the right thing to do. I need to prove that her fiancé was murdered, we can find out about Alice also. No one disappears suddenly. I promise."

She nodded, surprised by his intensity but supportive. "Take it easy, darling. I understand, and I'm with you. I'll help as much as I can." After a final goodbye kiss, she stepped out of the car, leaving David alone with his determination.

Inside the library, the cool and quiet atmosphere was a welcome respite for David. Everyone around him was immersed in their own worlds. He took a moment to survey his surroundings. In one corner, a woman was breastfeeding her child while reading a book. A little distance from the shelves, four teenage boys sat, engrossed in their reading, occasionally casting sidelong glances at some nearby girls. He went straight to the librarian.

The woman behind the desk looked up, matching David's

friendly smile. "Hello, how may I assist you?"

"Yes, I was wondering if you might have archived newspapers, specifically from around 1939," David explained, flashing her an smile.

"Actually, we do. They're kept in a special room, but you'll need to make an appointment first," she told him.

A look of concern crossed David's face. "I'm pressed for time, unfortunately. I don't really have the luxury of waiting..."

She studied him briefly, then smiled again, nodding at him. "I can make an exception this time." She slid a black book towards him. "You'll need to write your name here and present an ID."

David obliged, signing his name in the book and pulling out his ID. Upon seeing his name, the librarian's eyes widened in recognition.

"Yes, that would be me," he said,

She gave a thrilled gasp. "I knew it! Let me walk you to the archive room.

The archive was an impressively large room filled with tall shelves and cabinets, so much information in there. The librarian gave him a brief rundown of how the materials were organized, then left him to his work, offering her assistance if needed.

Left alone, David approached the shelves hesitantly. His heart pounded in his chest. This reminded him of his school days when he'd been too shy to ask librarians for help and instead chose to search for the needed books.

Taking a deep breath, David began his search through the microfilms, searching for any mention of Alice and her fiancé. He found a few relevant articles which seemed to confirm Harry's story. Some headlines said, "What Happened at the Mansion." Another said, "The Girl Who Went Missing." But the question remained: What had happened to her and her fiancé then?

David found an article about a body on a cliff. The title of the article was, "A Man Found Dead!" The details were vague, but something about it caught his attention. Could this be Alice's fiancé?

He printed out bunch of articles and returned the microfilms. He ran into the librarian in the corridor.

"Thank you. I found what I was looking for. I appreciate your help," David replied, expressing his gratitude for her assistance.

The librarian smiled in return. "I'm glad I could help. Let me give you a box to carry all you have printed in a box you have a lot of paper in your hand."

David exited the library with a grateful nod, leaving the cool quiet behind him. His mind was a whirl of thoughts and questions, but he felt that he has a puzzle to solve unraveling the mystery of Alice.

But still, a mounting frustration had settled deep in David's chest, a gnawing sensation that ached for more tangible facts about the tragedy. It was as though he was being needled by a firm conviction that both individuals had been victims of an unknown crime. David told to himself, "Why a successful person would kill himself?"

"I can't do anything more at the moment," he muttered. "Hopefully, the police can shed lighter, or I'll have to wait until I have the keys to that house - to Alice's room."

David's train of thought abruptly halted. A spectacle in the trees ahead snagged his attention, a sight few people were privileged to witness. Perched in the branches was a bird that bore a falcon's hallmarks. With a sharp cry, it launched skyward, its wings beating an almost audible rhythm against the backdrop of the silent landscape.

Initially, David speculated it was a peculiar mating ritual, but the presence of a prowling cat ascending the same tree suggested a more defensive motive. The falcon temporarily receded, luring the feline into a false sense of security before it descended in a swift, ruthless swoop. Its talons found purchase in the intruder, and with a jarring thud, the cat was dislodged from the tree. Landing on its feet - as cats are wont to do - it darted away, nursing its bleeding wounds and injured pride in the safety of the nearby bushes.

Captivated by the brief conflict, David fumbled for his phone, intent on capturing the unusual scene. Yet, the pace of the encounter defied his efforts, the entire incident concluding before his camera app even opened.

"Damn, what a pity! No one will believe this," he grumbled, his excitement replaced by a fleeting irritation. He started his car and pulled away from the curb.

His eyes flickered back to the printed articles scattered on the passenger seat.

"The cliff facing the beach," the article read.

A thought sparked in David's mind. "Perhaps I can locate this cliff, survey the surroundings, and construct a clearer image of what transpired." But the question remained - where was this cliff?

"Maybe André at the station can help," he mused, speaking to himself. "There must be information about the location."

His thoughts tumbled over one another when the shrill ring of his cell phone sliced through the quiet hum of the car's engine.

"David! It's Harry," the voice on the other end chirped. "Just wanted to let you know, if it's okay with you, you can sign the contract tomorrow. And, at eight o'clock tomorrow morning, you can meet the owner of the mansion."

"That'll be perfect!" David said. He thanked Harry, his thoughts already spiraling toward the prospect of finally gaining access to that elusive room.

David returned home; his anticipation of the evening tinged by the tension he found Lisa wrestling with. Engaged in a heated conversation over the phone, her frustration was palpable, even to David.

"We already talked about this, and I thought we agreed on it," she said, her words laced with annoyance. She flicked her gaze towards David, offering him a cursory greeting before returning to the call. "This has taken way too long. Don't you realize what you're doing to her?"

David listened to the dispassionate voice on the other end of the line, a man attempting to distance himself from the decision. "Hey now, I'm not the one who decided that. The other executives and board of directors agreed to fire her."

The news ignited a fiery response from Lisa. Her words tumbled out in a passionate defense of the person in question, arguing for her capabilities, her loyalty to the company, and the unfairness of the situation. Yet the man on the phone seemed unable to influence the decision.

After ending the call with a plea for him to reconsider, Lisa turned her gaze to the window. David watched as she stared at a group of children playing in the harsh afternoon sun, her eyes squinting against the glare. Her hand reached her mouth, her nails a target for her pent-up frustration.

Feeling the need to offer some comfort, David approached, his hands gently landing on her shoulders. "Do you want to talk about what happened?" he asked softly.

Lisa turned and welcomed the warmth of his embrace.

"It's Mary, my colleague. She's going to be fired," she confessed, her voice heavy with resignation.

The following explanation surprised David, but given the snippets of conversation he'd overheard, he wasn't entirely shocked. A lucrative deal had fallen through, blame had been wrongly assigned, and now Mary was being held accountable. She added "I want to help Mary. She is a good friend; she had helped me a lot in the past."

David searched for ways to alleviate Lisa's distress. "Babe, how can I cheer you up?"

"Don't know—tell me what you found at the library."

David's face brightened at the opportunity to share his findings. "Got it right here!" He handed over the box of documents, watching Lisa study them with curiosity and skepticism.

Lisa looked, and said, "if Alice is missing, then how, what happened. The articles don't say much about him. No name, just age."

David nodded in understanding. "I know, but I have a feeling they're the right people. We have to check with André anyway and maybe get more information about the incident," he mused, thumbing through the pages. After a moment of silent contemplation, he looked up at Lisa, a spark of excitement glinting in his eyes.

"What, what? Tell me!" Lisa urged, momentarily forgetting her earlier frustration.

"According to this newspaper, Alice's fiancé was found on a beach near a cliff. I think we could try to locate this cliff. We might get a better grasp on what happened if we could examine the area closely."

A glance at his watch spurred him on. "However, it might be

wise to wait for André – see if he's unearthed anything," he added.

But Lisa was all for immediate action. "We won't know unless we ask him. Just give him a call," she insisted.

David was reaching for his phone when the doorbell rang.

His gaze met Lisa's. "Were you expecting anyone?"

Lisa shook her head, moving to answer the door.

David watched in surprise as André presented himself. He looked exhausted. His face was flushed and sweat dripped off him in rivulets. "Please pardon, Lisa," he gasped. "Feels like my blood is going to start boiling soon."

Lisa, ever the gracious host, ushered him inside.

"I found what you were looking for," André replied between pants, patting his briefcase for emphasis. As he moved further into the house, he set it on the table, releasing a heavy sigh. Wiping the sweat from his brow, he pulled out some crumpled papers and worked to smooth them out on the tabletop before handing them to David.

"You could have just given me a call, you know," David said, a smile playing at the corners of his mouth.

André delved into his bag, retrieving another piece of paper. "I'd had enough of all the paperwork back at the station. Coming here to visit you two was a good excuse to call it a day," he said.

David's eyes scanned the police report. "It's dated the twenty-eighth of June 1939," he noted, proceeding to read the contents out loud: "Murder or suicide. The police were called to the scene following a report of a bloodied person on a beach north of town near the lighthouse and a stone's throw from a cliff. The deceased, identified as a male, prompted suspicions of suicide, or perhaps murdered. The scene was cordoned off and investigators dispatched. The police questioned the caller who isn't under any suspicion at this time." David paused momentarily. "The deceased had sustained head injuries and was identified as twenty-eight-year-old Jay Murphy." He looked up, his gaze meeting Lisa's. "It's him! Alice's fiancé! What about Alice? Did you uncover anything on her?" he asked eagerly, turning back to the report.

André's fingers idly traced his hairline as he glanced at his bag. "Uh – yeah, of course, here it is," he replied, passing a document to David.

"Alice Walker, twenty years old, reported missing from Silver Road, north of town. Left her home at eleven o'clock with her dog to visit a relative but failed to arrive and did not return home. Reported missing by her family around five o'clock. Described as wearing a long black dress, a black hat, and white shoes, and accompanied by a black dog." David set the paper down. "There they are! The black dog matches the one in the house picture." He sipped his lemonade before walking over to a table fan blowing at full force. "Do you know where Jay Murphy's body was found? Where is this lighthouse or beach cliff?"

"They found him next to the lighthouse?" André queried.

"The cliff is near the lighthouse, perhaps a couple hundred feet away," André estimated.

David's eyes widened slightly. "I've visited that lighthouse multiple times. I like to write there. I had no idea that such a tragedy occurred nearby. And it's not far from the house we're buying," he mused.

A sense of unease washed over him as he stared at the police report. There was a certain gravity to knowing that he wanted to figure out more, yet he felt compelled by these newfound revelations. David thought to himself if I know more about what really happened to Jay then I may be closer to find out what happened to Alice.

"I have to head out now," André declared, gathering his bag, and heading towards the door. He paused, glancing back at David. "You can keep the documents, David. And please, call me if you need anything." With a nod, he departed.

Closing the door behind André, David turned to Lisa. "Before I came home, I received a call from Harry. We're set to sign the contracts and meet the owner tomorrow. Once that's done, we can visit the cliff. Perhaps by exploring the area, we might gain a deeper understanding of what happened."

"That sounds like a plan. I wouldn't mind seeing what the view is like up there," Lisa said.

"I'm sure it'll be stunning. I've always enjoyed the sea view from the lighthouse."

Behroz Behnejad

Chapter 3

David awoke early and checked the time: quarter to five. He kissed Lisa's cheek and lay back, staring at the ceiling. Thoughts filled his head. What had happened on the beach cliff? Why did Jay commit suicide? David remembered the tree writing, "Alice+James", Who was James? How long was James working at the garden? What was his role in all of this?

David felt overwhelmed. He glanced at his watch and panicked - it was five minutes past five. To get moving, he sat on the bed's edge, rubbed the sleep out of his eyes with his thumb and forefinger, then walked onto the covered terrace, where a cool breeze welcomed him. The sky had no stars, just clouds, but birds chirped in the distance. "Blessing of blessings," he thought as he stretched and yawned. "Finally, some rain."

David went to the kitchen to fix some sandwiches and coffee. He then he hurried to the bathroom, seeing that it was pouring rain. A few minutes later, rain smattered against the windowpane, and in the sky, lightning flashed intermittently. The violent and mighty thunder raged between the houses, lightning striking the city below. And a gusty wind caused wet leaves to swirl up into the sky.

David stepped out onto the terrace and surveyed the early morning sky. The trees were parched, and the ground was a deep shade of brown - both desperate for moisture from the heavens. He breathed deeply and closed his eyes, imagining the raindrops on his skin.

A loud clap of thunder roused Lisa from her slumber. She raised her head from the pillow, wide-eyed with surprise. She drew closer to take in the sight, and David snuck up behind her, wrapping his arms around her waist. Then got up and walked to the terrace.

"Finally, some rain, my love," David said close to Lisa's ear.

Lisa spun around in his embrace and smiled at him, "Some? I'd say it's pouring!"

She pressed one hand into his chest and kissed him lightly on the cheek before pulling away. "Well while we wait, I'll make you breakfast."

David smiled, relieved that his early morning efforts. "It's already done," he said.

He watched as delight transformed her expression. "Really? When did you get up?" she asked in amazement.

"Quarter to five," he answered with a sheepish grin, a wide yawn accompanying the end of his sentence.

Lisa shook her head in disbelief. "Why so early?" she said in a slightly whining tone.

David shrugged. "Don't know! Couldn't sleep I guess."

After breakfast, Lisa said, "I'll go get ready. We can't miss the contract signing."

David peered out onto the terrace and noticed the rain had subsided.

"Nature must be at its most beautiful now, right after the rain," she said.

David loved when she spoke like that. He held her, taking in the smell of her hair. "Yes, it's wonderful! Now nature smells ALIVE."

As they drove off, David could feel the tension emanating from Lisa. She kept her eyes trained out the window, fiddling with her fingers. Noticing how jittery she was, he asked her what had gotten into her.

"I'm feeling a bit nervous," she replied, barely audible above the engine's din.

"Why?" David asked.

"I don't know," she said. "This whole situation feels off, I have a bad feeling."

David held her hand after they parked in front of Harry's office. "It's okay, love. Just close your eyes and take a few deep breaths," he said, getting out of the car. Hand in hand, they went inside and took the elevator to the second floor.

They stopped outside Harry's office. David looked at Lisa and smiled as he knocked on the door. After a moment, Harry opened it and greeted them cheerfully.

"Hello, my friends," said Harry with open arms. "Ready to buy a house?"

As David and Lisa walked into the office, David noticed a thin man with gray hair and wrinkles around his eyes. Beside him, a woman with black, unkempt hair was waiting. Neither of them looked at David or Lisa.

Harry introduced everyone. "Caroline, Philip, David, and Lisa."

Philip was the first to greet them. "It's a pleasure," he said, shaking David's hand. "Since I heard you were interested in buying the house, I've looked forward to meeting you. I've even been lucky enough to read some of your books. Some great stuff you write."

David's expression changed as he heard the kind words. "That means a lot that you appreciate my work," he said.

They sat on the sofas opposite each other. David could sense Lisa's discomfort as Caroline stared at her. She nestled closer to David, then she turned to Harry and said, "It was good we had some rain. It's been so hot."

"It won't be long until it gets hot again," Harry said, walking away to get some drinks for the table. He grabbed some documents from his desk and came to sit on the couch with a smile.

"Before you sign," he said, "do you have any questions or concerns?" He glanced at Lisa and David as he passed them the stack of papers.

David looked at Lisa and then turned to Philip. "I'd like to know more about the room behind the bookshelf. Do you know anything more about it?"

Philip seemed hesitant, but a nod from Caroline let his words loose. "What do you want to know?"

"We're curious about what happened in the house. Harry told us a little bit, but we wonder if you know anything more. Considering we're not allowed to enter the room; I really want to know what happened there."

Philip furrowed his brow and paused before speaking, quickly glancing at Caroline. He took a small sip of his drink and waved an old newspaper before him to cool himself off.

"When we purchased the house," he began slowly, "the previous owner warned us that the family who lived here once had requested no one ever enter their private room - and those who succeeded them had held this promise until a stranger showed up at our doorsteps. He said he was related to the family residing there seventy years ago."

David's eyes lit up when Philip mentioned the old man. "Who was he? Any relation to the family who were the original owners?" he asked, leaning forward in anticipation.

"His father was a cousin of Alice's father who lived nearby," Philip said, then added with a nod, "A cousin."

David raised an eyebrow skeptically. "How old was the man?"

Philip looked at Caroline before answering.

"He was probably over eighty, more or less."

Caroline nodded in agreement. "At least, he looked very old," she said softly, her mouth curved into a careful smile.

Philip continued. "He had old photos with him that he showed us. The pictures were of the family and the house."

Excitement bubbled inside David. He wanted to take advantage of this opportunity to learn about Alice and her family from one of its own. "How can I find him? Do you have an address or a phone number?"

Philip shook his head. "I have a phone number and I tried to call him once before. I learned that he had passed away. It was his son who answered the phone."

Despite this answer, David still had hope. "Do you still have the number? Maybe I can try calling?"

"I do," Philip replied with a nod. He gave it to David, who promptly keyed it into his phone and asked excitedly, "What do you know about the family or Alice who lived in the room? What did the man tell you about her or the family?"

"Alice had a fiancé who died by suicide and her body was found down on a beach by a cliff. The police believed it was suicide and Alice ran away. Her parents decided to keep her room untouched and locked the door, placing a bookcase in front of it. They sold the house with the promise that future owners would respect their wishes not to enter the room."

"I saw a tree in the backyard of the house, and it had the names Alice+James carved on it. Was there anyone in the family named James?"

"I don't know, but Alice's little brother was named Albert."

Caroline began to gasp and rummage through her bag.

"It's okay," said Philip. "Calm down. Look, here it is." He opened the lid of a container of medicine.

After several moments Lisa asked, "Are you okay? Is it asthma?"

Caroline gave a faint nod, the fear still apparent on her face. "It scared me, as always," she admitted, inhaling, and sipping her soda. She then slouched back in the sofa; eyes closed in relief.

Phillip glanced at David again and inquired, "What did I say before that?"

"I asked a question about James," David reminded him.

"That's right. When the man showed us his photos, one of them was of a young man wearing work clothes and holding gardening shears in his hand. He said this was their gardener who had some disability but had an extraordinary talent for growing plants. I don't recall what his name was though," Philip supplied the information and said "I know there was a Gardner" as Harry set more cold sodas on the table.

David then asked about Alice's fiancé, Jay Murphy.

"Jay was a twenty-eight-year-old guy who fell head over heels in love with Alice at first sight. Before he met her, he worked in a post office. One day, he got the brilliant idea to deliver mail and packages using an airplane. Without hesitation, he borrowed money from his family and took out a loan from a bank so that he could begin an air cargo business."

"A smart guy," David remarked.

"He bought his first plane and started working. He wanted to become a pilot and began his flight training. At the age of twenty-four he finished his pilot's license, and with his aircraft he delivered important mail for the city and the military. Eventually he bought a second plane, and it went so well that in two years he had acquired a total of five planes. He also had plans to start the same business in other cities. Jay named his company after his girlfriend, "Alice and Jay Airlines."

"I didn't know there was airmail seventy years ago," Harry said in wonder.

"But if he was so in love and such a successful businessman, why did he commit suicide?" David asked.

Philip shrugged his shoulders. "The man who came to see us asked the exact same question."

"What was his name?" David asked.

"Alan," Philip said to David "here is Alan's phone number. David took the note and thanked him.

"I hope I've been able to help you," Philip said.

"You've been really helpful," said David. "The only big unanswered questions are about Jay's suicide and James' identity—who was he, and what role did he play? Do you think calling his relatives would help me find out more?"

"Why do you care so much?" asked Philip.

"As an author, I'm naturally fascinated by mysteries," said David.

"We'll soon be living in a house with a room that hasn't been touched for seventy years. Now that I know something tragic happened here, there's no way I can resist looking into it further... And sure, if the story has all the right elements, maybe it could be my next book."

Harry laid out the papers for the house sale on the large mahogany desk. He picked up a pen, ready to sign, when David interjected, "But before we sign, I have a small requirement. I was wondering if we could move in within a week?"

Caroline and Phillip glanced at each other; their faces unreadable. Phillip cleared his throat and ran his hand through his thinning hair. With an expansive gesture of assurance, he smiled, "As I said earlier, it is a great honor for us to be able to do business with you. I have a truck and can have you settled into the house within a day. You can move in before the money has been transferred to my account. I'll leave the keys with Harry tomorrow, and you can pick them up from him. Fine enough?"

David signed the papers, shaking hands with Phillip, Caroline, and Harry.

"We are very grateful that we have found this house with a lovely view right on our doorstep," Lisa said with a warm smile. "And to think it came with its own mystery!"

"Alrighty then, everything is taken care of," Harry announced as he stood up.

The others followed suit, and Lisa stepped towards Philip and hugged him.

"Thank you," said Lisa.

As they made for the door, Caroline approached Lisa and looked her in the eyes. She smiled and said, "I'm not an unfriendly person. A long time ago, I experienced a tragedy, and since then, I don't like close contact with strangers. It's a challenge for me to connect with people. I hope you will accept this as an excuse." She smiled wider. "This time, I'm making an exception." She hugged Lisa and continued, "I can feel that you are good and nice people, and I apologize so much for my behavior."

"I can understand that" said Lisa, and David was glad to see the tension between them ease. "And you don't have to apologize."

On the way out, Phillip called out to David. "The lock on the gate is not great. I'll have it changed before you get the keys."

The street was almost deserted, except for a few kids nearest the couple's car. They were sitting on the pavement around a pair of broken flowerpots, splashing each other with water pistols, the bright sunlight glinting as they laughed. David and Lisa looked at them fondly before getting into their car.

David pulled his seatbelt and said, "Let's go to the cliff."

CHAPTER 4

On the way there, it started to drizzle. Water droplets landed on the windshield, forming tiny tendrils of water as they crested down the window. Lisa was silent. She looked out the window, twisting her hairs between her fingers. Soon the dark sky turned into a bright blue shimmer, and the sun broke out from behind the clouds.

Soon, they arrived at a dirt road. David steered the car onto the bumpy road and drove slowly forward. There were puddles everywhere, but the road was still manageable. All around it were farms, and a little further on, they came to a wind power plant. Rainwater gushed down from a steep cliff.

After a few minutes of driving, they arrived at a narrow gravel path. David parked the car by the roadside and said to Lisa, "From here we have to go on foot."

He exited the car and started walking. Lisa followed a few steps behind. It was windy. Every time the wind caught the plants and trees next to the path, little sprays of rainwater fell over them.

At last, they arrived at the shoreline, where a towering cliff rose from the ground.

"When Heaven and Earth meet like this, we're close to God," David said with awe.

The ocean's harmonies blended into an ethereal symphony that awed them both. They were struck by the grandeur of it all.

David shook himself out of his trance and tightly grasped Lisa's wrist.

"Let's go up the hill, and then we'll be there," David said as he climbed up the slope, tugging Lisa behind him.

It was only a short time before they were at the top of the cliff. The wind was strong. The water sparkled brightly, almost blinding. The lighthouse and some verdant hills were visible from a distance, the scene sprawling out in all directions.

David walked past the trees, their broad branches like a canopy above his head. He stopped and looked around at the wildflowers strewn across the meadow, feeling like he had entered another world. "It's so peaceful and freeing here," he said.

Lisa followed behind him, her gaze scanning the undulating hills.

She was about to ask what they were looking for, but David beat her to it.

"Just for the view," David said.

Lisa frowned back at him. "I thought you wanted to come here and look for clues?"

"I just wanted to come here and look around," said David. "Maybe we can understand something."

She stood straight and cocked her head as if studying him. "Understand what?"

David sighed deeply and ran a hand through his hair in frustration. "To understand what in the world was he doing up here alone, or if it was really suicide."

Lisa sat down on a rock nearby and looked at David. "David, what do you think happened here? What's your intuition tell you now?"

David scanned the landscape, his gaze resting on the gentle waves of the sea. Thoughts of Alice and Jay, if they were around probably, they would have kids and grandkids, rose to his mind. He sighed, ran a hand through his hair, then lightly brushed a fallen lock away from Lisa's face as she watched him intently.

A gust of wind gave him courage, and David slowly dropped to one knee. His voice trembled with emotion as he said, "I knew when we first met that you were the one for me. I want to spend the rest of my life showing you how much I love you."

Lisa dropped her freshly picked flowers on the ground. She brought her hand to her mouth, and tears formed.

David's voice shook as he spoke, his gaze pleading with her. His fingers curled tightly around the box, and as he opened it, he saw Lisa's mouth open in awe. "Lisa, I can't express how much I love you," said David softly. "I want to spend my life with you. Will you marry me and come on this amazing journey with me?"

Lisa stood there, unspeaking, unmoving. Suddenly, she howled with joy. "How can I say no? You are the love of my life, and with you there are no limits. You are my safety and the joy of my life. With you, I know what love means. Of course, I will be your wife. If I die and am born again and again, I just want to be yours. I love you so much." She threw herself into David's arms and gave him a long kiss. "You have no idea how happy I am. I don't have words for it. But...Did you plan this?" she said, looking at him in amazement.

"No," David said. "I had the ring in my pocket all this time and felt moved by this place on the cliff. I thought now or never," he said.

"I can understand the right time, but I'm a little doubtful of the place... this could be a murder site," Lisa said, laughing.

"Yes, but it's a beautiful murder site," he replied, smiling, and hugging her tightly.

"Anyway, I'm glad you did," said Lisa. "And when we get home, we'll celebrate."

"What do you have in mind?" David asked.

"Let's go to our favorite restaurant tonight," Lisa said.

As they held each other, they looked out over the sea. The two of them stood there a while, the whistle of the wind their only company.

"Shall we go, honey?" asked David.

"No, I don't want to go yet," said Lisa. "It's so beautiful here. I don't want this moment to end."

"But we could come back another day," he said, taking her hand and gently pulling her towards him. "Come on, let's go."

They climbed down back to the car and got in. Lisa giggled and looked at David.

"What is it?" asked David.

"Now that we're down here, I have an idea," said Lisa. "When we get married, we can have the wedding in our new house. It's so huge. I think it would be amazing."

"That's a great idea," David said and drove off.

Back at their old house, Lisa hurried inside to change to go to dinner with David. He spent time admiring the sun and felt the breeze before being interrupted by Lisa calling out as she left.

David picked up his phone and before going out he called the number that Phillip gave him.

A tired man answered, and David introduced himself then asked for Alan. He said, "I am Edward, what can I do for you?" David then nervously said, "I want to find out some information about Tim Walker the father of Alice, and also about James and Alice, if know anything."

Edward on the other end said, "Oh, yes Phillip told me that you may be calling me", hesitated slightly and answered, "All I know is from my father's story. Tim Walker was my uncle. There was a man named James, a gardener liked by all children. He had a disability, a brain malformation that made him speak slowly and stagger when walking. He was also illiterate but good at gardening."

"What else do you know about James?"

Edward said that James had butterflies in his stomach when he saw Alice, and after the cook told her father, James was forced to move to a shed. He became depressed and worked hard to avoid getting fired, which would mean homelessness.

"Could you tell me more about James?" David implored.

"My uncle found James in an orphanage," Edward said, "He was talented and knowledgeable and a born gardener. He was seven when he was placed in the orphanage and fifteen when he moved in with my uncle. Everyone, including him, was interrogated by the police regarding Jay's death and Alice's disappearance, but nothing stuck."

"What happened to him when your uncle sold the house?" David asked.

"James moved to another city and got a job on another farm, where he was given his own accommodations. It wasn't just Alice who disappeared from this house," Edward said. "There are others who were gone without a trace."

"Others?" David asked eagerly. "Who are they? When did the disappear?"

"In 1948, a family moved in, and the man of the house was a professor and scientist. People say he was working on a secret experiment, and after five years he disappeared without a trace. As soon as he disappeared, rumors spread that he had carried out a type of experiment that brought demons to life and that they took him with them to the other side," Edward said, laughing.

David hesitated, "But is it true that he went missing?"

"Yes, that's true. His wife disappeared a year later. Whatever happened, to him and his wife remains a mystery," Edward said.

"Did he work from home?" asked David. "Did he have a lab at home?"

"They say he had a lab in the house, but I do not know where."

"Who are the OTHER PEOPLE who have disappeared?"

"In the sixties, when the house sat empty while the family was on vacation, two burglars broke in. One of them climbed into Alice's room by smashing a window. The thief who climbed in was seen by a neighbor who, in turn, alerted the police. When police arrived at the scene, the one waiting outside was arrested, but the other thief was never found. Police searched the entire house but couldn't find him. He was just gone," Edward said.

David finished his glass and thanked him warmly, but before he hung up the phone, Edward added, "If you have any more questions, don't hesitate to call me."

"I will, thank you," David said and hung up the phone.

David sighed pensively as he returned to the terrace and sat in an armchair. He stared at birds chirping overhead, murmuring, "People can't just disappear. There must be an explanation."

Was he jealous of Jay's interest in Alice?

Suddenly, Lisa called from the hall after her run. "I'm home."

He looked at Alice's photo, perplexed by all the mysterious disappearances.

Lisa snuck up behind him, wearing a tight white dress that sparkled in the sun, her hair dyed dark brown. He stared, unable to express himself but enjoying what he saw.

"What DID you expect?" Lisa asked.

"A sweaty, smelly, tired girl," said David. "But where have you been? I thought you went for a run?"

"I saw this dress yesterday," Lisa said as she spun around on display. "And when we decided to go out, I bought it immediately. Then I hurried to the salon where my friend works. She's fixed up my hair. What do you think?"

David stroked her hair. "I love your taste. You have the best sense of style," he said, passionately kissing her. "But I can't go to dinner like this when you have THAT dress on. I have to change."

As David went to go and change, Lisa called out to him. "What did you do while I was gone?"

"I called that number I got from Phillip," said David. "It was a man whose uncle owned the house. The uncle being Alice's father Tim Walker, that is."

"Did you find out anything new?" Lisa asked.

"Yes! Lots of interesting things, but I'll tell you more at the restaurant."

Lisa sighed with a part-silly part-whiny voice, "Come on, you can't tell me a little bit?"

"No! I don't want to," David said.

"You're so mean," she said, making a childishly sour face that made David laugh. "Anyway, I'll call the taxi."

"I'm ready," David said, strutting out of the bedroom.

"Looking quite dapper, Mister," said Lisa. They stared at one another in the hall. "I love the blazer and pants. All black, slick. Waxed your hair, I see."

He put a toothpick in his mouth and grinned.

Lisa laughed and walked up to him.

"You are not nice today. Mmm-hmm. That cologne smells amazing," she said, and kissed him on the cheek, then she looked at her watch. "Whoop! I think the taxi is here."

They hurried to the taxi, and David opened the door for her and sat beside her in the back seat. He placed his hand upon hers.

When they arrived at the restaurant, a cheerful tune greeted them from the speakers, and their noses were tickled by an array of savory aromas. Some children chatted excitedly across the room near a towering aquarium packed with vibrant fish.

The waitress smiled warmly.

"Good evening," she said, gesturing for them to follow her.

She handed them menus and led them past tables of other couples, arriving at their favorite corner spot, screened off from the rest of the room but affording a view of the greenery and sea beyond. The waitress stepped back, giving them space to sit down before inquiring politely, "What can I get you?"

Lisa looked at David and made her request. "We'd like to start with a cold champagne – brut, please. The best kind you have."

"Yes, ma'am, and I'll have that right out to you."

David looked at Lisa in their private moment at the table. In admiration of her, he said with a charming smile, "You truly are a ray of sunshine, and everywhere you go, you spread so much joy. I'm so lucky that you showed up in my life." At the same time, he took out a rose from his jacket pocket and continued, "Not even a rose can compare to your beauty." He gave it to her.

Lisa smiled gently and smelled the rose before putting it in her hair. "I will never forget how we met. Mary set us up. She lured me out on the dance floor while you danced behind us. Suddenly she pushed me, and you caught me," Lisa said, laughing.

The waitress brought the champagne and opened it. The cork flew into the air with a bang, and the bubbles poured out of the bottle.

"Let's make a toast to ourselves and to a long and happy life together," David said and drank.

"Would you like to order now?" the waitress prompted.

Lisa looked at the menu and said, "Yes, we're ready, and I'll have the house special, please."

David noticed Lisa kept her gaze on him. He smiled. "I'll have what she's having."

"Excellent choice."

From the corner of his eye, David saw someone approaching the table. He looked around cautiously and saw a young couple coming towards them. The guy stopped halfway, but the girl introduced herself to the table.

"Hi, my name is Alice," said the woman. "This is my brother Alvin. I saw you when you came in. I wasn't going to bother you, but I felt compelled to ask... You're David Hamilton, right?"

David nodded. "That's me. You said your name is Alice?" David glanced quickly at Lisa and back to Alice.

"Yes!" She nodded and showed him a book she had in her hand. "I actually bought your book, DANCING WITH DEATH, last week and was wondering if you'd sign it?" she said, extending the book toward him.

David smiled. "Of course." He took the book and wrote on the inside of the back cover.

"I'm also writing a book in my free time," mumbled Alice, "but it's going kinda slow. Do you have any advice?"

David handed the book back to her and leaned back in his chair. He thought briefly and said, "You have to believe in yourself. If you are passionate about what you do, keep going. If someone says it's a waste of time, don't listen. Just do what you love."

"Thank you," she said graciously and hurried away.

Lisa looked at him and grinned. "Well said, darling." Her congratulations were replaced with worry. "Speaking of Mary, yesterday I was told she was let go. I called her immediately. She was so depressed and completely beside herself. She thought the whole incident was incredibly abusive and unfair, and I agree with her." Lisa sighed. "She has a new baby and a new house, and the future looked so bright and full of hope, but without a job it's looking pretty bleak. I wish I could help her somehow."

David heard the tremor in her voice. "I have friends who work in different pharmaceutical companies," he told Lisa. "One runs his own business. Perhaps he could help her out." He took a sip of the champagne, and it had a dry, bubbly flavor that was crisp and refreshing. The champagne was also slightly sweet, with notes of citrus and honey.

"It would be wonderful if we could help her," said Lisa. "After all, she brought us together."

"Okay," said David. "I promise we will help her." He smiled at Lisa and leaned forward across the table. "Earlier you wanted to know what I was talking about with that man whose father was a cousin of Alice's father—Tim Walker?"

"Yes, tell me," Lisa said.

"It was very interesting," stated David. "James was the gardener of the house, and he was in love with Alice. At one point, he told the cook who worked in the kitchen about his feelings for her, but unfortunately the cook told Alice's dad who got furious and made him move to a small house out on the land. Actually, the father rebuilt the small shed so that James could live there."

"Do you think his passion for her drove him crazy?" Lisa asked.

"Who knows," said David. "When we get keys to the house, maybe we can find out more."

"We'll have the keys tomorrow, right?" asked Lisa.

The moment the waitress arrived with their dinner, a quiet spread through the air. David and Lisa happily savored each bite of their meal starting with mix plate appetizer, then mix salad, followed by a beef wellington as a main dish. They were lost in their conversation when they saw two glass dishes arrived on their table, Golden

Opulence Sundae with 24 karat gold leaf on them. David said, "wow, never had anything with 24 karat eatable gold on it." When it was time to go, Lisa said: "I will always remember this evening - thank you darling."

David gave her an intense look and wiped his mouth with a napkin. "No, thank you, my darling. You enrich my life. Changed my way of thinking. Improved my way of working. I'm like a NEW MAN, and I promise the best I can to make sure you have a life overflowing with love. Let's toast to the future and eternal love."

Behroz Behnejad

Chapter 5

The phone jolted David awakes.

Harry's voice sounded on the other end. "Sorry if I woke you."

"What time is it?" David questioned, rising to a seated position.

"It's nine-thirty," said Harry.

"Shit! It's already that late? I went to bed late last night, so thank goodness you called," David said, rubbing his eyes.

"I wanted to let you know that Philip just gave me the keys," said Harry. "You can get them whenever."

"Really?" said David, "That's great! I'll come get the keys as soon as I pull myself together." David hung up the phone, stretched, and yawned. David and Lisa had not decided about their current house.

"Who was that?" Lisa said with a yawn.

"It was Harry," David said as he stood up, stretching his arms towards the ceiling. "Philip handed in the keys, so I guess we can go and pick them up."

David walked towards the terrace doors, opened them, and felt the cool breeze on his face. It was hot and warm outside. Warmer than before. David noticed the birds had taken shelter in the shade of bushes. Puddles of water were occupied by thirsty cats, puddled into dipping ponds by the rain from yesterday.

"Come and see, Lisa," David called.

"What is it?" she asked, joining him on the terrace.

David smiled at her broadly. "Lovely morning."

"Darling, why are you awake full of beans?" Lisa asked.

"I'm just excited about solving the riddle of that room behind the door," David said.

"Are you actually going to go into the room?"

"I just want to look for clues," David told her. "It's our house, and I won't touch anything or move anything out of its place."

"I'm not sure about this, we have signed a contract and we should follow the contract. We should not go into that room." Lisa said.

"Stop worrying, I won't touch anything in there." David said.

After he got himself ready, David told Lisa, "I'll go to Harry and get the keys, then make my way over to the house."

"You're going there today?" Lisa asked.

"I don't want to wait any longer," said David. "I want to look before we settle in. I have a strange feeling in here," he said, pointing to his chest.

Lisa gave him a puzzled look.

"Every time I look at Alice's picture on my phone, I feel like she's calling for help, like she wants to be free. I feel like she wants the truth to be revealed. It feels like I need to do this."

Lisa frowned. "You don't need to do anything, sweetie."

"Lisa," said David. "I do. It's a feeling deep inside me. Please understand."

This time, Lisa gave him a long, hard look. "I understand. Come get me when you have the keys."

"What? You want to help?" David asked. "And here I was thinking you were too scared."

"Oh, I'm scared," she said, and afterward, she giggled, "but I used to love playing detective when I was a kid."

"Fabulous! Thanks, darling. It's great to have your support in this," David exclaimed with a smile before kissing her forehead. Striding towards the doorway, he added, "I'll phone you as soon as I head over to fetch you. Let's do go there now!"

On the way to the car, David noticed an elderly man snoring loudly, sleeping on a park bench. Some teens circled him, making fun of him until he woke up and swore at them. When they ran away, David couldn't help but laugh, but when the man saw him, his angry glare made David turn away quickly and hurry to the car.

On his way to Harry, he pondered why the case had gone unsolved for seventy years. Could secrets in Harry's room point him toward clues? Was the truth hidden out of fear? Had Jay run away, or was he dead? David couldn't accept Jay had killed himself. It was inconceivable; a successful businessman with an adoring companion wouldn't take his own life.

David gripped the wheel and furrowed his brow as he drove, pondering the mystery before him. He had heard rumors of a love triangle between Alice, Edward, and James, but could it have ended in such a tragedy? He thought of the stories he had heard about James—how he was desperate to win Alice's love. Could jealousy have driven him to murder? David shuddered at the thought.

Lost in his thoughts, David felt like a pinball machine as hypotheses came in at different angles. Before he knew it, he had pulled up to Harry's office. He took the time to sit and reflect. His brain was still whirring with ideas. He took out his phone and gazed at Alice's photo, whispering to her as if she were there with him. "I can feel it, Alice. You want to speak up but just can't. I'll be your voice and make sure justice is served." With new resolve, he got out of the car.

When David entered Harry's office, Harry was on the phone. He waved to David and continued his conversation.

David stepped up to the large window and took in the magnificent view. The old city sprawled out beneath him, with a grand red-brick church at its center, surrounded by lush green gardens. He imagined Alice and her family visiting this 19th-century landmark.

Harry's voice snapped him out of his thoughts. "What are you pondering, buddy?"

"I was admiring the old church across from us. It must have been built in the 19th century, right?" David questioned.

"Yes," said Harry raising his eyebrows. "My grandfather was

actually a priest there. He was part of their history, a figure in the community, as naturally comes with that position. As a teenager, I used to attend services there with my parents."

"How long was your grandfather a priest there?" David inquired.

"Just over eighteen years," said Harry. "From 1910 to 1928, then he moved to another church in another city."

David settled into a reflective mood and said, "I can't help but imagine what this city would have looked like centuries ago."

While Harry was handing David the keys, he said "I have seeing old pictures of the city, nothing like what we have now, glad that I didn't live in that area. "Here the key, you can move in now, everything else will be ready in a few weeks."

"Thanks for everything, Harry. I'm happy and can't thank you enough. I'll write a book about Alice's mystery in the future."

"Don't forget to stay in touch, David, and good luck," Harry said, shaking his hand.

"I will, and thank you again," David said, leaving with a glowing face.

On his way to their current house to pick up Lisa, he called Lisa, telling her he'd be there in five minutes.

When he arrived, Lisa was waiting outside with one eyebrow raised and lips pressed together firmly.

"Let's go!" David said, shaking the keys excitedly. "Today, we'll look for clues about Alice's disappearance and Jay's alleged suicide without touching anything unless necessary. We're hands-off detectives."

Lisa asked what items they should focus on. "Anything that could give us an answer about her disappearance or Jay's suicide," David replied.

Lisa beamed with excitement - a room untouched for seventy years looked as if it fascinated her. "It'll be exciting to see how people lived back then," she said.

"That's why we have to be extra careful about what we do there so that we can preserve the room exactly as it looked in 1939," David said, looking at her curiously and continuing. "How do you feel, about all this, about what's next, about walking in?"

"Nervous and a little scared," said Lisa. "We don't know what's in there."

"Don't be silly," said David, looking at his watch. He glanced back at Lisa. "It's almost half past eight, and we don't have to rush. A thorough investigation can surely give us some answers."

They arrived at the gate, and David hopped out of the car to see if Philip had managed to fix the lock. It opened right away, much to his relief.

"Nice - the lock is fixed!" he shouted back to Lisa in the car. Back in the car again, David felt nervous tension bubbling up inside. His hands shook as he wiped his damp palms against his trousers. His forehead thudded against the steering wheel as he closed his eyes and sighed deeply.

"What is it, honey?" Lisa asked tenderly.

"Just a bit shaky, must not have eaten enough," he said, trying to shake off the feelings.

Lisa rubbed his leg. "If you want, we can come back tomorrow."

"No," said David getting out of the car. "Let's do it. I can't back out now."

On their way up to the house, a mother cat lay in the shade of a bush licking her newborn kittens. Holding onto David's arm for support, Lisa followed him up the stairs, where he tried each key until he found the right one.

Upon a slow but light push to open the door, they were greeted by an empty house. Everything was gone. They walked around and looked, but David felt impatient. "Let's go to the room," he said.

They walked into the living room, and soon after, they reached the stairway that led to the room with a fantastic view.

The bookcase stood in the corner, untouched. The sun was shining in the room, and it was warm. He stared at the bookshelf and examined it thoroughly. Curious, he walked back and forth and said, "If we pull the bookcase forward a little, and then gently move it to the side towards the window, we can access the door." He looked at Lisa. "Alrighty, if you grab the top, I'll grab the bottom, and we'll push it together. Okay? Are you ready? One, two, three, push."

The bookcase was heavy and scraped against the floor. Dust swirled around them, causing David to sneeze several times. After he recovered, he said, "Come on, one more time, honey. It's moving. A little more. That's enough."

Lisa leaned against the wall and slid down to the floor. "That's a heavy bookcase," she gasped. "A beast."

"Yes, but we still need to move it a little more towards the window," said David. "Come on."

"Whew, okay," Lisa said, standing once again. She held the bookshelf, and David walked around and started pushing it.

"Come on, a little more, Lisa," said David urgently. "Pull. That's enough. Now we can access the door."

Chapter 6

The door did not look unique in its design. In fact, it looked less than extraordinary. If not for the concealed door behind the bookcase, David would never have guessed it to be anything more than a storage or linen room.

"Looks the same as any old door to me," said Lisa. She approached the door, grabbed the handle, and tried to open it. "It's locked," she said. "Well, at least now we can guess they didn't just use the bookcase as a lock. They really didn't want anyone going in." Lisa glanced at David. "Still want to go inside and look?"

David approached the door and began trying each key one by one. "Oh yes," he said, hands trembling with excitement. After several failed attempts at unlocking the door, he became increasingly annoyed. "Gotta be one of these things," said David. It was the second to last that finally opened the door. David grabbed Lisa excitedly and hugged her. Then, he turned the key.

The door was large and made of thick wood, with a rusty metal handle in the center. When David opened the door, it creaked loudly, like it hadn't been opened in a long time. A wall of thick cobwebs greeted them, blocking the entrance. Through the doorway, they could see a dark room illuminated by slivers of light filtering through a window. A long curtain hung before the window, trapping most of the light.

The air in the room was stale and musty. It was clear the room had been closed off for years. A faint smell of dust also hung in the air from their disturbance as they moved inside.

"Babe, I need some light here," said David, and with a nod, Lisa walked towards the window.

"Eww," said Lisa as she reached for the window curtains. "Each step I take feels like I'm standing on something squishy," she said, pulling the curtain open slowly. "Ready?"

David said yes. "Seventy years without light," he said. "Let's see how this place looks, shall we."

The new light in the room revealed its contents. On the bed were several stuffed animals, and a bookcase near the desk held several dusty books with webs between them. A portrait of Alice Walker hung on the wall framed in dark brown carved wooden frame, Alice had a while dress with small pink flowers, and she was sitting on a chair with a black god next to her. There was a stuffed animal was propped up against a wardrobe closet on the floor. David saw a cockroach crawling around beside his feet. He stood on it. The squelch was sickening.

"Wow," said Lisa. "It's as if time has stood still here." David lifted his shoe to reveal the squashed body and juices of the cockroach.

"Oh, how disgusting," said Lisa. "That thing is still twitching."

"They're vile," said David. "I've already committed murder in this room."

David watched Lisa tiptoe around various insects towards the wardrobe. "Let's look inside," she said, opening the doors. "Ooh, gorgeous," she said look at this, a bunch of dresses on hangers of varying colors, she had a good taste of clothing and colors."

David saw a bunch of hats at the top of the wardrobe. "Snazzy," he said. "But, honey, remember we need to be careful."

At the bottom of the wardrobe, she found some shoes and, among them, a box. "I've found something here," said Lisa. She pulled a cream-color box free; it was dusty but in an excellent shape and opened it. "Wow, let's see. Shoes." She moved them to the side.

David walked over and joined her. "Anything else?"

David stepped over to Lisa. She began to open the lid. "Easy does it," he said.

Lisa gripped the lid and pulled.

"You seem more nervous than me," she said. "Just a little bit...there."

When she pulled open the lid, the contents of it were a treat to David's mind.

"Letters," said Lisa. She took the letters in hand. "My gosh, there's at least twenty letters here, all enveloped and addressed to 'beloved Alice,' and I guess from...Jay?"

David nodded. "Those things," he said, taking several books in hand. "Bunch letters and notebooks. All from Jay to Alice, I wonder."

"We have to go through everything," said David, flicking through the pages of one of the notebooks. "Perhaps there's a clue inside, maybe some idea as to what happened to Alice."

"Do you think this is okay?" asked Lisa. "I mean, these are supposed to be private. Right?"

"I know, but if we want the facts to make things right, we must do it," David said firmly. He left the box on the table and went through the books on the bookshelf. He recognized some of the writers, William Shakespeare, Jules Verne, the Sweetness at the Bottom of the Pie Fire from the Rock, and Girl in Reverse.

At the entrance to the room, he saw a grandfather clock almost two meters high, and he did not believe his eyes when he saw that it was working. What was most extraordinary, however, was that the hands were turning in the wrong direction.

Amazed, David roared, "Lisa, look at this...What...How?"

Lisa took her place beside him. "The hands," Lisa said, pointing. "They're turning counterclockwise. But how and why?" She paused for a moment and looked at David. "Do you really think no one has been in here all this time?"

David shrugged. "That's what they said."

"But I wonder if it's the truth," said Lisa. She looked back at the clock. "Think about it. How could it still be running after all these years?"

David shrugged again. "Magic?"

Lisa laughed and held his hand. "Cute."

David walked over to the clock and began probing behind it. "I can see something back here." A cord was sticking out near the base of the grandfather clock. "There's a cord back here. It goes into the wall."

"I've never seen a grandfather clock that runs on electricity," Lisa said, joining him.

"Neither have I," admitted David. "It's kind of strange."

"There are no electrical outlets here," said Lisa. She started biting one of her nails, knelt, grabbed the cord, and pulled. "There's something behind the wall, it feels like..."

"What is it, honey?" asked David.

"I just don't get it," she said, pushing herself back. "All of this is so weird. Maybe we should leave."

David put a finger to his lips. "Hear that?" he whispered.

"What?" Lisa whispered back, her eyes wide.

"Just listen," David said in a strained low voice. There was a faint, rasping sound coming from within the wall and behind the clock.

"I hear it," said Lisa. "Where the heck is it coming from? Are you sure it is coming from the wall?"

"The wall, I think," whispered David, pointing to the grandfather clock. He walked around the clock and surveyed its lower part. "I can feel a vibration." He tried in vain to find a hatch or an entrance. The rasping sound became louder and more frequent.

"Well, if we move the clock..." Lisa started.

"Not now," finished David. "Another day. We have to keep going," David said. He walked around the room. In a corner near the window sat a square gold-colored mirror. The heavy frame was dusty. In the other corner hung a bronze-colored watch decorated with carvings. "Very beautiful," he said, nodding approvingly.

By the bed was a white-painted vanity, complete with a heart-shaped mirror and four old perfumes sitting atop it, each bottle adorned with pearls and seashells. Next to these sat a small makeup box containing lipstick, eyeliner, and other jars. In the corner of the vanity was another box David opened carefully to reveal jewelry—earrings, and necklaces.

He whispered, "Fascinating, our Alice," before turning to Lisa and saying, "Come here, my dear, you'll like this."

Lisa rushed to the dressing table; her eyes wide as she caught sight of the jewelry box. She could hardly contain her anticipation and let out a squeal of delight.

"Oh, my God," she said. "How beautiful!"

With glitter in her eyes, she looked at all the antique jewelry. Her hands shook as she opened a bottle of perfume and smelled it. "Strange," she said, "but not terrible. Look, David. These bottles are so nice. They could be worth a lot now. My my, what a fanciful necklace."

David discovered a curtain hanging from the ceiling down against the dusty floor. "How bizarre," said David. "There's no window here."

He walked up to the curtain and pulled at the heavy velvet. He pushed the curtain aside further and drew in a quick breath when he saw what was hidden behind it. In front of him was a darkness with a path leading far into the wall. The entrance was narrow and low.

"M—mercy," David said without turning around. He stepped in but stopped, stretching his hand out in front of him. "It's all dark in here."

"You have a flashlight on your cell phone," Lisa pointed out from behind him.

"Honey, you're hanging on me," David said as Lisa leaned over him with all her weight.

When Lisa backed up, David took out his phone and turned on the flashlight. He saw some stairs and warned Lisa. "Watch out for the stairs," he said, carefully going down one step at a time as Lisa followed close behind. The air in the newly discovered room was heavy to breathe in. It felt damp, smelled so stale, so still. With his flashlight, he looked around and noticed a wall clock.

"This one is spinning counterclockwise, too," said David, flashing the light on the clock.

"I can see," said Lisa.

"What's going on here?" said David. "Why are all the clock hands rotating in reverse?" David coughed. "The air down here is getting to my throat."

"Me too," said Lisa. "It feels creepy here." Lisa clung to David's arm, her body trembling. "Something strange is going on in this room, and I don't want to be here anymore."

Under the wall clock stood a table, and on it, David found several books and notebooks covered with dust. He picked one up and opened the cover carefully, then looked at the first page.

"Alice Walker," said David aloud. "These must be her diaries. This is the type of thing I was hoping to find. Maybe we can find clues inside."

"Look at this, David," said Lisa. She seemed to have gathered her courage and was over by a shelf. She pointed at the objects on the shelf. "Two lamps, and there's still oil in them. Do you have a lighter?" She took them down and held onto them.

David lit the lamps and set them on the table, flooding the room with light. There were a lot of objects scattered around that had developed an aged look. Some perfume, makeup stuff and hairbrushes on one table by the mirror. One old sewing machine covered in dust was in the corner of one of the tables, an unfinished painting of a man staring off into the distance covered with a layer of dust.

"Who could he be?" asked Lisa. "It doesn't look finished."

On the shelves were some bottles and boxes. "I'm just...surprised seeing all these things in here," said David as he walked around the room. "There are so many things in here. But I think that's enough for today. This is a lot, too much. We'll take the notebooks with us and look through them at home, and maybe we'll put some pieces of the puzzle together."

David put out the oil lamps and left them on the table. He grabbed some of the notebooks and headed for the exit.

"Wait for me," Lisa called, rushing up behind him.

"Don't forget to get the rest of the books," David said. He sneezed. "Darn dust."

Annoyed, she returned and picked up the rest of the books but left all the letters on the table.

When Lisa caught up to him, David asked, "Did you get the books?" Lisa showed him. "Come on, help me put this thing back in its proper place." David laid the books on the floor, and together, they put the bookcase in front of the door where it had stood before. "And we left it preserved, sort of."

Lisa sank to the floor and gasped, wiping the sweat from her brow. "God, David, that thing's heavy. No more, I really don't want to go to this room again, it feels too much for me."

David sat down next to her and pulled her head onto his shoulder. "I know, but you did so great. We should go home now. I want to review the notes today. I'm so anxious to go through everything. By the way, did you noticed as we decided to leave the light outside was changing, becoming lighter?" Lisa said, no, I didn't notice it."

Lisa stumbled out of the house, her books in hand, and David followed close behind. He wiped his sweaty brow and squinted into the sunlight. He stopped short when he saw the cat, they had encountered a few hours before. She was still sitting in the same spot on the terrace, gently grooming and caring for her litter. David's eyebrows shot up as he checked the time on his watch.

"What is it?" Lisa pried gently.

"Look," said David, pointing to the cat. "Don't you think it's odd?"

"What's so strange about a cat?" Lisa asked.

"The cat hasn't moved from earlier," said David. "It's still washing its kittens since we entered. How long have we been inside?"

"A couple of hours," Lisa replied, looking at her watch. "What the...this can't be right. It's only ten to eight?"

"It was almost half past seven when we arrived. It's been a mere twenty minutes?" David said, puzzled. The sweat rolled down his back.

"That can't be right," said Lisa. "We were in there for at least two hours."

David, sweating more now and stinking from how it mixed with the musty, rank dust, opened the car trunk and put the books inside.

Inside the car, Lisa sat silently and stared at her wristwatch. "seven fifty-eight," she mumbled. "Same as the car clock."

They sat in the car and stared ahead. David's hands cramped around the steering wheel, eyes squinting. He strained his mind to think and eventually turned to face Lisa. "My word, Lisa. Do you understand what the hell has happened? I can't even process how…" he said, trailing off.

Lisa shook her head and shrugged. "I feel like I've been drugged. Are we out of our minds?"

"When we got here, it was half past eight, and for about two hours we were in the room, and now it's ten to nine," David said. "So, babe, either we got the time wrong, or something happened in that house."

"Time passed...slower," Lisa said.

"Yes, exactly," said David, and started the car. "Like something you see in the sci-fi movies."

"I'm scared," said Lisa, her voice shaky. "What if something more has happened that we don't know yet?"

"Who knows," said David. "You have any ideas?" David backed the car out of the parking spot.

"There has to be an explanation," Lisa muttered without moving her eyes off her watch. She glanced at David and asked, "When we were here the first time with Harry, did you notice anything strange then?"

"No," he said.

"There's something weird going on in our new house, David. I love the house, but." David saw a little fear in her eyes.

David drove towards the gate and said, "That day when we came here with Harry, we went through the whole property. Nothing strange or unusual happened then. So, I think there is something mysterious about that room. I want to find out more about it later, but right now I just want to go through the notes." He stopped the car at the gate. "Don't worry. We aren't not rush to move into our new house, we haven't put our current house on the market yet, so we won't move in until we figure out what is the story with that room and Alice's disappearance."

Lisa got out to open the gate and then sat in the car again. David felt a slight tint of guilt at how shaken she seemed to be. Much of the drive was made in silence. David thought about all scenarios about what could have just happened. Still, it all seemed so far-fetched and unrealistic that he could not find the words to communicate it to Lisa. And so, David said nothing.

The Time Walkers

Chapter 7

David had gathered himself by the time they arrived home. "It's okay, sweetheart. We don't know what happened. Maybe we got the times wrong. Maybe some energy field stopped our watch and car batteries or made them malfunction, for goodness' sake. There must be some logical explanation. I'll figure it out. I promise."

Lisa looked at David and nodded. "I'm still uncomfortable." She held her hands out. They were shaking. "Look at my hands, David. Shit."

When they got out of the car, they carried the notebooks inside and set them on the table in the living room. "Honey," he said, "could you get us something cold to drink? This might take a while." David took a seat at the table and opened one of the notebooks.

On the first page was a dried leaf, and on it was a hand-drawn red heart. In the center of the heart was written, "Jay." David read,

TOMORROW I'M GOING TO MEET JAY AT THE LOOKOUT, AND I'M GOING TO SURPRISE HIM WITH A PICNIC BASKET OF HIS FAVORITE

FOOD. THIS MORNING I ASKED JAMES TO ARRANGE SOME ROSES I WANT TO GIVE JAY. TOMORROW WILL BE THE THIRD ANNIVERSARY OF OUR FIRST MEETING, AND I WANT TO DO SOMETHING SPECIAL FOR HIM.

David attempted to rise from his chair, but he was so entranced by the book in his hands. He stood gazing ahead for a few moments, absorbed by the words on the page. Lisa walked in and saw that David still reading.

David continued to read.

"Anything interesting?" asked Lisa.

David smirked. "Everything."

Lisa sat on the other side of the table and took out a notebook. "David," she said as she opened it. "Look, David. There are lots of numbers, calculations, and diagrams. All of the pages show numbers."

David looked. "Definitely not ordinary mathematics. This is something very advanced." He flipped through the book. At the back were some blueprints. "What have we here?"

"Do you think it belongs to Alice?" asked Lisa.

David scratched his head. "I don't know. But why would it be among her notebooks if it's not hers?"

Lisa breathed out loudly. "I doubt it belongs to Alice. How could a twenty-year-old master such advanced mathematics?" She shook her head. "But...if not her, then whose is it?"

"It's beyond us," said David. "We have to turn to someone who knows more more about the formulas." He closed the book and reached for another. "Put it away and see what else we have here."

At first, the shock overwhelmed him. He started to browse the book more intently. He examined each page with growing excitement.

"This looks like...," he whispered, falling silent again. The book contained pictures and explanatory texts showing how different parts of the structures were connected. All of them were interconnected by a cord that led up to a particular piece of furniture in the room. When David saw what it was, his heart rate began to race. It was the grandfather clock from the room whose features -- marble dial and solid oak body – were depicted accurately on the book's pages. "Lisa, come see! It's a machine!"

Lisa looked. "A grandfather clock paired with a cord to a... I don't know, it could be... no, I can't come up with anything. What do you think it could be?"

"I don't know, but I suspect something…" he muttered, staring at the picture. He leaned out onto the terrace and lit a cigarette to ponder. Further away in the park, David saw some people playing ball and chasing each other with water pistols. Suddenly, Lisa snuck up behind him and put her arms around him.

"What's on your mind?" whispered Lisa.

"If I only knew," said David puffing out cigarette smoke. "This mystery is just getting weirder and weirder. I don't understand any of it."

"Is it the blueprints you're brooding over?"

David nodded. "Among other things. How could she have such

knowledge?"

"Maybe she was keeping the blueprints for someone."

"Maybe."

"Throw away the cigarette and come inside," said Lisa, grabbing his arm.

David did. "I'm going to keep the blueprints for a while. Maybe I can show them to an expert."

David re-read Alice's diary, searching for clues. In one line, Alice confessed that she suspected James had feelings for her and found it flattering, but still felt sorry for him.

"Okay," said Lisa. "So, Alice suspected that James had feelings for her."

"There is nothing that can explain their fate," said David. "Nothing about the blueprints either. On some lines I saw Alice wrote about things disappearing in her room. She wrote of feeling that someone was watching her. I wonder if James had something to do with all the items disappearing from Alice's room."

David rubbed his eyes. He wanted to call it a day, eat dinner, and slip into the comfort of holding Lisa in bed. Just be with her and let the rest of this slide till tomorrow. "We're not getting any wiser. That's enough for now. We have gone through everything and haven't found anything. Tomorrow I'll go return the diaries."

"If only we could find the shed James moved into," said Lisa. "Maybe we'll find something interesting there."

David sighed, his strength waning. "It should be easy to find if it's still on the property. We'll just search around the land close to the house."

Lisa glanced at her watch. "Oh shoot! It's almost six-thirty, so I'd better get started on dinner."

"What if the scientist hid the blueprints among Alice's diaries?" he wondered aloud, standing with his arms crossed.

Lisa shook salt on the meat and asked, "What happened to that professor? And that burglar?"

"Maybe the scientist invented a time machine and then used it to disappear?" said David.

Lisa looked at him in amazement. "Tell me you're joking," she said.

David chopped tomatoes, chewing a cucumber slice. "Maybe the scientist found a way to travel in time without the knowledge of others," he said. "I actually read in a science magazine that during WWII Hitler tried to build a time machine. The year the scientist moved into the house was 1948, shortly after the war, and I know several scientists left Germany."

"If these blueprints belonged to this scientist, there may be several notes he has hidden somewhere in the house or in Alice's room," said Lisa. "Maybe we should search the whole house for the blueprints?"

Lisa's phone beeped. David watched her read the message, her expression growing sadder by the second.

"What's wrong?" asked David.

"Mary says she's picked up her things from work, handed in her keys and her badge, and is on her way over here." As the fan blew her hair this way and that, she looked at David and said, "We have to help her. I just can't leave her alone given what she's done for us." She looked at David, tears in her eyes.

David got up from his chair and put his hands on her shoulders. "Honey, we're going to help her. I promise. I'll call around and check with my friends. Maybe they have something for her."

"It would be wonderful if we could help her," said Lisa. "Her daughter and the house she bought after her husband's death had brought her joy again. Now her dreams have collapsed."

David went out to call his friend Eric. He knew Eric was looking for people for his company, so that might be a good lead. Outside, a neighbor was having a barbecue bash, and their music filled the neighborhood. The scent of cooked meats and vegetables drifted into the air. David smiled.

As he sat, he lit a cigarette and dialed Eric's number. A moment later, Eric answered with a polite hello.

"Are you perhaps still looking for new people for your company?" David asked.

"Yes, I am," Eric answered. "I've interviewed five in two days, but none of them are qualified for the job. Most don't have the leadership skills or experience needed."

"I think I have what you're looking for," said David.

"Really?"

"Yep, and worth at least an interview."

"Tell me more."

David cleared his throat. "Her name's Mary. She's thirty-one years old. She has an MBA with ten years of experience. Four years in marketing and six years as sales manager in a pharmaceutical company. She's a sharp negotiator." David took a drag of his cigarette. He exhaled and said, "What kind of roles are you looking to fill?"

"A sales manager and a human resources manager," said Eric.

"She'd fit both, but she's better at selling."

"Is there anything you want to add before I meet her?" Eric asked.

"A couple of months ago, France showed interest in a new category of antibiotics that the company had developed. If the deal had gone through, it would've been worth a quarter of a billion. After many weeks of negotiations, everything looked promising, but for some reason France backed out and canceled the deal. The top executives blamed her and after much pressure she had to quit, but she was not alone at that negotiating table. Mary has made billions for the company in the past. She has sold many products, and I guarantee it will cost the company dearly when she quits."

He glanced at his watch before continuing, "She's reliable and trustworthy. I'm telling you this as a friend. If you grant her the opportunity, you won't be disappointed." His gaze shifted to the other side of the street, where his neighbor was busy flipping burgers on a sizzling barbeque grill.

"I understand," said Eric. "Did you say Mary? Is she the one at the

Christmas party at your house last year? The woman whose husband was killed in a car accident?"

"Yes, that's her," said David. "There were a lot of guests there. I'm surprised you remember her."

"She was the only person there who I hit it off with," said Eric. "We talked mostly about work and a little about her late husband. She told me after the death of her husband, she tried to forget by working as much as she could."

"Yeah," said David, "she's had a real hard time. She's doing well as a single mother. Both personally and professionally, she is a tough person, Eric. She's a determined and awesome negotiator. If you hire her, you'll be a winner. You have my word."

"I trust you," said Eric. "Give me her number and I'll call her today."

"She's already on her way to my place," said David. "As soon as she comes, I'll have her call you."

The second the call was ended, the doorbell rang. Lisa opened the door to a Mary. She looked at Lisa with her brown eyes, wet with. Her blond hair was damp with sweat. When she started to cry, Lisa hugged her. "Calm down, sweetie," said Lisa. "It'll be okay. Trust me." Lisa led Mary inside and closed the door.

"I've put so much time and work into this company, and what do they do? They treat me like a piece of shit. Colleagues are pushing me away. Today when I was in my office to pick up my things, the boss came in. I begged him to reconsider, but he just looked at me and said no. He accused me again of lack of trust." As Mary wiped her tears, David felt bad for her.

Lisa sat next to her as Mary sobbed. "I think about my child and her future," said Mary. "The house I bought. Are we going to be homeless? I'm so scared, Lisa. I feel like I'm falling apart. Yesterday I sat up all night thinking about my life and where it went wrong. I twisted and turned everything and tried to understand what went wrong at that table, but I didn't understand it. And now I'm the bad guy."

"Mary, you have to be strong for your daughter," said Lisa. "David and I will do whatever we can to help you." Then she turned to David.

David smiled gently as he walked toward Mary. "Hi, Mary."

Mary stood up and hugged him. "Okay, let's take a deep breath," He gave Mary a smile and said, "I've got something good to share. I want you to call a certain someone and introduce yourself. Say that David recommended you." David handed Mary his phone. "Call that number now."

"But who will I be speaking to?" asked Mary.

"You'll see," David said. "It's about some work I think you'd be perfect for. Just make the call."

As Mary called the number, David heard Eric answer from the other side.

"Hello, my name is Mary. David told me to call you, and I apologize, as I don't really know what this is about."

While Mary was talking, David made a glass of cold lemonade for everyone.

David and Lisa sat in the living room and waited for Mary. "How's the lemonade?" asked David.

"Just what I needed," said Lisa. She took a gulp of it and kissed him on the cheek.

"What was that for?" asked David.

Lisa looked at him, and her eyes sparkled. "For being so lovely and helping Mary like this."

Mary glided through the terrace door and into the living room a few minutes later. She was quiet, and sadness spread across her face before she broke into a smile. She leaned against them both, hugging them close. In a soft voice, she attempted to thank them but struggled to find the right words. After taking a deep breath, her voice steadied.

"What you did is inexpressible," she began.

David interrupted, "No. What you did for us is indescribable. You helped us find each other. You led us to one another. What we did for you pales in comparison. You deserve only the greatest things life can offer because you are a fighter." David spoke with his hand over his heart.

When he finished speaking, tears streamed down Mary's cheeks, and she sank onto the couch.

Lisa moved forward with a tissue in hand. "Don't cry. Everything will be fine now. I told you everything would be fine."

Mary nodded in agreement and smiled back. Her face shone with joy as she took Lisa's hand. "Thank you for the help and all the support you have given me," she said, crying uncontrollably again. "These are just tears of joy," she said, laughing.

David picked up his glass and announced, "Let's toast to a happy ending."

They happily toasted to Mary several times until finally, it was Mary who ended the toasting. "I have to go prepare for tomorrow's meeting with Eric. Thank you again, both of you for your help," she said, walking towards the door. She turned and hugged both David and Lisa once more, then left.

"I'm so glad we were able to help her," said Lisa closing the door.

David's phone began to ring. "Honey, I'm going to take this in the other room." In the other room, David answered, "Hello?"

"David! It's André. How are you?"

"Just fine," replied David.

"I hope I'm not bothering you," said André.

"No, not at all," said David. "What did you find out?"

"Well, it's about Jay Murphy, who died in 1939. I found something that you might find interesting."

"Please, do share."

"While I was going through the old case file, I found something about a police report."

"What kind of police report?"

"Sabotage."

"Sabotage?"

"Yes," said André. "It says here that Jay ran a company in the airline industry and that it's suspected someone had sabotaged one of the planes. Jay was the designated pilot, but someone took his place at the last moment."

"Go on," urged David. He felt blood rushing through his body again.

"Turns out someone had tampered with the plane," said André. "It crashed; you see."

"Oh my God!"

"Unfortunately, the pilot died. Jay reported the whole thing. Apparently, the fuel hose came off, or that someone had cut it off. That's what it says here anyway."

David rubbed his chin. "You said that the crash happened a month before Jay's death. Right?"

"Yes, yes," André replied.

"Could there be a connection between the events, do you think?" David asked. He could hear André thinking.

"It's possible, sure," said André. "But it could be mere coincidence. Why was it again this story is important to you?"

"Personal interest," said David.

"Ah yes, curiosity, same for me."

"Yes, exactly. I appreciate everything you're doing for me; thank you, truly."

"It's my pleasure," said André. "If I find more, I'll let you know."

David paced around the room, his hands raking through his hair as he muttered in deep thought. His gaze shifted between the window and the notes across the coffee table. He went out onto the terrace, a cigarette already between his lips. The sun was setting behind the trees, with large billowing clouds providing much-needed protection from its rays. Taking one final drag of his cigarette, David stepped back inside.

Lisa greeted him with a smile and steaming cups of coffee, which she sat on the table. He flopped down on the couch with an exhausted sigh and sipped his coffee, lost in thought. Not taking his eyes off Lisa, he related what he had discovered: "Jay apparently reported to the police a plane crash that happened at his company, just a month before he was found dead, but there was nothing in the Alice's diary notes about it."

Lisa took a bite out of a bun. "Maybe Alice wrote the diaries before the crash?"

"You may be right," said David. "I'll see if there are dates on the books." Sure enough, going through the books revealed more. "Here it says February 1939. Here is the last diary, and the date is the twentieth of April.

"So, there is a diary MISSING between the crash and his death, and after his death there are no more. I see that Alice was careful to write every day, and she wrote in her diary that something strange was happening in her room, as two of her diaries had disappeared in the past." David put the books back in the box and sat back down. "In the morning I'll go back to the house and return the diaries. I'm going to go through the room one more time. Maybe we'll find something like footprint, maybe some other notebooks, or something about Jay."

Behroz Behnejad

Chapter 8

The sound of cats hissing on the terrace startled David awake. He glanced up at the clock and decided to investigate. When he stepped out onto the balcony, the cats scattered. Taking a deep breath, he looked out into the morning sky. He appreciated the cool air and peacefulness that nature provided.

"Finally," he thought, sighing relief over winning this battle against the heat.

David crept back inside and quietly walked over to Lisa, who was still asleep. He leaned in and whispered sweetly into her ear: "Honey?" No response. Smiling, he kissed her cheek, then bounded to the living room to pick up the box and bring it down to the car.

David looked up at the sky and saw a looming gray cloud, its edges gradually darkening as it slowly approached. A gust of wind battered his face, scattering leaves from the nearby trees.

He reached for his keys in his car and scrambled up the stairs with a box tucked under his arm. ~~He~~ added a flashlight to the box just in case—better to be prepared this time. Finally managing to open the door, David stepped into an empty living room and surveyed the scene with a heavy sigh.

As he descended the stairs, he saw a small picture of Alice sitting on the bookshelf. He hadn't seen it there the day before when he and Lisa had visited. As he stepped closer, he felt a tingling sensation in his stomach. The picture seemed different from how it had appeared last week, but he couldn't put his finger on exactly how.

He couldn't shake the feeling that something strange was afoot, though he couldn't explain what. His frustration mounting, he spun around and decided to investigate further by checking the time before entering the room - so he could later compare it to whatever time he saw when he left.

He clutched the box to his chest, glanced at his watch – 8:30 am– then took a deep breath before stepping into the room, as though he was crossing an invisible threshold. David placed the box on the floor and flicked on the flashlight. When it illuminated the room, he froze in shock. His heart raced.

"What happened here?! Who did this?!" he yelled. He shone the light around the furniture and walls and noticed an unmade bed with stuffed animals scattered all over the floor. The wardrobe was open and in disarray. "Someone has been rummaging through here," he thought as a knot formed in his stomach. Upon closer inspection, he saw that every item was just as dusty and covered in cobwebs as if they had remained untouched for years. "This is impossible! Everything was in order yesterday when we were here, but now it looks like someone has torn through everything! Even the bed is messed up…this is so weird… what could have happened?" he murmured.

David swept the beam of his flashlight across the desk. He noticed a book lying there. It looked as if it had been untouched for years. It was covered in dust, and a pencil lay next to it. His heart raced, and he stepped closer. He ran his finger along its spine and lifted it gingerly, astonished he had never seen it before. He peeled away the cobwebs that clung to its cover and slowly opened the book. On the first page, scrawled in script long forgotten, he read:

Today I saw an unfamiliar figure in my room. They have taken all my diaries from me – every single one! I feel robbed of my memories, my thought, my childhood events, and all the date nights I had with Jay – everything is gone! Desperately searching through the mess, they left behind, I can find no trace of them. They are gone forever… Who could do something so cruel?

David's breath came out in shallow gasps as he wiped the sweat from his forehead. He clicked on his flashlight and pointed it at a box, his brow furrowed in concentration. His eyes flashed over the words scrawled across the lid: no date or any other identifying mark. With a trembling hand, he turned to the wall clock and noted that it was still ticking away with accurate time.

"This is insane," he muttered under his breath.

He picked up the box and set it next to the desk before turning around to leave. In an absentminded gesture, David left the bookcase askew. On his way out, he grabbed Alice's photograph from the bookshelf and tucked it into the crook of his arm.

Out in the fresh air of the yard, David inhaled deeply several times before glancing at his watch. "Seven forty-five". He shucked off his sweat-soaked sweater and tossed it into the car alongside the picture. Lifting his gaze skyward, he noticed that the sun is disappeared behind dark clouds, and a wind had picked up. Large raindrops splashed down against his bare skin. Thunder roared in accompaniment, followed shortly by a lightning strike just a few yards away.

David gasped as he saw a tree top engulfed in flames, sending sparks into the sky. He flung himself towards it, grasping a large leafy branch from the ground and beating at the blaze with every ounce of strength. Fear raced through his veins as he thought of what would happen if the wind took hold of this fire and spread it toward the house. The rain was pouring by now, but David kept striking at the flames until he was sure they were completely extinguished.

Unexpectedly, something flew at David, missing him by only an inch.

"Shit!" he screamed, protecting his head with his arms as he jumped away. He landed badly on a rock and writhed in pain. David peeked between his fingers to see what had happened and saw that a small chunk of roofing had fallen on him. WHERE DID IT COME FROM? THERE WAS NO HOUSE IN THAT DIRECTION. Carefully he looked in the direction from which the piece of roofing had come flying and saw that something was hidden behind the bushes. David crawled forward and discovered a shed that stood apart from the rest of the yard.

The thunder rumbled as the clouds began to disperse, allowing a streak of sunshine to peek through. David's eyes widened in amazement at the shed, and he whispered under his breath, "This must be where James lived."

He limped slowly towards it but was blocked by a large fallen tree. His hands stretched out hopefully to push on the door, only to find it locked tight with an old rust-covered padlock. He grumbled in frustration and ran a hand through his soaked hair.

"I guess I'll have to come back tomorrow with my toolbox and a chainsaw!" With a resigned sigh, he fastened his torn shirt around him and plopped lightly into his car, taking off down the dirt road.

At home, a concerned Lisa was waiting. "Oh, David! I've tried calling you a dozen times! What have you...?" She stopped when she saw him and stared. "What's happened?"

David walked in and closed the door behind him. He shook his head. "You're, you're not gonna believe this."

"Okay, come on, tell me," Lisa said.

"You remember what Alice's room looked like yesterday, don't you?" David asked, limping towards the kitchen.

"Sure," Lisa replied.

"Tell me what you saw there," David said.

Lisa rubbed her forehead. "On the bed, I saw some stuffed animals in a row. In the wardrobe, I found nice dresses and a few boxes of hats and shoes. In one corner was a dressing table with a bunch of items and some perfume. But where are you going with this?"

David frowned. "When I was there today, the BED WAS UNMADE, and all the stuffed animals were ON THE FLOOR. The wardrobe was OPEN, and some of the drawers had been pulled out. Some of Alice's dresses were on the bed. The room was A MESS. Someone has very clearly been there, looking for something."

"Ok? What do you mean someone was there? How could it be?" Lisa said. She busied herself and went to make coffee, but David could see she was shaken. She placed the coffee on the table.

David explained. "I could have been a burglar, but if a burglary occurred there, it must have happened a long time ago. Oddly enough, each piece alone looked untouched. No one has been in the room for a long time. Cobwebs were on everything, even on the stuffed animals on the floor. So, there was no evidence of a recent disturbance of those items. If someone had entered, there would be evidence, but I found no such thing."

"But why didn't the room look like it did yesterday?" Lisa asked.

David held his coffee as he spoke to Lisa. "Also strange was that I found a notebook on the desk, and I didn't see it there yesterday. In it, Alice wrote, that someone took all her diaries. She had looked everywhere and turned everything upside down."

"If the diaries were gone, how could we have found them in the wardrobe yesterday?"

"You're right about that." David stood and headed for the

bedroom.

"Where are you going?" Lisa asked.

David began changing into dry clothes. "I have to go back to the house again and find out what's going on there. I would be eternally grateful if you would come with me. Most likely, I found the shed James lived in as well."

"Are you sure it's the right shed?" Lisa asked.

"Not one hundred percent sure, but I have a strong feeling it's the right one," he responded, limping out of the bedroom. David went to the door, turned to Lisa, and said, "Come on, let's investigate."

Lisa looked hesitantly at David and asked, "Shouldn't we have your leg checked beforehand?"

David shook his head. "It's not that bad. We'll do that later, but before we go, could you please get the toolbox?"

Lisa nodded and did as asked.

The gust of wind that passed through the city was almost like a friendly embrace, carrying the sweet smell of rain with it. The sky was clear and bright everywhere he looked, but he could still hear a few distant rumbles of thunder. His skin tingled as the sun's heat touched him.

"Incredible! Can you imagine? One second, a heavy thunderstorm, and now this," said a surprised Lisa, standing behind David. "David, look at that man across the street. He's looking at us – and smiling."

David looked but saw no one. "Where?"

"I...I saw him right there, just now," she said. "He was standing there, right under that tree. He had a beard and sunglasses." She looked at David. "He saw a man, with a beard, but I just can't place him, at all."

David shook his head. "No, Lisa, there's no one there, not right now at least. Maybe he went into the house over there."

"In that case, he's really fast. It's a long way between the tree and the house. You believe me, don't you?"

"Of course, I do, but right now we have other things to think about." David took her arm and led her towards the car. Lisa picked up the photo from the seat and asked, "Okay, what is this picture doing here?"

"I found it in the house in the room next to Alice's room," David replied.

"I don't remember it being there yesterday. It was in the living room when we were there with Harry Why didn't the previous owner take the photo with them?"

David just shook his head, shrugged, and started the car.

"But how strange. The picture looks a little DIFFERENT from the one that we saw the first time," Lisa said.

"I think so too," David said, turning on the air conditioning.

"You took a picture of the photo with your phone when we were there with Harry," said Lisa Look at that and see if it's the same picture."

David handed his phone to Lisa. "Look for yourself."

Lisa brought up the picture, and when she compared the two, she was surprised. She looked at David and said, "Stop! I'll show you."

David drove onto the side of the road, took the car out of gear, and leaned against her.

Lisa pointed at the picture. "Look at this. She has her hair pinned up with a flower and is wearing a patterned dress. But on your phone, though, her hair is down."

"What do you think? Could there be several pictures in the house?" David asked.

"We'll see when we get there," Lisa said.

Behroz Behnejad

Chapter 9

David stepped on the gas pedal and drove as fast as he dared. When they finally reached the house, what they saw was a disaster. Near the main building, several roof tiles were scattered around, and one windowpane lay shattered with glass strewn everywhere.

David shook his head and whispered, "A monstrous storm."

When they entered the house, they stepped on broken pieces of glass. A few pieces of wood had flown in through the window and caused minor damage to the living room. Rainwater had come into the house and destroyed the floor. Lisa bent down, picked up a piece of wood, shook her head, and said, "A good start to our new house." She threw it and sighed.

David walked around, kicked some pieces of glass, and turned to Lisa. "We can't do anything about this now. What's happened has happened, but we can always fix it. Let's go down to the room and have a look." He took Lisa's arm and led them to Alice's room. David pointed to the bookshelf. "This is where I found the photo."

"Shall we go in?" asked Lisa, her voice shaky.

David smirked. "What is it? Are you scared?"

"No," said Lisa. "Well, maybe a tad. What if something happens and I panic. You go first."

David opened the door with a creak. He switched on the flashlight and searched the room. "What? It's not possible!"

"What is it?" Lisa asked. "Why are you shouting?"

David directed the light so she could see. "Look."

David watched her look around. "Do you see?"

"No...," she replied.

"Look," said David. "Everything is in order. It's been magically cleaned up in here!" David stepped into the room. Lisa followed him inside. "When I was here this morning, everything was on the floor and the room was messy, but now everything is back in its place again. Aside from us, no one has been here for years. Now look," he said, pointing his flashlight to the bed and desk. "Do you see all the dust and cobwebs? No one has been here, yet everything has been moved." David walked around with a pounding heart. He directed the flashlight back and forth, examining everything. Lisa held onto him tightly, following every step he took without letting go of his arm.

Dazed, David pointed his flashlight at the grandfather clock and curiously approached it. He saw some black cables on the back connected from the clock to the wall. He also saw a small flashing light behind the clock that lit up every three seconds. He leaned forward and peered at the lamp to take a closer look. He touched the cables lightly and tried to gently pull them out, but they were stuck tightly to the wall.

"Look, Lisa, a flashing light," said David. He breathed heavily to keep his flashlight steady. Nervously, he turned to Lisa. "What in the world could that be? And where could the cable lead?" He looked around the room. Sweat dripped down his forehead, and he tried to wipe it off with his shirt sleeve while pointing his flashlight at the desk. He moved the light faster and faster back and forth over the desk surface and the floor below.

"What are you looking for?" Lisa asked.

"The cardboard box with all the diaries that I left at the desk here. It's not there!" said David.

Lisa walked around the desk and looked under the table. "No, there's nothing here. Are you sure you left the box here?" she asked, looking under the table.

"Absolutely sure," he said, nodding emphatically.

"But the box isn't here now," said Lisa. She took the flashlight from David and walked towards the wardrobe. She opened it, paused, and then looked at David. "The box is here in the wardrobe."

David hurried over to Lisa. Lisa dusted off the thick layer of dust on the lid. When she opened it, David saw all the diaries in the box. David stared at the box in amazement and shook his head. "But I put the box over there," said David. He pointed to the desk. "How could the box have ended up here? And why is it so dusty?" He stood up and pointed his flashlight at the desk. "Now let me see..." He saw the same notebook on the desk that he had seen this morning. He examined the book with the flashlight in hand and found it covered in a heavy layer of dust. He brushed off the cover and removed the cobwebs, opened the book, and read:

> UNBELIEVABLE! I FOUND ALL MY DIARIES HERE IN A CARDBOARD BOX UNDER MY DESK TODAY, IT SEEMS SOMEONE HAS COME INTO MY ROOM AND RETURNED THEM, BUT THE QUESTION IS HOW! YESTERDAY THE DIARIES WERE GONE, BUT TODAY THEY'RE IN MY ROOM AGAIN. EVERYONE WAS AT HOME; I WAS ALWAYS IN MY ROOM, SO WHY HAVEN'T WE SEEN ANYONE? I'M GOING CRAZY.

Lisa and David looked at each other. "There must be a logical explanation," said Lisa, hands on her hips.

David nodded. "When we were here to pick up the diaries, she wrote that they were gone – and now that I have returned them, she wrote this. That means SHE'S BEEN IN THE ROOM," David said, chewing his lips.

"What are you talking about?" asked Lisa. "How could she have been here yesterday when she lived in the forties? Seventy years ago?"

"But what about her writing?" said David. "Is it just a coincidence that she wrote that the diaries were gone when we had taken them, or that she found the box when I returned it? It makes no sense." Suddenly he had an idea. He looked at Lisa. "I suspect that somehow, she makes contact with us, but without ultimately knowing whether we've actually found and read her comments. I'll leave a message in her diary to see if she responds. I'm sure something strange is going on in this room."

He took a pencil from his back pocket and wrote in Alice's diary:

HELLO! I BOUGHT THIS HOUSE, I AM DAVID. I WAS THE ONE WHO TOOK YOUR DIARIES. I'M SORRY I UPSET YOU. PLEASE WRITE ME SOMETHING WHEN YOU SEE MY MESSAGE.

David looked at Lisa and smiled. "This should be enough, so now let's hope for an answer. This feels a little silly, but I have no other choice, and I really want to try it." He closed the journal.

"Do you really think it's possible you can connect with her?" asked Lisa.

David hesitated and then cast his gaze at the grandfather clock. "That clock is no ordinary clock. Something is hidden inside it and behind the wall. Maybe a time machine?" he said, shrugging.

Lisa stared at David. "David, I'm freaked out. I want to leave now."

David squinted. "I'm thinking of that scientist who lived here in the forties and who disappeared without a trace. The neighbors called him a mad scientist because he was probably working on something secret, and people thought he had awakened demons, he never talked to the neighbors. I mean, that "burglar" got in and never came out... The blueprint we found! Everything indicates that something supernatural has happened AND IS STILL HAPPENING. What if the scientist was able to invent the time machine and travelled in time himself? And what if, after all these years, the machine still works?"

David once again examined the clock.

"If so, there is a risk that we are traveling in time right now without knowing it," said Lisa, looking around. "Again, it's so absurdly unreal, though, and is creeping me out."

"No, I don't think there's that risk," David said. "When we were here for the first time, we saw that the hands on the clock were turning in the wrong direction, and after spending what we thought was a couple of hours in the room, we noticed that only about twenty minutes had passed. There was also a beeping sound in here coming from the wall behind the clock. Something had happened, and the answer could perhaps be found behind the wall and in this grandfather clock."

"Okay, so how can you be so sure that we are not traveling in time now?" Lisa asked.

"As long as we do not hear a beeping sound and the hands on the clock go in the right direction, we are in the right time," said David. "If there is a time machine, it starts around ten and turns off automatically around half past twelve or one."

"Come on. How do you know that?" Lisa asked, staring at the grandfather clock.

"Hear me out. This morning I was here between half past eight and a quarter past ten and saw that everything was messy and untidy, and that hands on the clock were turning in the right direction, and now..." David looked at his watch, "... it's twenty past two and everything is in order, and everything is tidy. That means something has transpired here between ten and one."

David looked at the grandfather clock, turned to Lisa and continued. "That's enough in here for today. I just hope to get a response to my message." He took Lisa's hand in his and led her from the room. "Let's go check out the shed that James probably lived in. Maybe we can find something in there."

When they came out, the sun was shining, and there were no traces of the storm other than the physical destruction when they got to the house. There were cloudless skies above them, and the sun tickled their shoulders.

"Come with me and I'll show you where the shed is," said David. He took his toolbox with him.

"Why are you in such a hurry?" said Lisa in her attempt at keeping up with his stride.

"We have a lot of work to do," said David.

"I'm tired and need rest. And I'm thirsty" She fell silent when she saw the shed. "Is that the shed James lived in?" she said, pointing to the dilapidated building.

The red paint had fallen off, and the rest of the siding had been stained grey by weather during the years since Alice's father had built it. A piece of the roof had been destroyed by the storm, but despite all the years and bad weather, the little dwelling stood on steady ground. On one side was a window that was all black and couldn't be seen through. Lisa crept forward and cupped her hands against it.

"Can you see anything?" David asked as he walked to the door. He searched among his tools, hoping to find something to get the rusty padlock open and pull away the tree trunk blocking the entrance.

"No, nothing!" Lisa said, walking away from the window.

David examined the door. "It opens inward," he muttered. He stood at the door and looked at Lisa. "Hammer, please." Lisa handed him the hammer.

"What are you going to do?" asked Lisa.

"You'll see," said David. He struck the lock with the hammer. The lock fell uselessly to the ground. David jumped down from the trunk to kick open the door. Something flew out the door, and Lisa screamed in fear.

"What the hell was that?" asked Lisa, jumping back.

David protected his face with his hands and cautiously peeked between his fingers. "Just a few birds that probably took shelter inside from the storm." He reached out his hand to Lisa and, without looking at her, said, "Give me the flashlight."

Lisa gaped at him. "I think I left it in Alice's room."

"There might be an extra one in there," David said, pointing at the toolbox.

"You're right," said Lisa, handing him a flashlight.

David stepped through the door and turned it on. Every step he took made the floor creak. Stepping into the shed was like stepping into a place that time had forgotten. It had been almost seventy years since anyone had been there. The air smelled rotten and stale, was heavy to breathe and full of dust – so ungodly hot and stuffy, and cobwebs could be seen everywhere.

When David entered the shed, he saw garden equipment leaning against the wall. Above it hung a leather bag, as if someone had just taken it off. David could feel the stiffness of the leather when he touched it. Further into the room, he could see an old worn violin that looked completely ruined lying on a table. To the right of the table was a large hammer, and next to one of the windows hung a gold-colored clock which had stopped at half past two. David saw some old-fashioned bottles, measuring cups, and scissors on a shelf under the clock. Two oil lamps stood on either side of the shelf, and he could see traces of oil in them.

David found an old rusty sink in a corner that James had probably washed himself in. A basket suspended above the sink contained old razors and something resembling a bar of soap. Under the sink was some shoe polish in very old packaging.

At the end of the shed, Lisa pointed out an old broken bed and a worn chest of drawers next to the bed. The storm had made a hole in the ceiling, and rain had formed a large puddle in the middle of the decrepit mattress.

"Look what I've found," said Lisa, handing David an old photo.

David rushed forward and carefully took the photo to examine it. Half the faces in the photo were ruined, but it wasn't hard to see that it was Alice in the picture. He stared at it briefly but then put it back in the drawer.

Lisa turned to David. "The sight of all this is eerie and strange. I feel a little uncomfortable being in this place, as you know, but at the same time, it's fascinating to see all these tools and utensils. All the things that remain clearly show who lived here. I can even learn things about his personality." Lisa walked around and looked at the room. "It's like a masterpiece. I feel close to James somehow like he could walk in here at any moment.

"Being in this room is like walking with history close by," Lisa whispered. David watched as she stepped on a floorboard. It broke so forcefully underneath her weight that she fell into the hole below and screamed.

David hurried to help her up. "Are you okay? Lucky it didn't go deeper than your knees."

"I'm okay, I think, but I landed on something."

David pointed the flashlight at the hole and saw that she had fallen through a hatch in the floor. At the bottom was a metal box.

"Help me get it up," David said, putting down his flashlight. He bent forward to grab the handle. Carefully they lifted it up, but the handle came loose, poorly eaten by rust, and the entire contents of the box spilt out to the floor.

"It looks like notebooks, just like the ones we found at the house," said Lisa, and David noticed her perk up in that very second.

David didn't make a sound, just nodded. Slowly he reached out to touch the black leather covers.

"Could it be?" David said quietly. "Are these Alice's notebooks, or maybe James' journals?"

"But James couldn't read and write, could he?" said Lisa.

David held the notebook in his hand very still before putting it back in the box.

"David?" asked Lisa. "What is it?"

"I don't know," said David. He pushed the box away and looked at Lisa. "I have a feeling that James was hiding something. I don't know what. I can just feel it."

"Such as?" said Lisa. "After all, he was..." Lisa fell silent. "But what if he just hid behind his disability? What did he do?"

David's eyes did not let go of Lisa. He stared at her intensely. "We have to go home now. We found what we were looking for. We'll go through all the books at home. Maybe it'll shine some light on Jay's horrible murder and Alice's disappearance."

Outside they were greeted by the cool air. The sun had disappeared behind the trees, and some clouds were floating by in the sky as if in a hurry. No traces were left of the high waves on the sea from just a little while ago. The wind tickled David's sweaty back. He closed his eyes and took a deep breath. "A cold beer would be good now," he said, carrying the box.

"And I would give my right arm for a cold shower," laughed Lisa.

After a short walk, they came to the car. Exhausted and soaked, David opened the trunk and put the box inside. Weakly, he turned around and leaned against the car, fanning his face with a piece of paper. Then he heard something. Curious, he walked around and listened.

"What are you looking for now?" asked Lisa. "Let's get you back for that cold beer."

David glanced at her. "Listen. I hear something."

Lisa squinted. She pointed to a fallen tree. "It sounds like someone is panting, and the sound is coming from the fallen tree."

Over by the tree was a black dog with a large, heavy branch fallen over its body. It was whining and gasping from thirst and fear. The dog shook its tail and howled when it saw them.

David grabbed the large branch that had fallen over the dog and pushed it away. The dog was wearing a vest. "This looks pretty heavy," said David. " I don't think he's too hurt, maybe just dehydrated."

Lisa fumbled with the dog's vest. "It's stuck."

"He needs water," said David. "Quick, I saw a water tap over there. We'll carry him over." He picked up the dog, but the tap was broken.

He put the dog down gently and grabbed the tap. He tried to turn it on, but it was stuck. With all his strength managed to turn the stuck handle. It gave a squeak, and water began to flow from it. He poured water into the dog's mouth with cupped hands while Lisa rubbed cool water on its fur.

Slowly the dog came around and stood up. He drank his fill, and Lisa petted him and embraced him. David fiddled in vain with the vest. "It's too tight."

"Hey, there's something in the vest," said Lisa. "I felt a vibration when I touched it."

David touched the vest and looked at Lisa in wonder. "What could it be?"

Suddenly they heard footsteps approaching. A tall, heavy-set man with dark, messy hair swayed towards them. A dog walked beside him.

"Hello," said the messy-haired man. "My name is Peter, and I live a stone's throw from here. Are you the new owners who bought the house?"

"Yes," David answered and came forward to greet him. "My name's David and Lisa here is my fiancée."

"Nice to meet you," said Peter. "I heard a new owner had moved in, and I was hoping to say hello."

"Have you lived here long?" asked David.

"Twenty-five years," Peter replied.

"Have you seen this dog before?" David asked, hoping it belonged to someone nearby.

Peter looked at the dog. His face gave no expression of familiarity. "This little black dog? No, where did you find it?"

"It was here," said Lisa. "He was stuck under a fallen tree branch. David freed him, and we gave him some water."

The dogs began to sniff and lick each other gently. The black dog, still weak, sat down in the shade of a bush, and the other joined him.

"Did you see much of the previous owner?" David asked.

"Not much," Peter replied.

David leaned forward and patted the black dog. He glanced at Peter. "Anything you could tell me about the previous owners?"

Peter shook his head. "Not much. They were so secretive and mysterious. In all these years I only met him four or five times. They were almost never at home, and if they were, the lights were off. The family was invisible and never showed their faces outside. Given that I don't live very far from here, I could see activity and movement here in the house without seeing anyone," Peter replied.

"What kind of activity?" David asked.

Peter frowned as he patted the dog. In a low voice, he said, "Not to be rude, but I probably shouldn't be speaking about this."

"What do you mean?" Lisa asked.

"A lot of strange things have happened at that mansion," said Peter. "No one dares to talk about it anymore. Not even to the police."

"It's okay," said David. "Whatever is said will stay between us."

Peter looked around and stroked his forehead. He looked at David and then at Lisa. Large beads of sweat formed on his forehead. "One day at dawn I was out walking the dog. Suddenly I saw a giant lightning bolt strike down, but oddly enough, I didn't hear an explosion. At first, I thought it was a thunderstorm, but it was sunny and clear that day. To my surprise, I saw a large shiny object. It looked like a church bell, something dark brown, hovering over the yard. The object landed softly right over there," he explained, pointing to the stable. "I tried to hide, but the dog started barking. I tried to silence him and hurried over to hide behind the big tree." Peter fell silent, his gaze resting on the dogs.

David glanced at Lisa and back to Peter. "What happened next?"

Peter shook his head. "I can't. I don't want to talk anymore about that. I shouldn't have talked to you at all," Peter said, looking nervously to the left and right.

"We won't say anything, and no one is listening," Lisa said. "Come on, Peter, it's okay. We want to start our family here, have children, we need to know."

"Okay," said Peter. He wiped his palms on his pants and continued in a low voice. "When the object landed, I thought for a second that it was a UFO, but when the door to the object opened, to my surprise, I saw three human individuals in uniform who looked like they were getting out to walk around the yard. On their uniform was a symbol that reminded me of a cross or a swastika. One of them went to the house and looked through the windows, and then he shouted at the others, saying something in a foreign language that I did not understand. Soon after, they went back to the object. My dog started barking again. Quickly I tried to silence him, and when I looked up again, the object was gone. Oddly enough, I didn't hear any engine noise." Peter shook his head.

David blinked. "What language do you think it was? Did you recognize any of the words?"

Peter fixed his gaze on David and shook his head. "I don't know. Maybe Dutch or German. I couldn't even guess."

Lisa and David looked at each other. "What else happened here?" asked Lisa.

"I've said enough," Peter said.

"Please, tell us before we move in," Lisa asked.

Peter looked at her, and his voice was a whisper once more. "One afternoon two months ago, I was out with the dog at the jetty and threw him a stick. From a distance, I could see a light on in the house. I went there and thought I'd have a chat with my neighbor. But then something strange happened." He hesitated. "I saw a woman in an old-fashioned white dress, maybe from the thirties or forties, wandering around the yard. Carefully I approached her and saw that she was noticeably shaken by something. She looked around nervously and then saw me. Slowly, she stopped and took a few steps back. Unexpectedly, she burst into tears. Of course, I didn't know how to react or how to help her. She seemed stressed and absent-minded, somehow. With a trembling voice, she mumbled repeatedly, asking where she was. 'Why does everything look different here? Where am I?' she kept repeating."

Peter subsequently fell silent again. With a deep breath, he looked up to continue. "A car came running and stopped in front of the house. I saw my neighbor getting out of the car, rushing towards the woman. Stressed, he grabbed her and shouted, 'What are you doing out here? You're supposed to be in bed!' then he turned to me and said sharply that she was his niece, who'd come to visit them after a long journey. And then he roared at ME: 'What are you doing here on my land?' Turning to the woman again, my neighbor told her to go inside." Peter sighed. "I was curious, of course, and asked for the woman's name. She turned to me, her face all white, and said, 'Alice.' Then they went inside.

Peter proceeds: "As I turned to walk towards my house, the neighbor came running and called for me to wait. 'Wait a minute!" he shouted at me. I'm terribly sorry for what happened, and I wasn't myself at all. She simply shouldn't have shown up out here when she's sick, and I behaved inappropriately on top of that – I'm so sorry,' he said, begging my pardon. I nodded to acknowledge that. And still curious, I asked why she was wearing an old-fashioned dress. He shook his head nervously and replied tremblingly that she just comes up with many oddities. She dresses in old clothes sometimes because she is interested in vintage fashion. 'At home, she has many clothes like that,' he explained."

"Did you say she called herself Alice?" David asked.

Peter nodded.

David glanced at Lisa and quickly pulled out his cell phone. He brought up Alice's picture and asked eagerly, "Is this the woman you saw?"

Peter nodded. "Why, yes, that's her. Do you know who she is?"

"Not really," David said. "But I want to find out a little more about her."

"Why?" Peter asked.

"Writer's curiosity", David replied.

The sun was setting, and the wind had picked up, creating a pleasant atmosphere. "Is there anything else you can tell me?" David asked when he noticed Peter starting to leave.

Peter stopped. "One more thing," he said. "Another day, I saw her again, reeling around the yard. She gave me an alarming look, but as soon as I approached, she walked towards the house. Then, I also saw my neighbor sneaking up behind her. He grabbed her and before they disappeared, he looked at me with a threatening look. I mean, I was kinda shocked. My neighbor then closed the door behind them with a bang. I wasn't sure what was goin' down with that."

"Thank you for telling us all this," said David. "If you remember anything else, please, just call me," David said, handing him his business card.

Peter nodded. "I will, but I'd be much obliged if you don't tell anyone about our meeting." Slowly Peter walked back towards his house but then pivoted right back to them and muttered, "Oh, and when the men in uniform landed in the yard, two of them went into that stable. When they came out again, they had a yellow-colored box that shone in the sunlight and carried to the object. Look in the stable and maybe you'll find something," he said, then waved goodbye and left.

Lisa and David looked at each other for a moment. Lisa patted the do. "What have we gotten ourselves into? Swastikas, German-speaking men, and floating objects."

David pursed his lips. "Not to mention a girl who wore an old-fashioned dress and whose name was Alice, who also looked like Alice." David knelt and patted the dog.

"Frankly, I feel cold with fear," said Lisa. "Not in my wildest dreams could I have imagined being in a situation like this. Who were those uniform people, I am scared."

"Neither do I, but don't be afraid," said David, looking at her.

"What if the uniformed men come back and hurt us when we move in?" Lisa said.

"Calm down. I promise not to let anyone hurt you," David said.

"Okay," Lisa said softly.

"Come on," said David. "Let's go home. We have a lot to do. The first thing is to go through the diaries. And I guess we're giving a home to this little guy, right? He needs a name."

When they got to the car, the dog climbed into the back seat and sat down, completely calm.

"Any ideas on a name for the dog?" David asked as he sat down in the driver's seat.

"I don't know. Let's talk about that later," Lisa replied. "Do you think Phillip is the scientist who lived here in the forties?"

David shook his head as he drove away from the house. "It's not impossible."

"If he's the scientist that we've heard of there is a high probability that what we heard of could be true," Lisa said.

"You mean the stuff about the time machine?" David asked.

Lisa nodded.

They were silent almost all the way home. The setting sun was a comforting yet tiring sight, and within moments of it appearing, David yawned, with Lisa following. "What are you thinking?" David asked.

"I have a bad feeling," Lisa said.

"We will be careful," said David. "I promise. We'll move in when we know what's going on."

The Time Walkers

Chapter 10

It was dark when they got home.

"Let's get to work immediately," David suggested.

"Don't you want a nice hot bath first?" Lisa asked as she carried the notebooks to the house. "And I thought you wanted beer."

"I want to get started right away," David said, driven to push himself even further beyond where the crazy new findings had taken them today.

When they entered, David set the books on the kitchen table and quickly entered the bathroom. He washed himself off briefly, changed his shirt, and then headed for the kitchen to arrange a coffee and some sandwiches for dinner. As he sat at the table, his heart was pounding noticeably hard, and his hands trembled uncontrollably. He took a deep breath and opened the first diary, combing his hair back through his fingers. To his disappointment, he saw that some of the pages were unreadable. Dampness and mold had destroyed some of the text. Frustrated, he flipped through the rest of the diaries and realized that only a small part of what was written could be read.

He cursed to himself as he read what he could:

TODAY WE RAN AT EACH OTHER, BUT ODDLY ENOUGH, SHE IGNORED ME, HER GAZE EMPTY.
THE MAID CAME TO MEET ME WHEN I WAS IN THE BARN, AND WITH A STRANGE FACE THAT WORRIED ME, SHE CALLED THAT THE MASTER WANTED TO SEE ME IMMEDIATELY. WORRIED, I WENT TO THE HOUSE, AND WHEN I GOT THERE, THE DOOR WAS OPEN. I HEARD ALICE'S PARENTS TALKING OVER EACH OTHER, BICKERING SOMEWHAT LOUDLY IN THEIR EXCHANGE, AND IT GAVE ME SHIVERS. RATHER FRIGHTENED AND WITH TREMBLING HANDS, I OPENED THE DOOR. AS SOON AS I OPENED IT, EVERYONE FELL SILENT, AND THE MASTER LOOKED AT ME ANGRILY. WITH A WORRIED LOOK, HE PUT OUT HIS CIGARETTE AND MUTTERED SOMETHING BITTERLY. I ASKED WHAT HE HAD SAID, AND THEN HE JUST RAISED HIS VOICE AND REPEATED: "YOU'RE OUT. YOU CAN'T LIVE IN HIS HOUSE ANYMORE!"

The rest of the text on the page was unreadable, so David flipped to the next page.

WHAT AM I SUPPOSED TO DO? HOW COULD THE COOK TELL THE MASTER ABOUT MY FEELINGS FOR HER? I ASKED WHY I NEEDED TO BE EVICTED AND SAID THAT MY FEELINGS FOR ALICE WERE PERFECTLY INNOCENT. I'M JUST LOOKING FOR A LITTLE LOVE AND...

David sighed. The rest of the entry was so blurry it couldn't be deciphered.

Lisa appeared behind him. She embraced him. "How is it going?

Did you find anything interesting?"

David loved the smell of her shampoo and soaps, and he pulled her close for a second to put his nose against her. "Yes, I have, but due to mold and damp conditions, some of the pages are unreadable. It's the opposite of your lovely, seductive scent, dear."

"Eeew!" said Lisa. "Be careful. Mold can give you a whooping cough and your nose can start to run. Maybe you should wear a face mask."

"Well, I don't have gloves or a face mask, and this has gotta get done," David said.

"Wait a minute," said Lisa. "I think I have some in the first-aid kit."

When she came back, Lisa handed David a pair of gloves. "Put those on." Then she handed him a mask.

David put on the gloves and face mask and continued reading the diaries while Lisa fetched the coffee and sandwiches, he had made earlier.

"What have you found?" asked Lisa as she sat across him at the table.

David frowned. "That James was evicted from the house and that it was the cook who ratted him out."

Lisa handed David a sandwich and placed a coffee cup in front of him. Busy, he nodded his thanks without looking at her. With one hand, he moved the face mask and took a big bite of the turkey sandwich while trying to flip through the book with his other hand.

Somehow, he managed it. He returned to reading.

HOW AM I SUPPOSED TO LIVE IN THE SHED? I'M SO CONFUSED.

Then the text was unreadable again. After a few lines, David was able to read again.

THIS MORNING I WAITED FOR HER OUTSIDE THE HOUSE, HOPING TO CATCH A GLIMPSE OF HER AND BE ABLE TO EXPLAIN, BUT I NEVER SAW HER.
ONE NIGHT I SAW ALICE THROUGH THE WINDOW. SHE SAT IN FRONT OF THE FIRE WITH THE FAMILY AND JAY – HAND IN HAND, LAUGHING. AS SOON AS SHE SAW ME, HER LAUGHTER SUBSIDED, AND SHE LOOKED AWAY. IT HURTS ME TO SEE THEM TOGETHER. FOR YEARS I THOUGHT WE HAD SOMETHING SPECIAL. SHE ALWAYS ENCOURAGED ME WHEN I WAS DEPRESSED.
I WAS DEVASTATED WHEN I HEARD ABOUT THEIR RELATIONSHIP. HOW CAN I FORGET HER CHARMING SMILE AND LAUGHTER? BEFORE, SHE WOULD HOLD MY HAND AND SHOW ME THAT SHE CARED. SHE HAS A RADIANCE THAT I CAN'T RESIST. HOW CAN I FORGET HER?
ONE EVENING I SAT IN FRONT OF THE FIRE I'D LIT, AND I JUST THOUGHT FOR A LONG TIME. I REALIZED THAT REALITY ISN'T AT ALL LIKE THE FAIRY TALES. FOR A LONG TIME, I STARED DEEPLY INTO THE FIRE, AND SUDDENLY I SAW, WITH MY OWN EYES, THE DEVIL. THROUGH THE FIRE, HE LOOKED AT ME. HE TRIED TO PERSUADE ME TO HURT OR KILL JAY.

David looked at Lisa. "The rest is unreadable." David took a large bite out of his sandwich and chewed. After he swallowed, he said, "But by and large, I understand what he writes." David took out another diary hoping it could be read, but to his surprise, it couldn't be opened. The pages were stuck together. David looked at Lisa and exclaimed in frustration, "FUCK IT!"

Lisa recoiled in fear. "What the hell are you doing? You scared the shit out of me."

David glared at her, and with a tense look, he picked up the book and said, "It's completely and utterly destroyed. I can't even open it."

"Take it easy," said Lisa. "It's not the end of the world. We'll just find out if he's guilty. After all, we're not going to read a whole book about him."

"You're right," David said, taking several deep breaths. He sipped his coffee, leaned back in his chair, and looked at Lisa. "I'm sorry, sweetness. It's been a long day. Did you find anything?"

"Here it says that people expressed themselves very disparagingly," Lisa said.

PEOPLE HAVE CALLED ME A FREAK.
I HAVE TO RIG A TRAP. ONE DAY I FELT PROVOKED WHEN I WALKED INTO THE HOUSE AND SAW THEM KISSING.
I HIT HIM WITH A HAMMER I HAD WITH ME, AND THEN I BANGED HIS HEAD AGAINST THE STONE. I DRAGGED HIM OVER THE EDGE. OVER AND OVER, HE BEGGED ME TO SPARE HIS LIFE: 'PLEASE! SPARE ME.' FOR A MOMENT, I FELT BAD WHEN I SAW HIM SUFFERING, AND CONFUSED, I TOOK A FEW STEPS BACK. I STARED AT HIM AND SAW HOW HE WAS BLEEDING HEAVILY FROM HIS SKULL. I HESITATED A LITTLE AND THOUGHT THAT IF I LEAVE HIM LIKE THAT, I WILL BE EXPOSED. HESITANTLY, I WENT TO THE EDGE, LOOKED DOWN, AND SAW BIG WAVES HIT THE ROCKS WITH FULL

FORCE.

"Oh, my god…" Lisa said. "On the next page he has written this."

I PULLED HIM UP, THEN I GLARED AT HIM AND SAID, 'YOU DESERVE THIS. NOW THAT YOU KNOW MY SECRET, UNFORTUNATELY I HAVE NO CHOICE,' AND THEN I PUSHED HIM SO HARD THAT HE FELL.

"What secret?" David asked in wonder.

"Oh my God," Lisa said, putting her hand to her mouth.

"What is it?" David said, taking a bite of his sandwich.

Lisa didn't answer. She just flipped to the next page of the book as her eyes moved across the faint text.

"What does it say?" David asked.

Lisa read out loud once more.

WHEN I SAW HIM FALL AGAINST THE ROCKS, I FELT A GREAT RELIEF AT FIRST, BUT WHEN I SAW THAT A TREE HAD CUSHIONED HIS FALL, I PANICKED, THINKING THAT HE WOULD BE FINE. BUT THE TREE WAS TOO SMALL AND COULDN'T HOLD HIM, AND HE FELL OVER THE ROCKS.
I PANICKED AGAIN WHEN I SAW HOW THE WAVES SWEPT HIM AWAY. I WAS FLOODED WITH THOUGHTS, KNOWING IT SHOULDN'T HAVE ENDED LIKE THAT. I JUST WANTED LOVE.
FEAR AND CONFUSION TAKING HOLD, I WENT TO PICK UP THE PAINTING HE USED TO WORK ON HERE AND PUT IT NEAR THE EDGE, RIGHT WHERE HE FELL. THEN I LEFT ALL THE PAINT HE HAD WITH HIM BY THE SIDE. I OPENED A BOTTLE OF VODKA THAT I HAD WITH ME AND POURED OUT HALF OF THE CONTENTS BEFORE PUTTING THE BOTTLE AMONG THE PAINTS. AND BEFORE HE FELL, I

PUT A SMALL BOTTLE IN HIS POCKET, IN CASE THE POLICE WOULD FIND HIM, SO THEY MIGHT THINK HE WAS DRUNK WHEN HE FELL.

Lisa looked at David and shook her head. "Jay probably used to paint there, and James knew about it — putting his awful plan into action when he was there."

David nodded in agreement. "Perfect location and no witnesses. The motive was jealousy and bullying. People had looked down on him, and there was probably a lot of hatred just building up in him. He was obsessed with Alice! When he found out about their relationship, James still tried to start a relationship with her, and when he failed, his personality changed."

"One thing I don't understand," Lisa said, "is that for years he was a faithful servant and worked for the family and lived there. Lots of kids loved him and trusted him. What happened next? Why did people begin to express themselves derogatorily and bully him? Could Jay have something to do with the change, when he began his relationship with Alice, and what secret was he talking about?"

David shrugged. "A secret that was important to James and somehow came to Jay's attention that probably became too much for James, so he got rid of him."

Lisa rolled her eyes and shrugged. She leaned back and rocked her feet.

David took up the last diary, opened it, and flipped through the entries, but only two pages were readable:

MY HEART POUNDED WHEN I SAW THE POLICE IN THE YARD. I TRIED TO STAY AWAY, BUT THE POLICE WANTED TO INTERROGATE ALL THE FAMILY MEMBERS AND SERVANTS IN THE HOUSE. THE POLICE TOOK ME AND TWO OTHERS TO THE POLICE STATION. IN ONE ROOM SAT A POLICEMAN WHO LOOKED VERY SERIOUSLY AT ME. HE LOOKED WEIRD.

FOR A WHILE, I BECAME WORRIED WHEN I SAW THAT THE POLICEMAN WAS SCRUTINIZING ME AND ASKING A LOT OF QUESTIONS TO PUT PRESSURE ON ME. HE ASKED ABOUT THE WOUNDS ON MY HANDS AND LEG, AND I EXPLAINED THAT I'M A GARDENER AND OFTEN HURT MYSELF LIKE THAT ON THE JOB. IT WENT WELL IN THE END, BUT IT WAS UNPLEASANT TO SIT IN A DARK ROOM AND BE INTERROGATED.

ONE DAY BEFORE HER DISAPPEARANCE, I SAW SOMEONE I DIDN'T KNOW. HE WAS WOBBLING AROUND THE HOUSE. ANOTHER DAY AFTER HER DISAPPEARANCE, I SAW THE SAME PERSON I HAD SEEN BEFORE. HE WAS IN HER ROOM, RUMMAGING AMONG HER PAPERS AND CLOTHES. AS SOON AS HE SAW ME, THERE WAS A FLASH, AND HE DISAPPEARED INTO THIN AIR. IT SOUNDED VERY STRANGE WHEN HE DISAPPEARED, LIKE A CRACKLING SOUND.

David looked at Lisa and harbored a guess. "Could it be the scientist who abducted Alice, and could the woman our neighbor saw has been her? All these are questions that we haven't found answers."

"This story just gets stranger and stranger," said Lisa.

"I hope to get an answer to the message I wrote her," David said, putting aside the diary and stretching his legs. "That would be amazing, interacting with her somehow."

"Well," said Lisa. She picked up the diaries, placed them into an empty cardboard box under the table, and left it there. Then she went to the dog on the balcony. David watched as she patted the dog. "So, what shall we call him?"

"What about Storm?" David suggested.

"Storm?" Lisa replied.

"Yeah, because we found him on a stormy day," David said.

Lisa smiled and nodded. "What a fitting name. I like that. Let's try to get his vest off. There are four screws here. Looks like we're gonna need a screwdriver."

David looked closely at the vest. "That is no ordinary screw. Maybe get the electric one, and let's give that a whirl."

Within minutes Lisa handed David the electric screwdriver. "Okay, here! Try this."

The hatch on the vest opened easily with the electric tool, but David gasped when he got it open. "Oh, what the living hell is this?" A cylinder-like metal object sparkling brightly inside the box with a rotating rod. Three red, yellow, and green lights were located next to the cylinder.

"Sh—shit," said Lisa. "What is it? A bomb?"

"I don't think so," said David. "But whatever it is, I don't dare touch it."

Lisa nodded. "Wise decision."

David closed the hatch and screwed it back on. In shock, they just sat there and stared at the dog. Carefully, David glanced at Lisa. "I have a feeling that this dog does not belong to anyone in the here and now."

Lisa looked at David and shook her head. "Huh? What do you mean?"

"Alice had a dog, remember? She wrote in her diary about a black dog, and she had a black dog with her when she disappeared," David said thoughtfully.

"Strange that the dog began to wag his tail and lick you when he saw you. It felt like the dog recognized you and knew who you from before," Lisa said.

"But I've never seen the dog or had contact with him," David said. He took a closer look at the vest in case he could see a brand, a name, or a date – but to no avail. Exhausted, David leaned back and yawned. He stretched his hands straight and said, "That's enough for today. Mind-blowing day. Then he looked at the dog and patted him. "See you tomorrow, whatever you are. You can sleep on the terrace tonight in case something happens."

David could not let go of his thoughts on James' diaries in bed and whispered straight into the air. "What secret was he talking about? And why did people suddenly start to dislike him? Why was there so much hatred boiling up in James?"

"He went through a personality change when he found out about their relationship," said Lisa. "Then he tried to start a relationship with her but failed, and the guy took it way too hard. Their relationship aroused immensely strong feelings in him."

"He may have been completely obsessed with her," said David. "And the negative events around James plunged him into depression." David's eyes were heavy. By the time he finished speaking, he heard a gentle snore. "Honey?" he said, smiling as he realized Lisa had fallen asleep. David closed his eyes. "Great idea, babe."

During the night, the dog howled briefly but then fell silent. Tired, David opened his tired eyes but immediately closed them and muttered, "That stupid dog." With half-open eyes, he saw a thin-haired man with glasses wearing a backpack. He walked towards the dog, and then they left the bedroom together. Everything became quiet again, and David was too tired to react. Sleep took him once more.

The Time Walkers

Chapter 11

David opened his eyes and saw the neighbor's gray and white cat perched atop the terrace railing like a sentinel. As he stepped out of bed to stretch, he noticed the cat was unaccompanied.

"Where is the dog?" he wondered aloud.

He glanced around the surrounding area, but there was no sign of the pup. Curiosity piqued, he decided to investigate further. He walked into the kitchen, and what he saw made his stomach turn. The box of diaries Lisa had placed on the dining room table before bed was gone. Quickly, he returned to the bedroom and woke Lisa up.

David nudged Lisa. "Wake up Lisa. Wake up. Wake – up!"

Lisa moaned and looked at him with tired eyes. "What is it? Wh—uh, what?"

"The dog is gone, and I can't find the diaries you put on the dining table!"

"What are you talking about? I put them on the dining table yesterday, and the dog was on the terrace," Lisa said, getting out of bed. She rushed out onto the terrace and then to the kitchen. When she came back, she shook her head. "How is this possible? What could have happened?"

"Last night I heard the dog howling," said David. "I thought maybe it had seen the neighbor's cat, but then I saw someone with glasses and a backpack walking out to the living room with the dog in his arms! I thought it was just a dream, so I went back to sleep."

Lisa looked frightened. "You saw a person in this house without reacting?"

"Lisa," said David. "I was barely awake. It was like a dream."

Lisa was wide-eyed. "But the door was locked, and there are no signs of burglary. Why did he just take the dog and the diaries? Didn't you see who it was?"

David's brow furrowed in concentration as he recalled the suspicious figure leaving the house on the day, they had first viewed it, shrouded in a long coat and wearing glasses.

"No, it was dark," he said slowly. "Now I get the feeling we'll find out. I wonder if that was the scientist."

He glanced at Lisa, whose lips were pressed into a thin line. She held her arms tightly over her chest, attempting to protect herself from something unseen. He could hear the strain in her voice when she spoke.

"Can't we just sell the house and leave it all behind us?" she asked, almost desperate. "I dreamed of having a big place where my kids could run around and play."

David shook his head with a sigh. He knew this wasn't easy for her, but he also wanted answers.

"But honey, we haven't even moved there yet," he said gently, "and as I said before, if what we heard from that old man the neighbor were true and things become dangerous and if the Germans and flying objects pan out based on the neighbor's story." He paused and looked at her intently. "I just want to know about Alice's disappearance and her fiancé's suicide before we make any decisions about moving in."

Lisa shook her head and looked into David's eyes. "By then it might be too late," she told him. "What if we move in then strange things starts happening, have you thought of that? Do you really want to risk everything? Is our future worth nothing?" Lisa sighed, sat on the couch, and hid her face in her hands.

David got on his knees and held her. "Lisa, love, I think about you and our future first and foremost, and that's why I want to find out the truth before we move in. I want to ensure you're comfortable."

"Whatever," she said. The comment stung. "You just want to find out the facts so you can write a book about her. But you are not thinking about the risks."

"That's not true," said David. "Of course, I want to write a book, but I would not take unnecessary risks. I promise. Right now, I need you. We have to stick together. Nothing will happen to us."

Lisa looked up at him. "You can't guarantee that."

"I know. But we've fallen into a mystery. I can't - we can't back away now."

"Go and call André now."

"Are you serious? Now? Like right now?"

Lisa nodded and smiled. "You owe me a dog. I'm going to fix up some breakfast."

As Lisa went to the kitchen, David rushed to the bedroom and made the call.

"What can I do for you?" Andre answered.

"In 1948, a man lived in the house we bought. He was a foreigner and a scientist. Five years later, he disappeared without a trace. I wonder if you could find out anything about him– if he had children, and if so, if they're alive."

After reviewing some details, André promised his help and ended the call.

When David came onto the terrace to see Lisa, she was standing beneath the sun umbrella, shielding herself from the blazing sunshine. David smiled at her and gazed out onto the streets. Despite the little figures moving around outside, his mind was in overdrive. As he sank into his thoughts, beads of sweat ran down his forehead.

"What if he has children, and they're still alive today? Then I can get answers to my questions about Alice, Jay, and everyone living at that house, the fuller history of things."

"What are you thinking about?" Lisa asked.

"I need answers," said David.

"Take it easy," said Lisa. She rubbed his back gently. "You'll get answers. Just wait." She pulled him to the table and gave him a glass of orange juice. It was ice-cold. "You need breakfast. And, David, you understand that I am afraid, right? And afraid for you? I don't want anything or anyone to ruin things. Certainly not a seventy-year-old event."

"I understand that, and nothing is going to happen," David replied. He took a bite of the sandwich and chewed while glancing at Lisa. "You know, IF we know the truth, history could take a different turn."

"How do you mean?" asked Lisa, sipping her coffee.

"If there really is a time machine, we can travel in time and change things so bad things won't happen to Alice, jay, and her family. Adjust events a little bit, ones you're not happy with."

Lisa raised an eyebrow. "What would you change about your past?"

David eyed his sandwich and deliberated, "Not much, but I would love to do things that have been left undone, or not waste my time on people who didn't really care about me. I would have cared less about people who were around me for just one reason, and instead tried to devote more time to my loved ones. I would take better care of my family."

Then came a loud popping and crackling sound. The cat on the terrace growled and hissed in fear before running away.

David jumped up. "What the hell was that?"

David held Lisa's hand tightly as she hid behind him. Together, they went to the living room and looked around but saw nothing.

David walked around the kitchen. "Stay here," he told her as he looked around, there was a sofa, two armchairs on either side, a coffee table in the front of the sofa. When he had finished looking around, Lisa's face was pale. "I didn't find anything," said David.

Lisa gasped. " What happened? Where did the sound come from? And what was that spark?"

David's gaze set upon an envelope on the dining table. He glanced at Lisa and asked, "That's your envelope?"

David was sweating heavily, his heart pounding. He moved the envelope but didn't open it, trying to control his anxiety. Lisa shook her head as she looked at the envelope.

"Wait!" she cried. "What if there is a something dangerous in it, a chemical powder of some sort?"

David looked at her. "How? The envelope looks empty."

"Be careful anyway."

Trembling, David opened the envelope to find a small note inside. He took it out and read it aloud. "It says 'One should not mess with history, only learn from it. What has happened belongs to the past.' This looks like a warning. Now we have another mystery to deal with, only this one is aimed directly at us."

"David, shouldn't we be taking this warning seriously?" said Lisa. "It sounds like a threat. Like I said, let's just sell the house and put this all behind us."

"I don't want to back off, Lisa," said David. "I can't. I want to continue what we've started. Please, stick with me. I will take this as a warning and consider it seriously. But I want to solve Alice mystery, I am very curious. You don't have to join me if you don't want to. If you feel scared, go to your parent's place and I'll call you when it's all done."

Lisa shook her head. "I'm not leaving you now. One more try. Just one. Deal?"

"Deal!" David kissed her on the cheek. "I won't let anything happen to you. You're very important to me, won't let anything happen."

When David's cell phone rang, Lisa jumped.

"It's André," said David before answering the phone. "Hello André! How are you?"

"I have news, I want Alice's mystery to be solved, so I started information gathering." said André.

"Let me hear it, André," David said.

"I found the one you've been looking for. There was a person who lived here between 1948 and 1953 – William Schwartz, a physicist from Germany who had worked with Albert Einstein, among others. In the autumn of 1953, he was reported missing by his wife Maria Schwartz, who also disappeared a year later. Two years after her disappearance, the house was sold by their children, Eva and Erhard Schwartz."

David nodded eagerly. His heart was beating twice as fast as usual. He sat motionless as André spoke. When he tried to speak, his voice trembled.

"Do you know whether their children are alive, or are there grandchildren at this point?"

"Yes, both children are alive and live on the other side of town. Right next to the park. The brother lives on Happy Street no. 63, and the sister lives on Rainbow Road no. 84, not far from each other, actually."

David quickly wrote down the addresses. "If you find anything more, just call me," he said, thanking André warmly.

André told David, "Anything new you find please share it with me. I am very interested in this mystery."

After he hung up the phone, David breathed a deep sigh of relief and ran his hands through his hair. He turned to Lisa and smiled, eyes twinkling in anticipation.

"I just found out where the scientist's family lives. We can get our answers now!"

Chapter 12

David had changed out of his clothes and was waiting impatiently by the door for Lisa to join him.

David looked at his watch and called out loudly to Lisa. "Come on, honey, we have to hurry."

"I'm coming," Lisa replied. Several moments later and she was running towards him.

Inside, the car was steaming.

"Where do they live?" Lisa asked.

"Both of them live right next to the park by the beach. We'll visit the son first," David said.

Lisa rolled her eyes. "Wow. Nice places to live along here. Not just anyone can afford to live in these fantastic abodes."

As David drove toward the son's house, he was hit with a mixture of feelings. Lisa rested her head on his shoulder. He was anxious, but at the same time, he felt hopeful. He placed his hand on her knee.

"How are you feeling right now? You okay?

"I don't know!" Lisa said, shaking her head. "I'm worried that he won't want to see us."

"Why wouldn't he?" David asked.

Lisa huffed. "Well, because we are obviously a couple of prodding, nosy strangers, and he might not want to share his parents' story with us. And why should he?" She looked from David and out of the window. "Is this it? My gosh, it's so huge and... elegant."

They parked their car in front of the gate and slowly looked around the street. A little further away on the road stood two large flowerpots, posted there like guards, nearby some children were playing.

David walked towards the gate, enchanted by the lovely house, and Lisa followed. Through the gate was a large, well-kept garden with a lush lawn. The trees had branches heavy with fruit.

Lisa looked up at the security camera. "Ring the bell."

David stepped forward and pressed the bell. He looked into the camera. After a short wait, a woman's voice answered. "Who is it?"

"Hello," said David, not quite sure where to look. He kept his gaze on the security camera and waved. "My name is David Hamilton, here with my fiancé Lisa. We'd like to meet Erhard Schwartz, if possible."

"Erhard is..." the voice stuttered, then said, "Wait - David Hamilton? As in the famous author David Hamilton?"

"Yes, ma'am, that's right."

Lisa rolled her eyes at him and smiled.

"I see." There was a pause. For a moment, David suspected that mentioning his name might have put her off. But then the response came. "Just a moment, please," the speaker replied.

David turned to Lisa and smiled. "Sometimes being famous has advantages I guess."

Lisa caressed David's back and kissed him on the head.

David was startled when the gate opened, and the female voice welcomed them.

They felt pleasantly cool and comfortable when they entered the courtyard. A large pond sparkled in one corner. A cat sat nearby under an artificial waterfall.

"Look at this place," David gasped. "It's like we've entered a fairytale. The grass is so vibrant and lush, and the flowers in bloom are brighter than I've ever seen." Lisa nodded in agreement, still taken aback by the garden's beauty. They heard a light, feminine voice behind them as they continued to admire it. Turning around, they saw a woman with a beautiful red patterned dress and subtle makeup on her pale skin. Her smile was gentle as she approached them.

"My name is Victoria Schwartz. Erhard is my father."

Lisa shook Victoria's hand. David was still stunned. "This garden is like a piece of paradise on Earth. How is it so lush and green?"

"My father and his gardener have been planting everything for years, taking care of the garden. With constant irrigation and love, he's created his own slice of paradise," Victoria explained.

Lisa gestured with her hand. "It's wonderful here."

"But I don't think you're here to look at the garden, right?" said Victoria.

"No, ma'am," said David. "We were hoping to talk to Erhard."

"Erhard, of course. He's in the flower house."

Victoria went first, and David and Lisa followed. On the way there, they saw a cat growling and hissing at another, trying to attract the fish. It fell into the pond out of fear of attack. Drenched, it came out of the water and ran up the tree, with the other cat following in a chase.

Further away, they came to a glass house. Laundry was strung up nearby, drying on the line. At first, Victoria entered the glass house, and a short while later, she came out with a smile and said, "Come on in."

As David and Lisa walked in, they noticed a man wearing white and black glasses. He had a cleanly trimmed mustache. A variety of colorful plants and flowers filled the area around him. He was tall and had a strong presence about him. He was reading a book while sitting there, a ray of sunlight illuminating his pale skin and thoughtful gaze.

When the man saw them, he rose from his seat and greeted them with his deep voice. "I'm sure you already know this, but I'm Erhard."

David nodded. "Yes, sir. This is my fiancée, Lisa, and I'm David. Pleasure to meet you."

Erhard frowned at David and Lisa.

"We just bought the house that you and your parents lived in, in the forties. Do you mind if we ask you a few questions?" David asked apprehensively.

"Questions about exactly what?" Erhard responded somewhat

stiffly.

"About the house and the disappearance of your parents," David replied.

Erhard nodded sadly and sat back in his armchair, removed his black glasses, and rubbed his eyes. "I haven't talked about my parents for years." He stared at a small fountain where the water gushed forth. David found the sound of it relaxing.

"We wouldn't want you to tell us if it makes you feel uncomfortable," said David.

"It's okay," Erhard said, raising his eyes. "If you weren't the person, you are, I never would have let you in." He looked at Victoria. "Could you show them to the living room? I'll be there in a minute."

"Please come with me this way," Victoria said, walking ahead of them.

Lisa chewed her lip as they trudged up the hillside, past a small clump of trees. When she spoke again, her voice was tight with worry. "Are we making Erhard uncomfortable?"

Victoria patted her on the shoulder as they climbed the stairs and entered the rural house. The hall was lit by soft, warm lamplight, gleaming off cherrywood tables. There were ornately hand-carved oaken frames in every corner.

David's eyes widened to take it all in, impressed increasingly with each passing glance. The simple decor fused old and new together in a charming mix that made his heart swell. "What an incredible collection you have here," said David.

"Everything you see here is from the 1700s and 1800s," said Victoria. "Things my dad has been collecting for years." Victoria gestured for them to enter the living room. "And here he is."

Chapter 13

When Lisa and David entered the living room, their eyes widened in surprise. Standing tall in the corner was a grandfather clock that matched the one in Alice's bedroom.

Lisa glanced at David and mouthed, pointing at it: "Look at the clock!" He nodded.

Victoria asked if something was wrong.

"No," David said. Trying to lighten the mood, he added: "You don't see clocks like this every day. It's a real beauty – old yet wonderfully preserved."

Erhard stepped into the room from the hallway, his hands behind his back.

"It is very old," he said. "From 1785. My parents tried to save everything they could when they left Germany. They paid smugglers to get their antiques and possessions out of the country. Those plates hung on the wall over there are a hundred or two hundred years old. The clock here once stood in Hitler's study."

Lisa raised her eyes, looking at the grandfather clock. "Did your father know Hitler?"

"Not exactly, but as a scientist, my father worked for him as assigned duty, and sometimes, he and other scientists encountered Hitler. He had to obey and there were no excuses to be made," Erhard said.

He walked over to the armchair by the window and sat.

"What do you know about their disappearance?" David asked.

"If you'll excuse me, I'll go get some refreshments," said Victoria.

Erhard leaned back in his armchair and asked them to sit. For a moment, he hid his face in his hands, played with his gray mustache, and closed his eyes.

"Since I have read all your books, and I think Alice's mystery disappearance is going to be your next book, I will share what I know" Erhard said. For years, I have been wallowing in my thoughts, and they're still a heavy burden to bear. It was not easy for my parents to flee Germany with my sister and me."

"I can imagine. What happened to them?" David asked eagerly.

"I'll tell you what I know. As a scientist, he could not walk around freely in Nazi-occupied Germany. All scientists were under constant surveillance. At the war's end, there was chaos, awful confusion, and discord amongst the leadership. Hitler's ministers and commanders-in-chief were under significant pressure from Hitler. They were hiding in a bunker, as you probably know. They asked my dad to bring his family to the bunker. But Dad had a bad feeling about it and tried unsuccessfully to contact some of his colleagues and other scientists. He also tried to reach his parents but couldn't get hold of them. He decided, without thinking, to go with us on foot to his parents in Berlin' to help them escape.

"In Berlin, Out in the streets, there was only death, body parts, and blood. Dead bodies in piles, scattered all around. I saw young children crying over their dead parents. My mom and sister were crying incessantly. I clung to my sister's hand and tried to keep up. I, too, was in a state of shock when I saw all the dead around me. The bullets rained down on us. Several times we had to take cover so as not to be hit by the bombs that landed near us. A stone's throw away, a bomb struck, and a family on their way to the shelter was torn to pieces."

Erhard coughed and held his hand to his mouth. His eyes were empty. He looked at his green garden and rubbed his forehead.

"When we arrived at my grandparent's house, we saw a burnt-down house partly set aflame. Dad called to his parents but got no answer. Worried, he went inside, and we followed. Suddenly dad saw his father lying buried among the fallen debris. He lifted our grandfathers' bloody head and pressed him to his chest, shouting out his anger and sadness. My sister and I were desperate. At that moment, I felt nothing. No fear. I just looked without understanding." Erhard sighed and hid his face in his hands.

David sat without moving in his chair, listening.

Erhard wiped his tears. Victoria came in with a large tray of refreshments and set it on the table.

"Please, have some," Victoria offered and handed a glass to Erhard.

David looked longingly at the tray, leaned forward to take a glass, and took a quick sip of the drink. Surprised, he looked at Victoria. "This is delicious. What is it?"

"A secret recipe from my grandmother," said Victoria with a small smile. "My mother taught me when I got married. She said that this recipe should be passed on to family only, and no outsiders can ever learn the ingredients."

"It's divine, smell my favorite flower rose, and taste great" Lisa said.

David turned to Erhard. "Are you able to continue, sir?"

Erhard nodded. "Yes, of course." He put down the glass and clasped his hands together in his lap. "I remember how my mother went into the house to look around. Suddenly she screamed and pointed desperately on a direction. I looked where mom was pointing. There I saw that my grandmother was lying on her favorite sofa that my grandfather had bought for her. Her knees were pulled up tightly to her stomach. She was shot in the back and in the abdomen. I will never forget how my mother rushed to her side, wailing, or how my despondent father kissed his father on the forehead as he said goodbye. Softly, he laid him on the ground, and then rushed to his mother to pick her up, holding her. Again and again, he kissed her bloody cheek and cried out in grief. Suddenly, she opened her eyes, and we were all so shocked. Dad ran his fingers through her hair and assured her that everything would be fine."

Erhard leaned back in his chair, took a few breaths, and closed his eyes again.

Lisa put her drink on the table, looked at him anxiously, and leaned forward. "It's okay if you want to stop."

"It's quite okay," Erhard replied. "I always get emotional when I talk about this." Then he resumed. "My grandmother looked at him and smiled kindly. At that moment, grandma was so beautiful. Calm and collected, she looked at all of us, and then at dad. She was breathing heavily but was still quite calm. We immediately noticed that she was trying to say something. Eventually, she could get out that Nazi' were after us. 'Save yourselves, leave the city,' she warned. Then she looked at my sister and me and uttered, 'Save my grandchildren.' She slowly closed her eyelids, sighed, and took her last breath."

Lisa was wiping her eyes of tears.

Erhard eyes were watering. He removed his glasses, quickly wiped them, then rose and strolled to the window. He leaned against the windowsill and looked out at the garden. After a few moments, he turned to Lisa with a depressed look.

"For years, I have tried to forget. I sought help from a psychologist, and with therapy, I finally found some level of inner peace – but it didn't last long. I saw things and found things in the current house and the last house that reminded me of my parents."

David leaned in. "Like what?"

"One late night in 1971, I was asleep. Suddenly I was awakened by a strange sound. Barely awake, I raised my head, looking around with tired eyes. At first, I couldn't see anything, but then I saw my mother standing by the door to my bedroom. She was smiling. The light from the hallway let me see her face. She looked just like she had when she disappeared. With a friendly smile, she waved to me. Sweaty and dismayed, I searched for my glasses. But as soon as I had put them on, she was gone."

Erhard closed his eyes and ran his hand over his hair. He opened his eyes again and shifted his weight from one leg to another.

"Just at that moment, my phone rang. My sister called from her house and she was hysterical. She said something I couldn't understand. I tried to calm her down, and finally, she took a few deep breaths to tell me that she had seen Dad in her room. She said she was asleep when she heard a strange noise. And then she had seen dad in her bedroom. He waved and then disappeared with a smile. 'He just disappeared into nothing,' my sister cried."

"Could it have been a dream or a hallucination?" David asked.

"I would believe that if it had happened only to me," said Erhard. "But it happened to my sister that very same night. That was much more than coincidence, to us. A few weeks later, I received a letter from a bank that changed my sister's life and mine alike. The letter had information about the number of shares I of shares in a newly started telephone company. My sister received an identical letter. In six years, those shares went up, and by then the company had about two thousand employees. It didn't take long before we were millionaires. At the moment, the company now has about forty-five thousand employees around the world. My sister and I together own half of the company shares."

"Maybe your parents knew in advance that the shares in the company would go up. Or did you find out where the shares came from?"

Erhard nodded. "Yes, well, when we were young, we would often hear our parents talking about how they could ensure that we'd have a comfortable future. One day dad came home and told mom that he had hired a law firm and an investment firm. They were commissioned to help us invest in different companies and buy shares – and today they still help us with our investments."

"Have you ever thought about trying to find your parents? Or finding out what happened to them?"

Erhard grimaced. "I tried to get to the bottom of their disappearance. I dug and dug. For hours I sat and went through all the papers my dad left behind. A year after their disappearance, I found dad's diaries in a box in the attic. When I went through them and read, I realized what had been going on in their lives."

"And what was it? What happened?" David asked.

"He was persecuted and lived under most profound pressure," Erhard said. "His life was in grave danger, and mom's too." He took another puff of his pipe and stared at the clock.

"Why was he persecuted and under pressure?" David asked.

"First, my father was a scientist and a team leader. He worked with a group of scientists who were responsible for an experiment under Hitler. But at the end of the war, the experiment was interrupted as the Russians approached and everyone involved was executed immediately. Most of the scientists on the project were killed by the SS, and the whole experiment was discarded, but fortunately my father and one other scientist got away," Erhard revealed at last, taking the last puff of the pipe before placing it in his ashtray.

"Was there anything about the experiment in his diaries?" David asked.

Erhard smiled. "No, Dad never mentioned anything about the experiment."

"Tell me if you know anything else at all along those lines. Please," David begged.

Erhard's was annoyed and asked, "Why is my father's work so important? I have told you everything I know. Look around. I have created this paradise to be able to forget my parents' absence. For many years I have been burying myself in work and gardening. I have built up everything you see here just to be able to move on with my life. I know nothing more than what I have told you."

David decided to come clean. "His work is important to us because since we bought the house, a number of strange things have happened there. Neighbors I've met have had strange experiences in the area. They've witnessed flying objects above the house and people in uniform walking around the yard, speaking German. A neighbor saw a girl wandering around and absent-minded and confused. She wore an old-fashioned dress from the thirties or forties, claiming her name was Alice. A girl who lived in the house in the forties disappeared without a trace, and her name was Alice too."

David leaned forward and hid his face in his hands. He tried to put everything that had happened into words as clearly as possible, but he realized how crazy this all sounded.

Upon regrouping his thoughts, he continued, "In the sixties, a burglar broke into a locked room in the house and never came out. Yesterday we found a dog under a fallen tree wearing a vest or jacket, and in the vest, we found strange appliances, cords, and flashing lights. We also found some notebooks belonging to the gardener who worked for the family during the time when Alice disappeared.

"Then last night I was awakened by a noise. Half-awake and extremely groggy, I believe I saw someone snooping around our house, but I was so sleepy and could barely stir. In the morning, we discovered that both the dog and the notebooks were gone! One of those notebooks contained, by the way, very advanced mathematics with a bunch of strange numbers and diagrams. As you can see, we just want to know what's going on there before we move in." David sighed. He gave Erhard a tense look and then backtracked. "Wait. You just said that many of the scientists were executed when the Russians approached Berlin. What experiment was interrupted?"

Erhard raised his brow and stared at David with hooded eyes.

"Dad never talked about his work at home. The only thing he said that I ever heard because I was eavesdropping was that German agents were following him."

"Was the experiment about time travel?" David asked, taking a sip of his drink.

Erhard pursed his lips and glared at David.

"What are you talking about? I don't know what you're talking about."

David pushed on. "Many people have disappeared as soon as they entered the house or as soon as they put their feet in the locked room, including your parents and the burglar. Alice, whose room it was, disappeared without a trace," David said furiously.

"We want to have children," interrupted Lisa. "One day in our new house, and we don't want anything to happen to our family either."

Sitting curled up on the sofa with her feet tucked under her, Victoria shook her head. She looked at Lisa. "We don't know more than this. Dad told you everything he knows."

David spotted a family photo on the wall beside the grandfather clock. He walked over and looked at it. His heart began pounding in his chest.

"Who are they?" he asked.

"Those are my parents," Erhard replied.

David approached the photo to study it more closely. He looked at Erhard, incredulous. "But these are the same people we bought the house from!"

"What are you talking about?" said Erhard. "Those are my parents, William, and Maria Schwartz."

"But their names are Philip and Caroline," Lisa said as she joined David by his side.

"Maybe the people you bought the house from just look like my parents," Erhard replied.

David nodded at the idea, but inwardly he was getting increasingly frustrated. In his mind he asked himself why Erhard wasn't sharing more information. He scanned the photograph once more before looking up at Lisa with a determined expression. "Yes, I suppose so," he said, his voice even. "Well, we really should be going now, darling."

David stepped up to Erhard and offered his hand in gratitude. However, something seemed off about the old man. He could sense an underlying tension between them, almost hostility. It was too much for him to handle.

Erhard looked at David with raised eyebrows. "There's no use messing around with the past, David. Everything that has happened belongs to history. You can't change it." Then he shook his head. "What has happened cannot be changed. That's what my dad always said."

Victoria walked them out to the gate. David and Lisa thanked her.

Hesitantly, David looked at her and nodded goodbye, then got in the car. Lisa cranked down her window and hung out her arm. The sun was blinding. She nodded at the house. "I have a bad feeling about our new house. There's something hidden behind its beautiful facade. I'm sure Erhard knows what's going on in our new place."

David nodded and started driving. Lisa glanced at him. "You saw something when you looked at the photo," she said. "What did you see in it besides Philip and Caroline?"

He looked at Lisa before fixing his eyes on the road again.

"I saw a date. The photo was taken in 1957 – Four years after the disappearance of the father and three years after the mother's disappearance, but in the photo, they were all together. I am convinced now that Erhard knows the truth and that he is still seeing his parents. I am sure there is a time machine." He glanced in the rearview mirror. "Maybe Hitler and his followers also traveled in time and just disappeared. Maybe they live in another time and another place. Perhaps they are living today as refugees, lost in time."

"I had an unpleasant feeling when I saw the photo," Lisa said. "More than before. I don't want to move into the house when we know something like this is going on."

"We're not moving in yet," said David. "I'll find the time machine first and find out the truth."

"But shouldn't we listen to Erhard, about not prying into history?" Lisa said.

"We have ended up with a mystery. I can't just stop pursuing the truth," said David. "I just want to know what happened to Alice." David turned off the road. "It's not like I'm going against what Erhard said."

"Where are you driving us to?" Lisa asked.

David grinned. "We're going to the house. I'm going to find the time machine."

Chapter 14

With determination, David drove towards the house. Upon arrival, they spotted a figure darting into the barn, followed by an odd crackling noise. Swiftly, David parked the car and chased after the fleeing figure, Lisa hot on his heels. However, it was ominously empty when they breached the barn's threshold.

"Odd," he murmured, his brows furrowing in confusion. "Did you see that man?"

"Did you also hear that sound?" Lisa asked, staying close to him.

David nodded in agreement. "Yes, a peculiar crackling noise. But our main question remains unanswered: Where did that man go?"

They thoroughly inspected the barn, searching behind any object large enough to conceal a person. A memory sparked in David's mind as they ventured deeper into the barn. "Come to think of it, he resembles the man I saw at our home last night. Sunglasses, a backpack, and an unusual belt around his waist."

Locating a switch, David flooded the barn with light to aid their investigation.

As they scoured the barn, David desperately sought signs linking the mysterious man to William Schwartz since he used to live in the house. Despite their best efforts, their search within the barn bore no fruit.

"What are we looking for?" Lisa asked, her eyes mirroring his own confusion.

"I'm not exactly sure," he replied, his voice tinged with panic, "Some sort of footprint or clue, perhaps."

"Do you think it might have been William Schwartz?" Lisa proposed, raising an eyebrow in query.

David offered no verbal response, merely shaking his head at first. A few minutes later he said, "Our intruder entered the barn either to hide or escape us. If we're to uncover any clues, we'll need to extend our search outdoors."

Once outside, David gestured to the spot where he'd initially spotted the man. "I first saw him over there. Let's search the area and be cautious."

Separating, they scoured the yard diligently. Lisa broke the silence, gazing at David, "He seemed to have originated from where we found the dog. Maybe we should investigate there?"

After a moment's consideration, David nodded in agreement, making his way toward the toppled tree they had discovered the day before.

"Keep an eye out for anything unusual," he instructed. They

systematically examined the surrounding vegetation, leaving no leaf unturned.

Suddenly, a glint of metal caught Lisa's eye. "I've found something!" she exclaimed, digging a small, metallic cylinder out from the undergrowth.

Rushing over, David gingerly collected the item from Lisa. A closer examination revealed a subtle vibration emanating from it.

With a wary expression, Lisa observed the mysterious device. Heart pounding and voice wavering, she questioned, "What is it, David? Could it be dangerous?"

David was perspiring heavily now, his clothes sticking to his skin. He shook his head at Lisa, "We can't be sure. Please step back while I examine it."

Suddenly, they heard the crunch of footsteps. Before David could react, an unfamiliar voice echoed, "Don't move and don't turn around. That cylinder belongs to me. Toss it behind you. I don't want to harm you. Just let me depart in peace."

"Who are you?" David demanded, his grip on the cylinder tightening.

"I'm a relic of the past," the voice responded.

With a puzzled look, Lisa glanced at David. Stopped on their feet, she muttered, "The past?" She then addressed the unknown speaker with a hint of a smile, "Are you, Philip Schwartz or William Schwartz?"

"Hand over the device, and you'll get your answers," the voice bargained.

With a swift motion, David flung the object aside. The silence that followed was interrupted by a sharp, crackling noise. He spun around, but there was nobody there.

Lisa spoke up, her voice was unsteady, "David, that voice sounded so familiar. As soon as he mentioned the past, it reminded me the way of Erhard was talking about his father."

David nodded in assent, his hand lightly gripping Lisa's shoulder. The heat had made his shirt cling to his neck, so he pulled at the collar for relief, wiped his sweat-drenched forehead, and lit a cigarette.

He took a drag before addressing Lisa with weary eyes. "That's enough for today, Lisa. I'm not in the mood for any more surprises."

Lisa's mind was teeming with questions about the mysterious cylindrical object. Could it have been related to the dog or the elusive time machine?

David glanced back at the house and sighed in frustration, "If only I could find that time machine!" He stubbed out his cigarette and turned to Lisa. "Would you mind driving?"

Lisa filled their ride home with probing questions about the enigmatic William Schwartz. She rattled off her unsuccessful attempts to find information about him online. She wondered aloud why someone of such presumed intellect remained so obscure not for his own privacy but for his experiments.

In response to her barrage of queries, David mentioned Schwartz's involvement in clandestine Nazi experiments. David's musings conjured images of a world where Einstein championed humanity while Schwartz was unwillingly entangled with Hitler.

When they reached home, Lisa pulled the car into the driveway. David extracted himself from the passenger seat, each movement betraying his exhaustion. He made his way towards the front door, halting abruptly mid-stride.

Lisa shot him a quizzical look. "What's wrong?"

"Didn't we lock the door this morning?" David asked, a frown forming on his face.

"Of course! Why?" Lisa replied, her hand already on the car door lock.

David pointed out, his voice stammering with apprehension, when he tried to turn the handle, the door was unlocked. The sight left him gnawing that they were in for another round of unusual occurrences.

David moved toward the open door with Lisa following closely, her whisper barely audible, "Could it be a burglar?"

"We're about to find out," he said, nudging the door further open, his nerves strung taut in anticipation of the unknown.

Suddenly, a cat released a sharp meow, darted out from the shadowy interior, and disappeared into the night. Lisa jumped and let out a yelp, but David reassured her. "It was just the neighbor's cat." Gathering his courage, he cautiously ventured inside, Lisa on his heels.

To their surprise, the fan was running. "Who turned this fan on?" David exclaimed; his shock evident in his voice.

From the kitchen, the sound of a radio crackling with static reached their ears. With a quick look at Lisa, David hushed her and began to stealthily navigate toward the source of the noise. On entering the kitchen, they halted, rooted to the spot by what they saw.

A young man with hair slicked back in glossy waves sat at their table, an old-fashioned radio before him. A woman stood at the counter, diligently polishing silverware. Both were clad in anachronistic uniforms, and the woman's perfectly coiffed hairstyle harked back to the 1930s.

"We've been expecting you. You have quite a lovely home," the young man started, glancing at David with a puzzled expression. "Something strange happened when we stepped in here. My radio just stopped functioning properly. It's nothing but static now."

"That's an old model," David observed, trying to mask his surprise.

"Old? It was a Christmas gift just three months ago, back in Germany. It was perfectly fine until we arrived here," the man retorted.

Suppressing his bewilderment, David responded with a casual shrug and a lopsided grin. "If you're from around here, you'd know that Christmas was six months ago."

"Yes," the man agreed, his cheerful nod belying his disoriented state. "I lost track of the year, but the radio should still be working, right?"

A chill ran down David's spine, but he managed a nonchalant nod.

"Perhaps it's just poor reception."

Lisa, who had been silent until then, found her voice, "Who are you two? And why are you polishing our silver?"

"Just passing the time while waiting for you," the woman responded with a light giggle. "And doing you a little favor in the process."

Meanwhile, the man had procured a bottle of brandy, poured himself a generous measure, and downed it in one go. "Excellent brandy," he complimented, glancing at the date on the bottle with a smirk. "I'm considerably older than this brandy." He let out a chuckle at his own quip.

David attempted to steer the conversation back to their mysterious guests, "You're travelers, aren't you? From a different time, I presume. But this time-traveling concept is a bit difficult for us to grasp." His words hung in the air, a thinly veiled invitation for them to share more.

The woman laughed softly and moved to stand behind the man, her hands resting lightly on his shoulders.

"I can see why you're confused, but time, as you understand it, has become insignificant to us," she stated.

"Just a week ago, in 1945, we were married. We had a small, intimate wedding dinner with a few friends. But we couldn't linger; we had to leave before the party was over. You see, we can shift through time at will. We can freeze it, reverse it, or leap forward. Therefore, time and its constraints and consequences have lost their grip on us.

We've learned to master it."

"In a normal life, we would have loved to have children, but currently, we're on a mission," the woman added.

David nodded, a smile playing on his lips as he turned to the man. "Okay, but I highly doubt you chose our place for your honeymoon. What brings you here? What do you want from us?"

The man arched an eyebrow in acknowledgment, turning off the static-filled radio and leaning forward on the table. His tone took a stern edge, "You're sharp! You must have a clue about what we're after."

"Actually, we don't," David replied succinctly.

"Then I will aid you, but in return, you must assist us," the man offered, setting the ground for negotiation.

David exhaled a frustrated sigh, "What can we possibly do for you, sir?"

"Hold on a moment," the man requested, rising from his chair, and disappearing into the bathroom. He doused his face with cool water to combat the heat. Meanwhile, the woman busied herself with a peculiar belt she wore.

"That's an unusual belt. What's its purpose?" David queried.

She turned to look at David, a playful giggle her only response.

The man returned from the bathroom, declaring, "I feel better now," as he reoccupied his seat. "What were you saying?" he inquired, casting his gaze on David.

David moved toward the table, pulling out a chair for Lisa. "Sit down, Lisa," he requested, his voice soft before he refocused his attention on the young man.

The man resumed the conversation, "We're curious about your connection with the Schwartz family."

"We have none," David responded truthfully.

"But you did visit them today, didn't you?"

"Yes, we did. But that doesn't establish any familial relation," David clarified.

"Surely you understand I'm not a fool," the man retorted, a hint of irritation creeping into his voice.

"I do. And if you've deduced so much about me, you'll understand why we visited. If you know who I am, you'll comprehend my interest in seeing him," David articulated steadily, striving to clarify his intentions.

The man surveyed David, leaning back in his chair, a smile gracing his lips.

"You bought the house where they resided from 1948 to 1956. What piqued your curiosity?"

"It wasn't the Schwartz family that drew my attention, but the previous occupants from the thirties and forties. The murder mystery surrounding a family member and the subsequent disappearance of his fiancée intrigued me. As a writer, I thought perhaps the Schwartz family might have known something about their fate," David tried to explain as calmly as he could.

The man changed the subject abruptly, "You discovered a dog in your yard wearing a vest. Where is it now?"

"I have no idea. It vanished by morning."

"Didn't you see anyone?" the man probed.

"I heard something while asleep, but it's all a blur now. I was too exhausted to care," David sighed deeply, "What's the purpose of this interrogation?" His tone hovered between annoyance and despair.

"Do you realize that Phillip, the man who sold you the house, is actually William Schwartz?" the man queried.

Chapter 15

David shot a surprised glance at Lisa. He reclined in his chair and put his hands on face and groaning in exasperation. "Enough is enough! This is just too much to handle!"

The man turned to David, his brow furrowed in concern, his eyes flickering between him and Lisa. "What are you implying?"

"I'm just struggling to wrap my head around everything. It's all rather mind-boggling, isn't it? You're twenty-six but born in 1919. You got married a week ago, yet the ceremony was in 1945. You're on a time-travel mission, and now you're telling us that we bought a house from the Schwartz family. It's a lot to digest," David responded, a hint of hysteria creeping into his voice while playing a role to extract information from the man.

"You're aware we come from a different timeline. So why the shock?" the man countered, gazing at David.

"Well, it's not every day you encounter time travelers," David retorted, his voice rising slightly.

"I empathize with your bewilderment. We've been trailing the Schwartz family, but William Schwartz keeps altering his location and timeline. It's been a challenge catching up with him," the man sighed, his sincerity evident in his tone.

"And why are you after him?" Lisa asked.

"He's privy to critical information. Information that affects us all," the woman said.

"Who does 'us all' refer to exactly?" Lisa demanded.

"I meant us, our group. We're always on the move, seeking a stable temporal residence. However, Schwartz's knowledge poses a threat, so we must locate him."

"We mean him no harm, but we must find him before it's too late," the man concurred.

"I get that, but we can't assist you. We aim to uncover the truth behind Alice and her family's fate," David interrupted.

"While we'd like to trust you, our circumstances necessitate monitoring your movements because you're the current owner of the house. For every step you take, we'll be a shadow behind you. Consider this a friendly warning—disclose our meeting to anyone; the consequences could be perilous. Not even William Schwartz should know. Understand that we bear you no ill will. Our pursuit is solely focused on him. We could approach his children, as they frequently meet, but they've posed no threat so far. Thus, we've elected to hold back," the man elucidated, glancing at Lisa.

David nodded in acquiescence because he wants to be cautious.

"We understand."

"Splendid! I'm glad we see eye-to-eye," the man said, rising from his chair. The couple strapped on their backpacks.

"Oh, one more thing - might we know your names?" David asked, his curiosity piqued.

The man chuckled at David's inquiry. "My name isn't of much consequence."

With that, the enigmatic couple sauntered into the living room. As they vanished from sight, the room filled with a familiar crackling sound. David and Lisa darted into the room, but the couple had already disappeared.

"What on earth...Is it possible they work with Nazi?" Lisa speculated.

"The Nazis must be after William Schwartz and his wife," David mused.

"You failed to mention your knowledge about the time machine and the peculiar events in Alice's room," Lisa pointed out.

"Sweetheart, less talk means fewer problems," he advised gently, a grin playing at the corners of his mouth.

"But what's our next move? We've been put on notice by these time travelers. Can't you see how far out of hand things have gotten? I'm frightened by these bizarre turns of events!" Lisa's voice trembled with a mix of fear and anger.

"Look, nothing substantial happened. They were merely sizing us up. Now they know we're not on their trail," David assured her soothingly, trying to instill calm in the tense atmosphere.

Lisa continued, her voice shaky, "And at least we've confirmed the existence of the time machine. We can stop this hunt and get back to normality." She collapsed into her chair, leaning heavily against the table, and buried her face in her hands. "This is just too much. The whole scene feels like a macabre play. People are pursuing us. I can't bear it any longer and want it all to end."

"Believe me, my love, I share your sentiments. But this is our reality, and we need to approach it with clear-headed logic. It seems German scientists have created a device capable of traversing time and space, a secret hidden from the world. It's difficult to comprehend its actual functionality," David confessed, bending down to embrace the distraught Lisa. "Rest easy, my dear. Nothing will harm us. The Nazis are merely concerned we might expose them and their secret. I've made it clear we're seeking Alice and the time machine is in her room. And to prove our intentions, I aim to meet Alice, and possibly avert a disaster," he reassured her, gazing into her eyes.

Lisa looked at him in disbelief. "Are you joking? No, you can't be serious!" She pushed him away.

"Now that we know time travel is feasible, I'm eager to explore it and bring back a wealth of new experiences," David declared, his gaze drifting to the terrace. "My motivations extend beyond the scope of my book. Consider the potential benefits. Perhaps I can meet my ancestors, like my grandfather, who perished in a plane crash at forty.

Maybe I could even prevent that tragedy and save him."

Lisa seized David's shoulders, giving him a sharp shake. "Enough!" she exclaimed. "This isn't amusing anymore. Are you seriously willing to throw everything away on this reckless gamble? Don't you see the potential dangers? What if the time machine malfunctions and traps you in the past? What about our relationship? Are you prepared to risk all that we've built together?" Lisa's voice wavered as she started to sob. "David, you barely understand how it operates. You have no idea what awaits you on the other side. At least consider Erhard's warning! This is a courting disaster!" Her breath hitched in her chest.

"Darling, you need to let go," David said, gently prying her fingers off. "You're holding a bit too tight."

Lisa noticed her nails digging into David's flesh. "I'm sorry," she muttered and released him. "I was just... frustrated." She dropped her gaze. "So, you're seriously considering going once you locate the machine?" she asked, searching David's face for answers.

He nodded. "I only intend to make the journey once I fully understand how the machine functions. There shouldn't be any danger involved. Would you assist me in finding it?"

Visibly upset, Lisa turned to gaze out the window, her mind churning. She glanced back at David standing beside her, shrugged, and answered haltingly, "I've known you for many years, and now it feels like you've ensnared yourself in a predicament with no escape. You're so engrossed in her story and ready to jeopardize all we've built together. "I feel inclined to leave you to your detective games. It seems you and I are not in an agreement, I want to stop this detective work, and you don't, so, you are putting me in a difficult situation. I am sticking around so nothing will happen to you even though I am not happy about this whole thing," Lisa confessed, her voice heavy with resignation.

David reached out and held her gaze. "I promise not to do anything that might endanger us. I'll be cautious. I'm not obsessed with her. I merely find her story compelling and tragic. Remember my book, *Dancing with Death*? The way I immersed myself in that tale? It was a true story about a man facing death daily and eventually learning to live with it. I virtually lived with him, spending day and night at his home, recording his experience with death. You didn't find it peculiar then."

"Well, this is entirely different. We're dealing with a time machine. Actual Nazis are on our tail, meddling in our affairs," Lisa countered, her voice drained of energy.

"Absolutely, which is why I'm proceeding with extra caution. If we're under surveillance now, do you think they hear us?" David glared at the ceiling and shouted, "I'm interested in Alice and her fiancé, not pursuing Nazis!" He turned back to Lisa. "Grant me this one opportunity. It could become a massive success, even a literary goldmine for us. Maybe the most popular book globally. I promise to journey only when we've gathered sufficient information about the time machine. Please, Lisa?"

Lisa held his gaze for a beat, then sank onto the sofa, laying down her terms. "If I can accompany you, you can go, or else I'm leaving. If I mean anything to you, you'll let me join you. Don't abandon me."

"Taking you could expose you to danger," David warned, mindful of the harsh realities of the situation.

"Then you're not going either!" Lisa retorted.

"You drive a hard bargain," he remarked, a smile tugging at his lips.

"But just so we're clear, David, I'm not thrilled about this. I agree with this for you. We started this journey together, and we'll end it together, but the moment danger arises, we retreat," Lisa asserted fervently.

David simply nodded, placing a hand over his heart, promising her he would respect their agreement.

"When should we commence our search?" Lisa inquired.

"Tomorrow, at daybreak," David suggested. "I suspect there's more to that wall than meets the eye. Perhaps the clock conceals some contraption or mechanism that facilitates time travel."

Fear laced Lisa's voice as she confessed, "I'm still scared."

David responded with a nod and a comforting assurance. "I won't let any harm come our way. You have my word. Trust me."

"I do trust you, David. More than anyone else in the world, but I can't shake these unnerving feelings about our current predicament," she replied, sighing. "I can't seem to control it."

"Allow me to reassure you once more," David said. "I'm always cautious, especially when your safety is at stake. I would never act recklessly."

Drawing her into his embrace, David held Lisa close, offering her the solace of his presence, allowing the silence to soothe their shared concerns.

Chapter 16

David went to the storeroom to retrieve his toolbox. He popped it open to ensure all the necessary tools were neatly arranged inside.

"Darling, where did you place my hammer?" he called out.

"It's in the third kitchen drawer," Lisa responded.

Following her instructions, he found the hammer in the drawer and placed it in the toolbox. He then hauled the box out to the car. Outside, he spotted an ice cream truck surrounded by a cluster of eager children, all waiting to enjoy a cold treat. Nearby, a cat was lapping at a dropped scoop of ice cream, attempting to find respite from the heat. David arched an eyebrow at the sight, mumbling to himself,

"An ice cream wouldn't be a bad idea."

After storing the toolbox in the car, he strolled over to the ice cream truck, his eyes devouring the tempting images of ice cream plastered on its side while he waited his turn. Now happily clutching their cool treats, the children dispersed in the heat.

"Sir, what can I fetch for you?" the vendor asked, his voice resonant and jovial.

"Well, it's a tough decision," David replied, not tearing his gaze away from the enticing options.

Suddenly, a familiar voice behind him suggested, "Get one scoop of vanilla, one of blueberry, and one strawberry. In a cup. It's my preferred combination."

David swiveled around and, to his astonishment, found Erhard standing behind him, holding a bag.

"Erhard – what brings you here?"

"Ice cream, why not enjoy an ice cream?" Erhard returned, wearing a nonchalant smile.

Before David could formulate a response, Erhard silenced him and turned to the vendor: "Three of the same, please, my treat."

Dumbstruck, David simply watched as Erhard handled the transaction.

"Here's your tray, David. Let's head to your place," Erhard said, handling the payment.

Taken aback, David pointed the way, his gaze firmly on Erhard. "This isn't about ice cream, is it?" he asked, a note of suspicion in his voice.

"My sister and I have owned this company since the eighties. It was established in 1951 and is famed nationwide for its homemade ice cream. I hope my children, perhaps even my grandchildren, will carry it forward," Erhard responded, tactfully bypassing David's question.

"Step inside," David said, pushing the door open. "Lisa, we've got company!" he called.

Lisa peered out from the kitchen, surprised at the sight of David and Erhard standing in the doorway.

"What's happening?"

"We're about to enjoy some ice cream," Erhard informed her, his smile radiant. He strode towards the table, placing his bag on it. "Better eat it before it melts," he added as he began to pull an array of unusual devices from his bag, placing them strategically around the living room.

With the devices in place, he settled down at the dining table with David and Lisa. Turning to David, he finally spoke, "Guess you're wondering why I'm here?"

David nodded, his expression serious.

Gazing at the melting ice cream, Erhard began to indulge his sweet tooth. "I can never resist this," he declared cheerily.

The room fell silent as Lisa and David waited for Erhard to speak.

"We could potentially be overheard by spies," he divulged. "The devices I've placed around your living room ensure they won't be able to eavesdrop."

"Spies? Who? And who knows you're here? Your arrival was certainly unexpected," David said, sampling his ice cream.

"The individuals pursuing my father," Erhard stated.

"Your father? How are we involved?" David probed.

"My current house is under covert surveillance by the Nazis. They investigate every new occupant," Erhard explained.

"Phillip and Caroline, are those your parents?" David inquired; his eyes trained on Erhard.

Erhard acknowledged with a nod, enjoying another spoonful of his ice cream before reclining in his chair, his gaze drifting toward the window.

"My sister and I were oblivious to our father's actions. He remained tight-lipped about his job, experiments, and the time machine itself. It was only after our mother's disappearance, with a letter as our sole clue, that we discovered the nature of his experiments," he recounted, his tone calm yet authoritative. "In the letter, he detailed their plans to return to us soon. A few months later, they did, albeit with new identities as 'Phillip and Caroline.' To throw the Nazis off their trail, we sold them the house and relocated." Erhard paused, sighing heavy. "Our interactions since have been limited to covert meetings."

He took a moment to gather himself before continuing, "However, the Nazis somehow discerned their identities and our clandestine rendezvous. They visited us one day, demanding the surrender of our parents and the location of the time machine. We managed to convince them that we were in the dark regarding our father's activities." Erhard paused momentarily, taking another bite of his ice cream before meeting David's stunned gaze. "The Nazis tend to keep those close to my parents under scrutiny, and with your recent purchase of the house, coupled with your curiosity, you have inadvertently piqued their interest. My parents sold the house purely as a diversion. Had you remained indifferent to their history, you could have continued living unbothered. But now, the Nazis suspect your involvement," he concluded.

David and Lisa exchanged a glance, their curiosity seems to overtake them.

"Do the Nazis suspect there's a time machine in the house?" David probed.

"They hold suspicions about the presence of a time machine, but despite numerous visits to the house, they've come up empty-handed. The reason, perhaps, is that they lack knowledge about the machine's appearance or size. I, too, am unaware of its hiding spot within the house," Erhard admitted.

"Isn't there a risk that the Nazis might threaten you, compelling your parents to turn themselves in?" Lisa asked, her voice trembling slightly.

"The Nazis understand their threats will prove futile. If they were to harm us, my father could turn himself and the time machine over to law enforcement or other authorities and reveal Hitler's continued existence. That's a gamble they cannot afford."

"Where might Hitler be now?" David asked, polishing off his remaining ice cream.

Erhard smiled, shaking his head in response. "Should I possess that knowledge, I wouldn't be here conversing with you." He gazed out the window, a sigh escaping his lips. "Hitler is a time-wandering refugee, much like my parents."

"Time wanderer, an intriguing choice of words," David echoed, smiling in return. "But why do the Nazis desire the time machine, given they have their own?"

"My father's presence poses a threat to the Nazis, the potential exposure of their nightmare. His time machine surpasses theirs in both capability and advancement. He has constructed and secretively installed several time machines across multiple locations and time zones, known only to him," Erhard declared, pride resonating in his voice.

"Doesn't the prospect of the Nazis terrify you or your sister?" Lisa interjected.

"Provided we abide by certain boundaries, we remain safe. I recommend you do the same, or you won't last long. Refrain from delving too deeply into the past, lest things spiral out of control," he warned, dabbing his sweat with a napkin before proceeding. "My father informed me yesterday of your recent contact with them."

David regarded Erhard in astonishment. "I encountered them today, a younger pair. How could your father have mentioned that yesterday?"

"The time machine renders the impossible plausible," Erhard chuckled.

"Indeed! Still a bit difficult to digest."

"Exercise caution should you cross paths with the young couple again. Don't let their youth and charm deceive you! Their ruthlessness has been demonstrated numerous times. The man, Bruno Fischer, has been responsible for the deaths of nearly nine hundred Jews and disabled prisoners in just two years. Remember his name," Erhard warned before approaching an appliance he had placed on a table earlier. He glanced at David, "My father wishes to present you with a gift."

"A gift? Whatever for?" David questioned.

"Out of respect for you and admiration for your books. It's a device to prevent Nazi agents from eavesdropping on your conversations within this house," Erhard proposed.

"All I seek is the truth behind Alice's vanishing and her fiancé's cryptic death. I have no intentions of unmasking their secrets or revealing Hitler," David responded, agitated by the predicament he found himself in.

"I understand, but the Nazis aren't aware of that. Their fear and suspicion make them wary of anything related to my father and this house. They'll go to any lengths to avoid exposure. I'm simply asking you to tread carefully. Keep the devices, and don't allow anyone else to tamper with them. I must take my leave now, but I'll bring more ice cream when I visit next week," Erhard concluded on a cheerful note before heading for the door.

"Why reveal all this to me?" David called out just as Erhard was about to depart.

Erhard paused. "I saw a reflection of myself in you when we first met. Stubborn, fearless, but genuine. Your books have granted me insight into your thought process. Your intentions are pure. Take care of yourself and her. Don't disregard my words," he said, his voice heavy with emotion, before leaving.

David and Lisa were left in stunned silence, exchanging puzzled looks.

"Do you think he was being truthful?" Lisa mused. David nodded.

"I do, indeed."

"How can we be sure he isn't using these devices to spy on us now?"

"He had no reason to withhold anything." David replied, a hint of fatigue creeping into his voice.

"Nonetheless, I'm worried, do you think Erhard is not telling you the truth?"

"Naturally, it's not every day one gets visited by time travelers," David attempted to lighten the mood with a quip.

"Do you still intend to undertake the journey with the time machine?" Lisa asked, fixing David with a severe stare.

David returned her gaze with a smile, paused briefly, then responded, "I understand your fear and hesitation. But let's find the machine first, and then we can deliberate on whether to travel."

"Why the insistence on time travel, despite the warnings and my reservations?" Lisa pressed on.

"Wouldn't you seize the opportunity, Lisa, if you had a time machine within your grasp?" David retorted, offering her a hypothetical challenge.

"No, not if it carries the risks it appears to," Lisa responded, holding his gaze steadfastly.

"I vow to exercise caution, not to frivolously embark on time travel," David reassured her, taking her hand into his.

She nodded in approval. "You won't embark on this journey without me, per our agreement. Okay?"

"We ought to retire for the night, love. Today has been quite eventful, but come tomorrow, I will revisit this topic," he suggested, leading her toward their bedroom.

Behroz Behnejad

CHAPTER 17

David's arms enveloped Lisa, pulling her in for a tender kiss. Their bodies collapsed onto the bed, a swell of laughter filling the room. But their merriment was interrupted by the intrusive ring of Lisa's phone. David passed her the device, an amused twinkle in his eyes as she rolled onto her side.

"Hello?" Lisa answered, panting slightly from the exertion.

"Hi! It's Mary."

Lisa adopted a more composed tone, suppressing a chuckle.

"Mary! A delight to hear from you. What's the latest?"

"Did I interrupt something? Should I call back?" Mary's voice wavered, expressing regret for not sending a heads-up text.

"No, not at all. It's been a while since we last spoke. Did the job interview go well?"

"Indeed, I bagged the position. It pays a hefty salary, quite a leap from my previous one," Mary shared with a note of triumph in her voice.

"And what about Eric? How did things pan out there?"

"He's a gem," Mary replied, her voice delighted. We hit it off right away.

"That's fantastic, Mary! I'm genuinely thrilled for you!"

"Your words of encouragement were instrumental, Lisa. I was on the brink of despair," Mary said, her gratitude audible.

"You've done wonders for David and me, too, Mary. Your matchmaking introduced me to David! We owe our bliss to you," Lisa expressed her heartfelt appreciation.

"You two were a match made in heaven. I merely nudged things in the right direction," Mary deflected with a chuckle. "Yesterday, I revisited my old office. I felt a need to resolve some lingering issues before embarking on this new chapter." She inhaled deeply, her resolve echoing through the line.

"I admire your bravery!" Lisa interjected, her respect for her friend evident.

"The atmosphere was frosty when I stepped in. The secretary asked me to hold on when I asked to meet with the boss. There was an undercurrent of hostility as their old coworkers passed by. As I sat in the waiting room, the tension grew. Finally, I was ushered into the office where he sat lounging in his chair with casual indifference. As soon as he saw me, his eyebrows knotted, and he spat out, 'I don't have all day. Spit it out.' His cavalier attitude triggered me." Mary paused, letting out a sound that was half chuckle, half sob. "I looked him square in the eyes and fired back, 'Did you think I was here to grovel? To shoulder blame that isn't mine? You knew my dedication to this job. I've invested blood, sweat, and tears in this company. It was thriving before you took the reins. Your high-handed rule caused a staff exodus. The company's future is now hanging by a thread. It's high time you tore down your ivory tower!'"

"How did he react?" Lisa interjected; her curiosity piqued.

"He was blindsided by my outburst. I remember his face when I labeled him 'a pitiful fool,' which summoned the secretary and a few staff members into the room. They attempted to escort me out, but a wave of his hand silenced them. His gaze hardened as he assessed me, finally admitting, 'Your audacity, albeit rude, can be an asset to the company. I could offer you your old position if you wish to return.' Let me tell you, his dismissive grin did nothing to deter me as I told him, 'Without a doubt, you need me. Without my efforts, your company teeters on the edge of catastrophe. Your tyrannical leadership will be the death knell for this company. You're hurtling towards an abysmal future. It's time you faced the harsh truth for the company and yourself.' Oh, Lisa, his stunned expression when I turned down his offer was a sight to behold. I felt liberated! I proved my worth."

"That's incredible, Mary! Your audacity to confront him is inspiring. You've paved the way, Mary! I'm genuinely happy for you," Lisa said, her voice brimming with admiration. "Given all that's transpired with you, the team, and the company, you're an inspiration."

Hearing her proclamation, David's eyebrows shot up in surprise.

He glanced at Lisa, nodding in approval, his thumb shooting up in a gesture of endorsement. "Amazing," he cheered.

"Who was that?" Mary inquired.

"That was David," Lisa replied, a contagious giggle punctuating her words.

"Great! Pass on my best wishes and thanks to him. Take care now."

David muffled a yawn as he nestled into the bed. Exhausted yet content, Lisa snuggled into him. Cocooned in each other's arms, they stared up at the ceiling, the day's events replaying in their minds.

David tenderly stroked her hair, musing, "Isn't contemplating other realities and timelines intriguing? To escape the present only to land in the same place but a different epoch."

"It's quite a conundrum to visualize time travel, to imagine finding a passage to a parallel universe. The concept of freezing time and yet maneuvering through it is hard to grasp. It's surreal," Lisa reflected, her reverie disrupted by the sound of David's rhythmic snores. She smiled affectionately, planting a kiss on his cheek. "Sweet dreams, my love."

A ruckus startled David from his slumber. His eyes fluttered open, and he wearily swung his legs over the edge of the bed to see an assembly of squabbling crows on the terrace. Irritated by their early morning fracas, he shuffled out to disperse them, then squinted at his wristwatch through sleep-veiled eyes.

"Damn it!" He grimaced. "Only just past five. Cursed birds." A sigh escaped him, acceptance of the impossibility of regaining his lost sleep. Resigned, he ventured into the kitchen, the cold tiles a shocking contrast to the warmth of the bed and fired up the coffee machine. Returning to the terrace, he nestled into a chair, drinking in the cool kiss of the morning air.

The comforting aroma of brewing coffee filled the house, and David savored it. Much like the first drag of a cigarette, the smell alone could satiate the craving. He leaned back into his chair, absorbing the quiet charm of the day breaking. His gaze meandered across the road. A small cloud burgeoned in the sky, sunbeams straining against the night's remnants, reaching for the tree branches, eager to awaken the sun resting beneath the horizon. A distant rooster echoed its morning announcement from the neighbor's newly erected chicken coop. The natural cadence of life stirring with the day brought a content smile to his face.

He found his gaze drifting upwards to the stars, still stubbornly twinkling against the encroaching dawn. Fighting the weight of his eyelids, he decided to witness the sunrise. Gradually, the sun inched above the horizon, its gentle warmth bathing his face, casting an intensifying glow that dared to challenge his retinas.

His serene morning was interrupted by the erratic flight of a couple of flies hovering over something on a distant part of the terrace. Drawn by curiosity, he approached to find a deceased bird. Revulsion seeping through him, he utilized a nearby barbecue stick to pick up the tiny carcass, tossing it onto the street below.

"Breakfast is served, local felines," he murmured, retreating to the tranquility of the bedroom. With a gentle tease, he began to tickle Lisa's nose. Her disgruntled groan was drowned out by his mirth as he marveled at her sleep-softened beauty. Despite her sleepy protests, he persisted with his torment.

"Enough!" Lisa mumbled, forcing her eyes open.

"Rise and shine, Time to greet the day," David chuckled, unabated.

"What ungodly hour have you awoken me at?" Lisa mumbled, stifling a yawn.

"Half past six," he revealed.

"Oh heavens! It's far too early," she lamented.

"Perk up! Coffee awaits," David responded, kissing her cheek before venturing off to fetch the morning paper.

A groggy Lisa soon wandered into the kitchen, her sleep-heavy gaze fixating on David. His grin stretched wider at her sight, causing him to tease, "My, Lisa, you appear positively ghoulish - I mean, you look delightful, but I can tell you're feeling wretched."

"Indeed," Lisa responded, "My sleep was troubled with peculiar dreams."

"Were they nightmares?" he inquired, setting a cup before her, and filling it with freshly brewed coffee.

"Not exactly, but quite disturbing, nonetheless. It felt that we were stuck somewhere and couldn't find the exit door to get out. I'm still damp from the stress of it all," Lisa lamented, revealing her perspiration-stained pajamas.

"Do you want to discuss it?" David probed.

"No, the memory will fade, along with the discomfort it brings," she replied, lifting her coffee mug for a rejuvenating sip.

"Very well, darling. Get dressed. We need to move swiftly; time waits for no one!" He cheerfully bounded back to their bedroom, leaving Lisa with her thoughts.

David finished getting dressed. A sky-blue shirt and dark pants would do for the day. But the sense of urgency at the current mystery bubbled to the surface quicker than the care of his appearance. "Lisa, what are you doing?" David's called from the bedroom. "We need to get going, love!"

"I'm brushing my hair," she called back.

"Please hurry!" He advised her again.

David rifled through their bedroom in search of his elusive cigarettes. A sudden realization struck him, and he remembered leaving the pack on the terrace table the previous day. Retrieving his treasured vice, he hit a match against its flint strip, illuminating the end of a cigarette with its flame. He inhaled deeply, the smoke's soothing journey through his body making the rushed morning worth it. Lisa's voice rang out as he finished, "I'm ready. Where are you?"

"I'm on the terrace. Coming!" He shouted back, extinguishing his cigarette in the ashtray after a final, satisfactory puff.

David found Lisa in the living room, a look of apprehension clouding her beautiful features. "Stay calm, Lisa. Everything will go smoothly; there's no need to be anxious before we've even begun,"

David reassured her, opening the front door.

The world outside was a serene painting, devoid of noise save for the rustle of leaves and the wind's gentle exhale. Lisa basked in the tranquility momentarily, closing her eyes as the sun painted warmth on her face. Despite her effort to lose herself in nature's symphony, David could see the worry etched on her face. Reaching out, he tenderly grasped her hand, kissing softly against her knuckles. "Trust me, everything's going to be okay. You're not alone in this," he comforted her.

Lisa's hesitance was palpable as she gave a tentative nod. "David, I'm not backing out. I want to be there for you. But something feels off. I never anticipated this when we bought the house. Now we're embarking on this journey, and it's a strain," she confessed.

Together, they walked to the car, David's face a stoic mask as he attempted to allay her fears with a reassuring gaze. "We'll be safe. You have my word. Nothing will happen to either of us, and we have each other," he gently reminded her.

Opening the car door for her, he watched as she sunk into her seat, her gaze landing on a mother cat tending to her kittens. "It's overwhelming to comprehend everything that has transpired and what lies ahead. It feels like a relentless dream, but I yearn to awaken. It's too much to process," she divulged, sharing her inner turmoil with David again.

David responded with a nod as he turned the ignition. "Your feelings aren't lost on me," he comforted her with a reassuring squeeze on her thigh, guiding the car out of the driveway.

CHAPTER 18

During their drive to the mansion, David and Lisa observed people diligently repairing damages from a storm that had swept through a few days earlier. As they neared their destination, an odd object materialized similar to flying object and dark color like church bell in their view, hovering quietly over the road in the distance. The thing was dark brown, resembling a church bell - just as their neighbor, Peter, had described. As they drew closer, it mysteriously vanished. David shared a look of astonishment with Lisa, his lips pursed tightly, and without any delay, they swung open the gate and drove onto the property.

A few minutes later, as they pulled up to the house, they spotted the same object, now levitating over the ground. With awe and caution, David brought the car to a sudden halt and stepped out to get a closer look at the oddity. His mind was a whirlpool of possibilities. Still in the car, Lisa squirmed uncomfortably in her seat, her gaze transfixed on the object with growing unease.

"What in the world?" she whispered, her hands clasping together in nervous anticipation.

Quietly, the object descended to the ground. It wasn't long before a human figure emerged from a hatch and began surveying the surroundings.

From within the car, Lisa called out, her voice hushed and fearful, "Watch out! Don't get too close!"

David ignored Lisa's caution and continued his advance. Upon noticing him, the figure recoiled, quickly retreating into the hatch. The strange object then ascended swiftly into the sky, disappearing as suddenly as it had appeared.

Stunned, David spun around to face Lisa, his mouth agape. "Did you just witness what I did?"

All Lisa could manage was a silent nod of agreement, her pulse racing uncontrollably. She remained paralyzed, watching as David hurried back towards the car. He retrieved the toolbox from the backseat before sprinting off towards the mansion. "Wait! Wait for me!" she called out, trying to match his frantic pace.

"We need to find the time machine before anything else happens!" David replied, shoving the mansion door open and heading straight for Alice's room.

Together, they moved the bookcase, the books jostling. David shone his flashlight around the room, confirming it was untouched. With a gentle push, the door creaked open.

"The moment we've been waiting for is approaching!" David declared, moving towards the desk, hopeful of finding a response to the message he had left for Alice. Much to his surprise, the diary had been moved to the table's edge. His hands shook as he opened the book, revealing the reply:

Who are you? How are you able to get into my room without being seen? Why does no one else notice you? This house is always full. Someone should have seen you. I am terrified now. Please, tell me who you are.

"Poor girl," Lisa whispered, standing close behind David. "We've upset her."

"Upset her now? She wrote this seventy years ago," David retorted.

"But we have scared her, this Alice. She was a real person with feelings and thoughts," Lisa insisted.

"Fair point. You're right about that. And we need to find the time machine," David replied, cutting her off. He veered towards the grandfather clock, squatting down to examine its base, where he felt a peculiar vibration. "Hmm, there's a small gap here... it's buzzing. If I could get this open, I'd be able to see what's behind it. Lisa, can you bring the toolbox?" His voice trembled slightly, his adrenaline running high.

As requested, Lisa placed the toolbox next to David. He selected a screwdriver and attempted to wedge it into the narrow gap. He grumbled and cursed under his breath; his shirt soaked in sweat from the exertion. After several tense minutes, the hidden compartment finally gave way. Overjoyed, David looked up at Lisa and offered a victorious smile.

"This is it," David murmured, his fingers gently lifting the box lid.

To their surprise, they discovered a rapidly spinning cogwheel with blinking lights and four shiny cylinders orbiting each other. Intrigued, David kneeled and leaned back slightly, his gaze fixed on the enigmatic device. His hands trembled with nervous anticipation. The screwdriver he held clattered onto the floor.

Lisa also knelt beside him, her hands resting on David's shaking shoulders. Her voice trembled as she asked, "Could that be... is it a time machine?"

"What else could it be?" David replied, his voice equally shaky. "God, it's unbearably hot in here. It's hard to think."

David turned his attention to the wall. He muttered, "Now, I need to see what's behind this wall." He moved closer to inspect the wire disappearing into the wall, his fingers tracing over it. "There are cracks here, and the wall seems a bit thinner. It's vibrating." He retrieved the fallen screwdriver and started chipping at the plaster, which crumbled onto the floor. "Bring me a hammer, love."

Lisa fetched a hammer and handed it to David. He focused and began striking the wall, his blows firm but controlled. After a few hits, a hole opened, revealing three large, cylindrical, metallic objects mounted on a massive black box, shaking with five pulsating lights on the side. David and Lisa could only stare, astonished by the sight.

"Can you believe this crazy device? It's almost unimaginable!" David exclaimed, his eyes wide with wonder at their discovery.

He also uncovered a small hatch, slightly ajar behind one of the cylinders, concealing something. Reaching in, David retrieved a heavy backpack equipped with a large belt.

"What's that for?" Lisa wondered.

David examined the backpack more closely, finding a small note on the back that read *Return*.

"What do you think that means?" Lisa asked.

David furrowed his brow and rubbed his forehead, "Maybe, it means we go back using this."

The belt had two buttons, green and red, and was connected to the wall by a cable.

"It might have a rechargeable power source in the backpack and the belt," David speculated, carefully unplugging the cables. Suddenly, they heard a faint beeping sound.

In a panic, David glanced at the wall clock and saw the hands moving in the opposite direction. "Grab the toolbox and get out of the room. It's time," he told Lisa, his voice fraught with urgency.

Shaken, Lisa reached out to David. "What? Why? What's going on? We — we agreed, remember? I'm coming with you!" Her eyes filled with tears, mirroring her rising panic.

"Lisa, the machine is on!" David yelled, noticing her impending tears.

"I'm coming with you!"

"Alright, but stay close," he shouted back.

Lisa dropped the toolbox and ran to David. She clung to him, her frightened eyes searching his.

David quickly donned the belt and the backpack, preparing himself for the journey ahead. He looked at Lisa and warned, "This is serious, Lisa. There's no turning back now."

Crying and struggling to articulate her thoughts, Lisa blurted out, "I love you! We're in this together. We can get through this," her voice breaking, her gaze meeting his.

David leaned in to kiss Lisa. Despite the overwhelming emotion, a sense of excitement stirred within him. He managed to smile reassuringly at her.

"Hold on," he roared, and in an instant, they both disappeared, their surroundings fading away as a new dimension enveloped them from all sides.

CHAPTER 19

The incessant beeping reverberated inside the room, the clock's hands spinning in rapid reverse. David watched Lisa peek through her fingers, her eyes fixed on the vortex of swirling energy around them. Time was running backward. Overcome, she cried out, "This can't be real. This must be a dream. We're going backward!" Her grip tightened around David's arm.

A whirlwind of fear and exhilaration consumed him. He shouted, "It's working! It's working!"

As they moved through the fabric of time, the grinding noise of a machine echoed around them. It reminded David of the spinning of gears before they abruptly halted, giving way to a deafening silence. Lisa glanced around, noting a subtle transformation in their surroundings. Everything was the same, yet pristine. There was no layer of dust, no cobwebs. Small, scattered lights lent a warm ambiance to the room. They were in Alice's room.

Suddenly, the room echoed with laughter. Both David and Lisa spun around, startled. A woman sat at a desk dressed in white. David instinctively pulled Lisa closer and stepped back, motioning for her to keep quiet. The floorboard creaked beneath them, attracting the woman's attention.

On spotting David and Lisa, the woman's eyes widened in surprise, "Goodness gracious!"

"Please, don't be frightened," David quickly responded, keeping his voice steady. Lisa stepped forward, adding, "We don't mean any harm. We can explain."

The woman seemed skeptical, "Who are you?"

"I'm David, and this is my fiancée, Lisa," David introduced, indicating Lisa. "You're Alice, right?"

Alice stared at them, her face showing clear horror, but she nodded in confirmation.

"Do you recall the message I left for you?" David asked.

Alice was speechless. She took several shaky breaths, closing her eyes to regain her composure. Once she had gathered herself, she asked, "How did you get in here?"

David shrugged, admitting, "I don't completely understand, but we have a machine that enables time travel."

Alice's wonder was evident. "How do you know my name?" She let the book she'd been holding drop from her hands and rushed towards the door.

"Wait!" David called, extending a hand toward her. "Stay for Jay's sake."

Just before she could open the door, Alice stopped, her grip on the handle so tight her knuckles were white.

"What do you know about Jay?" She asked, her back still turned towards them. "What do you want from me?"

David could tell she was fighting back tears.

"We're not here to harm you, only to warn you," he assured her.

"Please, let us explain," Lisa implored. "We're here to help." Carefully, she approached Alice and placed a gentle hand over hers.

Slowly, Alice's grip on the handle relaxed. She let herself be guided towards the bed and sat down, avoiding their gaze.

"The machine I mentioned allows us to travel through time. That's how I've learned things about your family," David explained patiently, knowing her shock might prevent her from understanding their intentions.

"What will – what will happen to my family?" Alice asked, fear tinging her voice.

"We'll tell you everything we can. We come from a world and a time where the unimaginable is real. In our time, your past has led to disastrous consequences for your future, which we need to correct," David explained.

Alice fixed her scrutinizing gaze upon David, her eyes narrowing as she processed the information. She slowly rose from the bed and cautiously approached him. "You're here with no intention of harm, am I correct?" she asked.

David nodded, his reassuring smile softening the situation.

Alice posed another question, "What brings you here?"

David confessed, "We're genuinely here to help you, Miss Alice, to avert a looming misfortune."

The idea baffled her. "To help me?" she echoed. "What is going to occur in my future? And how does my past factor into it? You can't possibly predict my future. This is all so bewildering."

David calmly responded, "It's not solely about you. It involves your fiancé as well."

She began to pace around the room. "How could you foresee my future? What's destined for Jay?" she asked, her fear palpable.

"The information might be challenging to digest, but if you bear with us, it will all make sense. It concerns both you and Jay. Promise us not to flee at when we tell you what we need to tell you, "he urged, his expression serious.

Alice regarded him apprehensively but managed to offer a hesitant nod.

"We've journeyed from the distant future, an era filled with marvels. Our origin is the year 2009, which is sixty-nine years ahead," David said slowly.

Alice didn't respond, her confusion evident as she stood there, her gaze shifting between him and Lisa.

David empathized with her skepticism. Lisa recalling her disbelief when encountering the time machine. "Science is on a rapid trajectory of advancement. In the near future, scientists will construct a device capable of manipulating time, facilitating travel to the future and back," he said.

"A time machine? I thought those were confined to fairy tales and novels."

Lisa chimed in, "We thought the same, Alice. But the reality is time travel is real. We are living proof of that."

Growing more confident, Alice challenged them, "But how can you prove you're from the future?"

Caught off guard, David hesitated. He remembered Lisa's misplaced flashlight and asked, "During one of our visits, Lisa left a flashlight on the desk. Did you come across it?"

Alice looked at David, her surprise apparent. "That belonged to you?"

David confirmed with a nod. "Yes, what became of it?"

"I showed it to my father, who then took charge of it."

David gave an understanding nod. Then, he remembered his cell phone. He fished it out from his back pocket and presented it to Alice. "This is a phone of the future. These are the buttons used for dialing calls. This tiny feature here is a camera for capturing photos," he demonstrated, scrolling through images. "This is Lisa and me. Here we are seated in the living room of our home, and this picture was taken when we purchased our new car," he explained, his enthusiasm contagious.

Alice pointed at the screen, "A car? Is that what's in the picture?"

David confirmed. "Yes!" A wave of relief washed over him and Lisa. The flashlight and the cell phone were solid evidence, lending credence to their claims. They had successfully managed to establish their credibility while offering Alice a glimpse of the future.

Alice was visibly calmer now. "Such splendid images, and all rendered in color as if painted. I've seen colored portraits of people. Can you describe what your world looks like?" she asked, her curiosity piqued.

Lisa began to describe their world, her face lighting up with enthusiasm. "The world retains its beauty, albeit accompanied by constant noise from vehicles. A considerable number of people endure stress due to their work life. Rapid technology development sweeps the globe, and keeping pace becomes a challenge. Everything runs on computers — devices akin to typewriters, yet capable of storing data and performing calculations. Now, these computers connect through phone lines, resembling the telegraph system. Messages can be exchanged, and bills paid right from home, eliminating the need to visit a bank."

Alice listened attentively; her eyes transfixed on the images on the cell phone screen. Suddenly, she identified a familiar face in one of the photos: Her own.

"How did you acquire this photo? It was captured only a month ago," she exclaimed, pointing to a corresponding photo on her bedside table.

"That picture was in the house when we toured it in 2009. We purchased it. Your story intrigued me, and I was drawn to your photo, so I used my phone to capture an image of it."

Alice shook her head, overwhelmed by the revelations. She sank into the chair at her desk. "I feel so disoriented." She buried her face in her hands, then lifted her gaze to meet David's. Her voice trembled as she asked, "What is my fate?"

David tried to soothe her concerns. "I'll explain everything, but we need to meet your parents first. We'll handle everything else in due time," he assured her.

Alice asked a troubling question. "And what if they refuse to believe you and decide to involve the police?"

David conceded, "We don't want trouble, in such a case, we'll be forced to return." He shrugged, attempting to convey nonchalance.

Decisively, Alice commanded, "Then follow me." She headed towards the door, leading them onward.

Lisa leaned towards David, her heart pounding with anxiety. She whispered, "now what?"

David, feeling a similar surge of anxiety, attempted to comfort her. "We'll be alright." He clasped Lisa's hand in his, offering silent reassurance, and together they followed Alice up the stairs to the hallway.

Once they reached a small room, Alice suggested, "You can wait here while I fetch them."

In the small room, David watched as Alice wrestled with thoughts of her future. He observed her chewing on her nails, a clear sign of the anxiety coiling within her. Questions danced around her, as frantic and numerous as a swarm of bees. *Was death her inevitable fate? What did the future have in store for Jay? Were these people attempting to hoodwink her?*

Could time travel actually exist? Were their words sincere? A familiar voice jolted Alice from her internal reverie.

"Sweet Alice, are you doing alright?" Her father's worried voice reached David's ears.

"Yes, but I have something important to share," Alice replied, glancing over her shoulder to ensure that David and Lisa were still there. Alice's father, intrigued, abandoned his newspaper, and stretched within his armchair.

"Tell me, what's on your mind?"

"Some people are here, and they'd like to meet you.

"Who?" he asked, matching his daughter's anxiety with his own.

Outside, Alice's mother was busy repotting a houseplant. Seeing her, Alice knocked on the window and motioned for her to come inside. Her father's curiosity was now piqued.

"Follow me," Alice guided her father towards the room where David and Lisa were waiting.

Rising from his seat, her father crossed paths with his wife in the hall.

"What's all this about?" she asked, confusion etched on her face.

"Alice has someone she wants us to meet," he explained.

"Some people," Alice corrected him before opening the door. "You can come out now. Meet David and Lisa."

Wide-eyed, Alice's father studied David and Lisa with their unfamiliar attire and hairstyles. He then turned a baffled gaze toward Alice.

"Their different appearance scared me initially, but they clarified their intentions — they're here to help." Alice paused to regain her breath. "You must believe them and trust what they say," she emphasized, the weight of her revelation lifting off her shoulders.

Extending a hand towards David, Alice's father introduced himself, "I'm Eric. You're David, right?"

"Yes, sir. I'm David Hamilton, and this is my fiancée, Lisa," David confirmed, returning the handshake. "Could we move to the living room to continue our conversation?" he suggested.

Eric's brow furrowed as he shot a worried look toward David.

Alice's mother spoke up. "How did you get in without us noticing? Did Alice let you in?"

"You must be Elena," David recognized her, moving to shake her hand.

Surprised, she eyed David as he extended his hand.

"How do you know my name?"

"We'll explain everything, I assure you. But first, promise not to overreact to our story. It may seem unbelievable, but it's all true, and we have evidence to prove it. We're here to help Alice and Jay," David explained, his speech interrupted by the sight of a man peeking through the door.

"Is that James?" David asked, motioning towards the figure.

"Yes, that's him," Elena confirmed, uncertainty creeping into her voice.

"James – could we have some privacy, please?" David asked before

James could enter the room. "Close the door on your way out."

James responded, "why should I leave?" David said, "Please, we want to talk in private, closed the door behind you." David saw him from the window, continuing his way towards the barn.

"Forgive my asking, but how did you know his name too?" Elena asked, her surprise palpable.

"I'll explain all, ma'am. Let's sit and talk more comfortably," David proposed, pulling out chairs for Elena and Alice.

The tension was tangible as they all sat, waiting for David to speak. David placed an oddly shaped device and his backpack on the table. He leaned forward, elbows resting on the table. Eric examined the strange device — a peculiar rectangle akin to a picture frame.

"The information we're about to disclose is vital, and the decisions you'll make based on it could drastically impact Alice and Jay. The choice is yours, but I implore you to hear us out and try to believe our words," David began.

He turned to Alice. "Both your and Jay's lives are in danger."

Chapter 20

Alice's eyes widened. Elena drew in a deep breath. David continued. "First, a tragedy is going to occur in Jay's life, and then you will vanish without a trace, never to be found by the police."

"How can you know this? How dare you come here and frighten us! Absurd!" Eric said, not bothering to hide his anger.

"Sir, because we've already been there and read about what happened to her and Jay in the newspapers," David said.

"Happened? Nothing has occurred or is in the papers. I can't comprehend any of this," Eric said, glancing nervously at Elena.

"We are travelers, and we don't belong to this time period. We come from the future, believe me," Lisa interjected, her gaze intense.

"The future? You must be joking! How can the future exist when we're here, in the present? We aren't there yet. We can never reach the future because it hasn't transpired yet. Right? And if so, how could you have been there? This is quite blasphemous, I must say," Elena replied, her laughter strained.

"Clearly, whatever you're both saying is utterly extraordinary," Eric said, his tone laced with indignation.

They exchanged a glance before turning to Alice, their heads shaking as if to dismiss these outrageous claims.

"I can attempt to explain, but it will be difficult to comprehend. We had a hard time understanding it ourselves, but then a series of events occurred that proved time travel is possible. In the future, because of Hitler's actions, science progresses, and some scientists manage to devise a way to travel in time, all conducted under utmost secrecy. Nobody is fully aware yet. The time machine we traveled in is within this very house," David explained.

"In our house?" Alice queried, a note of fear in her voice.

"Yes! In 2009, my fiancée Lisa and I will purchase this house, and to our surprise, we will learn about what befell Alice and Jay. The house's history will pique my curiosity. Then a series of peculiar events will convince us that advancement in technology occurrences is genuinely taking place here. I eventually unravel the mystery and discover the presence of a time machine in the house," David narrated, "and that happened to us today - being transported through time within this very house."

"Where is the machine?" Eric questioned.

"In Alice's room."

All eyes swiveled to Alice.

"How can we believe you?" Eric challenged, turning his gaze back to David.

"In 2009, we entered her room where we had left my flashlight, which Alice found and handed over to you. Correct?" David inquired.

Eric recoiled. "Well, that's correct, yes, about a light device."

"I also have my phone as proof," David added, reaching for his phone on the table before them. "It functions as a camera, and I have plenty of pictures from the future which I've already shown to Alice as evidence."

Alice nodded her agreement. "They're in color, like they're painted, Dad."

"For instance, here is a picture of Alice's portrait." Her parents gaped in astonishment. "I can also show you the time machine in my backpack. If this isn't enough proof, then I've done all I can. Now it's up to you whether to believe us or not."

They exchanged silent looks. Lisa cleared her throat and said, "Let us at least tell you what's going to transpire. Then we can return to where we came from, and you can decide how to proceed."

"Tell me now! What's going to happen to me and Jay?" Alice pleaded, her voice trembling with anxiety.

David nodded, met Alice's gaze, and began, "Someone in this house has developed an innocent crush on you, and your relationship with Jay is causing him anguish. After a sequence of events, he will murder Jay. The police will find no evidence and will conclude that Jay committed suicide, but I managed to unearth evidence linking that individual to the murder. Now that there's a time machine, we wanted to use it to avert this calamity."

"What will become of me then?" Alice asked, her voice shaky.

"According to historical records and newspaper articles, you vanish under unclear circumstances. The police believe that Jay's supposed suicide emotionally devastated you, and one day you run away from home, never to return. But my suspicion is that the same murderer might have killed you. Regrettably, nobody knows what happened to you. Eventually, the police closed the case," David explained.

Alice appeared exceedingly shaken. Tears trickled down her cheeks as she sat motionless in her chair, her gaze fixed on David. "What can we do? Who is this person? Are they here now?"

"Before I expose him, there's one thing I need to clarify. He hasn't committed any wrongdoing yet. We can't condemn him prematurely, as we don't possess a complete understanding of the circumstances," David said, mustering his utmost sincerity and goodwill.

"But you asserted that he murdered Jay or will do so in the future," Eric interjected.

"Yes, I did. But he hasn't committed the act yet. Together, we could alter the course of history and save Jay, Alice, and him. He, too, is a victim, and it's within our power to act upon that from now. We merely have to guide him towards a different path. Perhaps he's unaware of his looming murderous intentions. Our immediate aid is crucial," David said, his fist pounding on the table.

"Who is he?" Alice asked.

David hesitated for a moment. The room was heavy with

unbearable tension, the air thick and suffocating, reminiscent of the dust from Alice's room they first entered it. He was on the precipice of revealing critical information to the family. It was akin to striking a match – once ignited, the fire couldn't be undone, and decisions were imminent.

"We can assist him too. It's... it's James," David finally divulged.

"No! That's impossible. He's so harmless and kind. Everyone adores him," Alice protested, backed by her parents.

"But according to James, he is victimized by many here, and Jay isn't exempt from this," Lisa countered. "That's why James is also a victim."

"But Jay? He's always been kind to him when he's here," Alice responded, her voice wavering.

"Sure, when he's in your company. But the real question is, is he equally kind when he's alone with James?" David posed the question.

"Did James convey this to you directly?" Eric asked, arms folded defensively across his chest.

"No, but he chronicled it in his diary, which we've examined. He wrote about his experiences in this house, his relationship with Jay, and the bullying he suffered. He wrote about his feelings for Alice," David confessed after a deep breath, surveying the room. "Many were dismissive of him, including Jay. I believe that the bullying and other negative incidents, compounded by depression and your relationship with Jay, elicited potent feelings in him that drove him to murder," David explained.

"I can't make sense of this!" Elena exclaimed. "This doesn't match his character at all. James can't read or write. How could he keep diaries?"

"Literacy is his well-kept secret. I suspect that Jay somehow discovered James' talent, and James wanted to eliminate him to protect his secret emotions and secure Alice for himself. Jay had become a thorn in James' side that needed to be excised," David elaborated.

"How did you find out about his diaries?" Alice asked, her voice tremulous.

"We discovered them in the shed where he resided."

"But he lives here in the house," Eric replied, astounded.

"Currently, yes. But you will eventually expel him when he exposes his feelings for Alice. At that point, you, Eric, will decide that he is no longer welcome in this house nor allowed near Alice or her room. You'll renovate a distant shed on your property for James to inhabit. Following this relocation, he undergoes a transformation and succumbs to depression," David explained.

"What is happening here? It all feels like a nightmare!" Eric's sense of stability seemed to crumble with the shock of learning what had transpired under his roof involving his own daughter.

Lisa reached out and squeezed Alice's hands. "But there is hope," she assured. "You, along with others like Jay, will cast James into uncertainty. Jay poses a threat to him, and the only one who stands by him is you, Alice. But now, you can change your actions."

Suddenly, the living room wall clock chimed. The hands indicated eleven. The sound spurred David into swift action. He glanced at his belt, ensuring everything was in order, and then, a hint of panic surfaced as he looked at the others in the living room. He grasped the urgency of dealing with this matter swiftly.

"What can we do?" Elena questioned, noticing David's growing perspiration.

David laid out the new plan: "It's straightforward. Treat him as a family member. Everyone must respect him and his feelings. You all need to change, Jay included. As soon as anyone bullies James, you need to intervene, defend him, and not abandon him," David stressed. "If the cook exposes him, remain calm and don't take it out on James. Instead, instruct the cook or anyone else not to meddle in his life. James may have some form of mild autism, but he is a fully grown man. Everyone is entitled to fall in love. It's perfectly normal to fall for a pretty girl. Love is the most beautiful thing there is. With some understanding and assistance, he can move forward. He lacks parents of his own, and now you have the chance to assume that role. And Alice, you can be like a sister to him, so take care not to send him the wrong signals." David exhaled. The most crucial point had been made.

"What do you mean by the wrong signals?" Alice asked, her brow furrowed.

"James typically picks roses for you and places them in your room," David said. "Isn't that correct, Alice?"

"Not just my room. He also selects them for the living room," Alice responded.

"My question is, why do you suppose he does it only for you and not for the others in the house? Your younger brother, Albert, does he receive flowers as well? Or your parents? Have you ever asked him for flowers?" David queried.

"No," Alice mumbled, her gaze fixed on her mother. "I recall that once, two years ago, he entered my room with a bouquet and wished me a happy birthday."

Suddenly, she fell silent, shifting her gaze to David before continuing, "And I still receive flowers at least twice a month, and now that you mention it, I realize he might have developed feelings for me. I didn't realize then." Alice said.

David nodded in affirmation.

"He was hurt when Jay openly professed his love and proposed to you. James was watching. As soon as he overheard your intention to get engaged, the conflict escalated, and James saw red. He began devising a plan to alter that – one method being eliminating Jay."

Alice furrowed her brow and confessed, "We haven't informed anyone about the engagement." Her face flushed crimson as she glanced at her mother and swallowed hard.

Suddenly, a voice called outside the hall: "But we can do that now!"

Chapter 21

All eyes turned to the door as a well-dressed young man entered the room. Jay stood there radiating confidence. David observed the man's charming smile and how he looked at Alice. Holding a bouquet of flowers, Jay strolled towards her, removed his hat, and dropped to one knee.

Alice stared at him in surprise, unable to utter a word. Jay handed her the flowers and took her hand, looking deeply into her eyes and confessing his feelings. With tears streaming down her cheek, Alice struggled to speak. Instead, she nodded, a gesture of acceptance and joy.

"Is that a yes?" Jay asked, laughing.

Alice nodded again and laughed. Elena and Eric exchanged glances, their eyes welling with tears too. David noticed Lisa silently sharing a smile. But as Lisa spotted James's peering through the window, worry etched her face. She nudged David, "James is out there, and he doesn't look happy..." she whispered.

David simply nodded in response, feeling powerless to change the situation. He moved to the window, his gaze tracking James as the man rushed away, disappearing behind the distant bushes.

Jay took out a small black box from amongst the flowers he held. He opened it to reveal a sparkling diamond ring. Alice sank to her knees and embraced him, confessing, "I love you."

Jay placed the ring on her finger and kissed her. He then moved on to Elena, embraced her, and promised, "I will take care of her." He shook hands with Eric and then turned to Lisa and David, asking, "Have we met before?"

"I don't think so. My name is David, and this is Lisa, my fiancé. We're acquaintances of the family. We're travelling and won't stay long, so we'll need to leave soon," David replied.

Jay extended an invitation to his wedding, to which David responded noncommittally.

"What's your relationship to the family?" Jay asked.

"Just acquaintances, really," David answered, gesturing to Alice. "You tell him, Alice."

"What is she going to tell me?" Jay inquired, his smile fading.

Alice led Jay to one of the chairs. "You better sit down," she advised, her voice heavy with sadness.

As Jay sat, David saw curiosity piqued by the grave expression on everyone's face. Alice started speaking, alluding to the future and its realities.

"Life is short. Every day could be our last day. We mustn't take life for granted," Alice said, leaving the statement hanging in the air.

Jay squirmed in his seat. "What is it you need to tell me?" he asked, his gaze locked onto Alice.

"Our love will – *could* end in tragedy," Alice said, her voice trembling.

Jay looked taken aback, "Alice? What are you saying?"

Alice seemed to struggle to put her feelings into words, so she stepped up to Jay, posing a hypothetical question about altering the future to ensure the survival of love.

Jay looked puzzled, "Of course, but what do you mean by this?"

"You haven't forgotten what happened to your plane last month? When your pilot died in the plane crash? That day, you were supposed to fly the plane, but fortunately, you fell ill. The police concluded it was sabotage, right?" David managed to take Jay by surprise.

Jay looked amazed, "How do you know all this?"

"I know almost everything about the future, and for you, it might not look good," David replied, leaning back in his chair.

"You can never predict what will happen in the future!" Jay retorted.

David kept calm. "That might be true, but I know something's not right between you and James."

Jay squinted. "Please speak plainly," he said.

David explained his observations about the strained relationship between Jay and James, but Jay interrupted him, denying any issues with the gardner.

Lisa stepped in, positioning herself in front of Jay. "I see that you're hiding something, but you're just making things worse. We have good reason to warn you. We suspect that James might have been involved in the plane crash last month, but as of now, there's no concrete evidence. It's crucial that you reconcile with him before it's too late," she advised.

"How would you know such things?" asked Jay.

"Because we are from the future" Lisa replied, a knowing smile playing on her lips.

In response, Jay rolled his eyes and let out a sigh.

"There was a night, I wandered past his chamber. The door was ajar, and I took a quick glance inside. He was seated at his sewing machine. Initially, I thought he was simply sewing, but on closer inspection, I realized he was scribbling in one of the many notebooks before him. A few days later when he was absent, I ventured into his room and discovered the books, though I left them untouched," Jay recounted.

Alice directed a demanding gaze at Jay. "What possessed you to do that?"

Jay's voice was low when he answered. "Shock and anger consumed me simultaneously when I found him with the books, a pen clutched in his hand. He's been deceiving you for years."

"So, that's why you initiated the bullying, isn't it?" Lisa queried.

Jay cast his gaze downward at the table, sighing deeply before lifting his eyes to meet Lisa's. "Jealousy took hold when I realized he harbored feelings for Alice, and when I found the flowers, he had left in her room. I attempted to use his secret against him."

Alice reached for Jay's hand; her voice filled with disbelief. "How could you harbor jealousy? Do you question the sincerity of my feelings?"

"I... I apologize," Jay admitted, his eyes on the cat that had taken residence at his feet. He stood abruptly from his chair, walking over to the window.

The world outside was in motion, the wind wresting leaves from their trees. He glanced at the incessant ticking of the wall clock.

It was Elena who broke the silence. "Jay, is James aware of what you've discovered about him?"

"Perhaps," Jay responded, shrugging nonchalantly. "One afternoon, upon my arrival, Alice was bathing in the lake. I sought her out, and suddenly, I spotted James, hiding behind a tree, knees submerged in the water. He was shirtless, his gaze locked on her. Angered, I confronted him, asked him to depart, but he only grew angry, lunging at me with raised fist. I retreated, pleading once more for him to simply leave."

Eric sighed heavily, countering Jay's accusation, "You didn't catch him in any act. He has always set his fishing nets there, retrieving them a few hours later. Perhaps he spared a glance or two at Alice while she was swimming. It seems you've misread James, angering him unnecessarily. We must put an end to this before it escalates."

"And how are you so certain he intends to murder me?" Jay

demanded, turning to David.

David explained, "In the time we hail from, it is known that a man named Jay Murphy, aged twenty-eight, the owner of an airline, was discovered deceased on a beach near a renowned lookout. The official statement suggests he might have been intoxicated while painting, likely losing his footing and falling onto the rocks below. However, our independent investigation tie James to the crime."

David paced across the room as he continued, "Luckily, an individual introduced us to a relative of Eric's. He informed us of James's eviction from this house, his subsequent move to a shed situated further away on the property. Upon locating the shed, we rummaged through his belongings and found his diaries. Within those pages, he'd penned his feelings towards both Jay and Alice, detailing his intent to end Jay's life. The situation worsened when James witnessed your proposal to Alice."

"But he wasn't present during my proposal," Jay argued, as though he had caught David in a lie.

David laughed. "Perhaps we've slightly altered the course of history, but it holds little relevance."

"Earlier, I noticed James peering through the window," Lisa said. "Watching as you kneeled. He appeared troubled."

Jay seemed to mull over their words. "If this is true, it's too much like a dream. Where are you from? How can I be dead in your time while I'm here, alive, standing before you?"

David's voice echoed around the chamber. "You have to decide for yourself whether or not to believe us. We can leave here and never return; our mission accomplished. But remember that your decision will affect more than just you - it will decide the fate of many people. The clock is ticking - what do you choose?"

Chapter 22

David watched as Jay shrugged off his jacket and leaned forward. Jay rolled his eyes, then buried his face in his hands, peeping at David through his fingers. "So, can you show us the time machine? Not to make us believe you. Everything you said may be true, and I want to believe it, but I still want to see the time machine."

"Certainly," David responded, reaching for his backpack. The zipper was rusted, putting up a stubborn fight. Still, after a couple of determined tugs, he managed to pull it halfway open. Every eye in the room strained to glimpse into the pack. Inside, they caught sight of a large black box with flickering lights. Two silver, cylinder-like components vibrated on its sides, interconnected with cords to a smaller box within the backpack.

David hastily zipped up the backpack, a triumphant smile on his lips. "Convinced?" he asked. He turned to the room. "We've done our part. Now, armed with the facts, you can make everything right and save the future."

Alice, looking anxious, questioned, "But where should we start?" Her eyes flicked briefly to her father, seeking guidance.

The answer came from Lisa, her gaze steady on Jay. "Start by not going painting on the lookout," she advised.

"I'll keep that in mind," Jay nodded.

Alice fell silent then, her eyes locked on Jay, a sigh escaping her lips. Words seemed to elude her, her mind churning in quiet turmoil. She was thinking Jay should go with someone or not go at all.

The room was infused with tense energy until Eric finally suggested a course of action. "I'm going to get to the bottom of this. I'll find James's diaries in his room. Then, we can all talk to him and express how important he is to us. Maybe we can defuse his anger and change his mind by directly talking to James. If he was involved in the plane crash, we will, of course, report it to the police," he declared resolutely.

David interjected. "But please, this has to be handled discreetly. Remember, trust is a two-way street. It requires confidence and mutual respect. Jay, consider that all the negative events in James' life are a chance for redemption, a chance to befriend him. Consider the repercussions on your future, and if you want to save it, challenge fate. And finally, respect his feelings for Alice. Good luck."

Eric squinted suspiciously at David. "Who are you, really? What is your true intention behind this visit?" he asked.

David returned Eric's gaze unwaveringly. "I'm a renowned writer. Several of my novels have been adapted into movies. When I purchased this house, I was intrigued by the story of Alice and Jay - a tale of love but also sadness. I yearned to unravel the truth, to uncover what really transpired. My quest led me to the time machine, its creator, and even the man who constructed it," he explained.

"Who is he?" Alice asked.

"He is from Germany. Ever since he built his time machine, he has been on the run - running through time, eluding those who seek to possess him and his invention," David replied.

"Have you ever encountered a stranger near the grounds?" asked Lisa, turning to Alice.

Alice recalled an encounter immediately. "Yes, a man and his wife visited one day. They introduced themselves as Phillip and Caroline."

"Did they ask you anything?"

"They were new to the area, they said, and they were looking to make friends. However, something strange happened a few days later..."

The room listened intently as Alice recounted her strange, experience, her parents affirming her story with solemn nods. David and Lisa exchanged glances as they listened, their expressions mirroring their shared understanding. They knew this neighbor Alice spoke of, and his unexpected reveal further and the puzzle pieces became more tightly together.

Alice continued her story, adding more details that she had omitted earlier. "Suddenly, I heard someone. When I turned to look, I saw a man in a strange outfit I'd never seen before. He was with his dog, and they were both calling out to me. Scared, I sprinted towards the house and tried to open the door, but it was locked. When I peered through the window, everything inside seemed unfamiliar. Then, I heard something behind me again and was instantly overwhelmed by dizziness and fatigue. I staggered over to a bench that I didn't recall being there before and collapsed onto it, immediately drifting off to sleep. When I woke up, I was still on the same bench, clutching a book in my hand. It was surreal, almost as if I'd been dreaming. Still, it felt incredibly real," Alice narrated, her eyes full of confusion as she looked at David.

David probed further, "You don't remember anything else? And you didn't see anyone else?"

"No, but now that I think about it, I do remember hearing someone or something talking around me... It could have been a dream, right?" Alice asked.

David shook his head, denying her hopeful suggestion. "Philip and Caroline, the couple you met, are the owners of this house. And Philip is the inventor who built the time machine." He paused momentarily before adding, "It's highly likely that you traveled through time."

"Why would that happen?" she asked, her voice confused.

"I don't have an answer for that," David admitted. "Only they would know."

"What year was it then?" Alice asked.

"When you encountered my neighbor, it was the year 2009."

"So, you're saying I really traveled through time?" Alice's voice trembled with the enormity of the revelation.

"Absolutely! And you lost your dog during this period, didn't you?" David inquired.

Elena chimed in, confirming David's suspicion. "Yes, she did lose her dog, and it hasn't been found yet."

"Fascinating! After a storm, I found a black dog in the yard. It was trapped under a tree, panting heavily in the summer heat. Lisa and I managed to free him and found a peculiar backpack strapped to his body. We took him home, fed him, and gave him water. When we checked the backpack, we discovered a strange machine." He cleared his throat before continuing, "In the middle of the night, I heard some noises outside our house. When I went to investigate, I saw a figure leading the dog away, and then they vanished. The dog hasn't been seen since."

Alice's eyes widened, her hand moving to her forehead. "So, you're saying my dog also traveled in time?"

David nodded, confirming her suspicion.

Jay, who had been silent all this time, finally snapped. "This is all too much! I should have just stayed home today." He undid another button on his shirt, which was evidently making him uncomfortable.

With a sense of finality, David reached for the backpack, hoisting it onto his shoulder with practiced ease. He glanced at the group gathered before him. "Now, it's time for us to head home. We've done what we came here to do. We came to secure your future. Now, the choice of how you wish to live is yours. Seize this opportunity and, perhaps, effect some positive changes," he urged.

Alice's voice broke through the quiet, her inquiry tinged with warmth and curiosity. "Will we ever meet again?"

David merely shrugged in response, his gaze steady. "Well, Alice, that's not entirely impossible."

Elena, her eyes welling up with emotion, asked, "How can we ever thank you?"

"By rectifying all the mistakes that have been committed so far."

His cryptic response sparked curiosity in Elena, prompting her to ask, "What year and what day did you come here from?"

Lisa interjected then, her voice echoing in the room. "The twenty-eighth of July, 2009. It was in the morning."

Suddenly, the room was filled with different energy as Eric bustled in, a small package cradled in his arms. He locked eyes with David and handed it over with a smile. "This belongs to you."

David accepted the parcel. As he unwrapped it, he was greeted by the sight of Lisa's flashlight that she had accidentally left behind in Alice's room. A shared look of amusement passed between him and Lisa before he allowed himself a hearty laugh.

Jay came forward then, readjusting his hat. His gaze alternated between the flashlight and David. David cautioned, "Remember, James is a wolf in sheep's clothing at the moment. He will go to any lengths to reach you. Befriend him, respect his emotions." He continued, his gaze sweeping over the room, "Treat him like a part of the family, not just an employee. He needs all of you."

Eric, silent till then, nodded in agreement. He lit his pipe. The smoke rings he exhaled floated languidly above the table before they slowly descended and vanished.

David's gaze remained steady as he issued a warning, "Never go to the lookout to paint, as discussed. Stay away from it. If everything goes as planned, a new chapter can begin," he then extended his hand towards Eric, firmly shaking his.

Alice giggled. "If we have a son and a daughter, we could name them after you two."

David turned his attention to Jay then, who had been largely silent until now. He watched as Jay approached Alice; doubt etched in his features. Jay placed his hands on Alice's shoulders, a toothpick casually tucked in the corner of his mouth. His gaze met David's. "You look doubtful. You still don't believe us?" Jay's words brought a thoughtful silence, broken by his skepticism. "Everything you've said seems credible, and I would like to believe you. However, only the future will tell. No one can predict what life will throw at us."

In response, David echoed his earlier sentiment. "Don't take life for granted. We are the future, and you won't make progress unless you take action. Rectify the past and leave nothing to chance. Make the most of this unique opportunity."

Alice reassured them, gazing steadily at Jay, "We will fix it. I promise."

David nodded, "I believe you will, especially when you see us disappear right before your eyes. And Alice, if you're alive in 2009, I would like to give you my home address and phone number so you can find us. We'll likely be living in this house by then."

David reached into his wallet, drawing out a small photo of Lisa. On its back, he scribbled his phone number, Alice watching the scene in amazement.

He handed the photograph to Alice, his voice firm, "Here's my phone number. Reach out to me on the twenty-ninth of July 2009 but remember to keep this a secret. Share it only with your loved ones, those who trust you and believe in you."

His mission was done; all that remained was for the seeds he had planted to grow.

Alice raised her eyebrows. "Could I live to be that old?" she queried, her tone light.

David replied with a reassuring smile, "Why not? In 2009, you will be exactly eighty-nine years old, and that's not that old. Many people are still healthy and well at that age. For instance, my dad is eighty-five in sixty-nine years, so there's a good chance you could have a long life."

A bright laugh burst from Alice's lips. "Then I suppose I'll see you then." David gave her a gentle nod. "It's time for us to leave."

David moved towards the exit with Lisa at his side, their footsteps heavy. Before stepping out, David turned around and wished them good luck. The door closed behind them with a soft click, their departure prompting everyone to rush towards the window, their eyes tracking David and Lisa's retreating figures.

Outside, the wind had picked up. It tugged at Lisa's hair, turning it into a wild, untamed mane. David and Lisa turned around one last time, their hands interlocked, and waved at their friends in the house.

With a sense of urgency, David pressed the button on his belt. His arm was linked with Lisa's, his eyes filled with nervous anticipation. He heard the beep from his backpack, ringing in his ears. The belt started to vibrate, its light pulsing with an intensity that matched his heartbeat.

Then, David and Lisa vanished in a flash. Despite this, a part of David remained tethered to the scene, his perception registering the sight and sounds as if he still physically existed among them.

David watched as Jay rushed outside, his eyes wide as he scanned the area where David and Lisa had just stood. He reached out, brushing the ground as if he could somehow touch the now absent pair. Turning to Alice, his voice shook with panic, "He...they just disappeared. How the hell did that happen?"

Alice, who had followed Jay outside, mirrored his shock. Her gaze was fixed on the spot where David and Lisa had been. He knew not how, but David heard her heart pounding with such force that it seemed to eclipse all other sounds.

From the house's interior, Elena's shaky voice echoed out, putting their shared disbelief into words, "Would you look at that? They just...vanished."

Eric blinked. "I guess that's proof they were telling the truth. They came from the future. We need to take their warnings seriously and act."

Jay spoke with determined grit, "If James really caused the plane crash, he needs to pay for it. He won't get away that easily, I promise."

Jay's gaze remained fixed on James, who seemed almost rooted to his tractor, slowly unloading bricks. David sensed an impenetrable energy hanging between them. He thought he saw a glimmer in James's eyes that said more than words ever could. What that glint might mean was now his burden alone to untangle.

Chapter 23

David and Lisa journeyed through time, a whirlwind of emotions swirling within them. They watched as life sped by in a blur. Days melded into weeks, weeks into months, and months into years. Seasons passed in the blink of an eye, the chilling winter giving way to warm summer days, which faded into vibrant autumn hues. Suddenly, a beeping sound emanated from the backpack, the green light on the belt flashing as it signaled the end of their journey.

David sighed in relief upon spotting his car parked by the stable. His eyes welled up as he turned to Lisa, "We're home now."

They were disheveled and dripping with sweat from the ordeal, but the overwhelming relief of being home overshadowed their discomfort.

David's phone sprang to life, its screen lighting up with missed calls and messages from friends who had reached out over the past five days. Among the barrage of notifications, a message from Alice caught his eye. She had sent her home address.

"Amazing. She's fine," David breathed, turning to Lisa. "We traveled on the twenty-eighth of July, but it's the second of August now." His expression turned to one of bewilderment as he continued, "We were there for just a few hours, but according to my calendar, we've been gone for five days. How is that possible? Something's gone wrong."

An icy fear gripped him, and without a second thought, he bolted towards the car with Lisa trailing behind.

"Where are you going?" Lisa called out.

"To the car. I want to check the time and date on the car." Upon reaching the car, however, David was met with an unsettling sight. The car was damaged. Bewildered and upset, they stood silently, taking in the extent of the damage.

Lisa finally broke the silence, "Who could have done this?"

Suddenly, a strange noise echoed from behind the stable. David and Lisa ventured to investigate. What they found was astonishing. Alice's black dog, sans its vest, bounded towards them, its tail wagging in delight. It leapt onto David, covering him in eager licks. Chuckling, David responded, "Hey there, buddy! Good to see you too. But what are you doing here all alone?"

While they were preoccupied with the dog, Lisa heard the crunch of gravel underfoot. Before she could pinpoint the source of the sound, a voice rang out, "Dogs are grateful creatures. They never forget kindness."

Spinning around, they were met with the sight of a hooded figure sporting a grey-black beard. His gaze was fixed on them, a hint of amusement playing on his lips. As he moved closer, his hands tucked casually in his pockets, he asked, "So, how was the trip? Don't you recognize me?"

David rose slowly, his brow furrowed in thought. "Should we? But wait, your voice. Is that you, Philip? Or William Schwartz?"

"Clever guy," William responded, lowering his hood.

"That's Alice's dog, isn't it?" Lisa inquired.

William nodded.

"She missed her dog. How could you do that to her?" David asked with a hint of accusation in his voice.

"I needed a test subject for my mission. I thought she would have moved on after nearly seventy years. I've only had the dog for a month actually," William responded with a shrug, a lopsided grin on his face.

"Are you planning to return him when you go back?" Lisa questioned.

"When the time comes, she'll get her dog back," William assured her.

David remembered Alice's experience of falling asleep while reading outside and waking up to a different landscape. "She was preparing for the big trip. I knew about her fiancé's fate, and I knew she was going to be murdered by James," William confessed, his face solemn.

"Something was going to happen, but we found nothing about a murder in James' diaries," David responded, taken aback.

Lisa asked was there a reason that you think something was going to happen to Alice.

"It was an accident. James didn't plan to murder her," William started to explain. "One morning, after Jay's murder, Alice went to the lookout, and James followed her. Likely he confessed his feelings, and when Alice rejected him, she slapped him, stepped back, and fell off the cliff."

William sighed. "I found it tragic. I decided to intervene, to prevent a happy couple's future from ending in such a tragic way. So, I travelled back in time, sedated Alice before she could go to the lookout, and took her to 2009 using the time machine."

"And now what?" David asked.

William's grin was bright as he spoke, his words carrying a light tone of triumph, "Now that you've changed the whole story, the risk to her life is over. You stopped Jay's murder and made sure she changed her future and her destiny."

The dog, having roamed around and sniffed at everything, suddenly barked at a cat attempting to make a meal of a dead bird.

"Why did you save only Alice – not Jay? You could have just used the time machine and traveled there to warn them, just like we did," David pointed out, his gaze never leaving William's.

"I wanted to change as little as possible in history by saving just her. I think science should be used to improve the future of humanity, not to play God and change history to influence the future," William countered.

"But you played God and changed things for Alice, giving her a second chance at life," Lisa chimed in, her gaze sharp.

"Yes, I did, but I changed it only for a single individual, and not for the whole history of the world," William retorted.

"Why didn't you save Jay? He was just an individual," David persisted, his gaze steady on William.

"You've saved him now. Look at what happened. There are a lot of people involved. Their children and grandchildren, it's world-famous small airplanes company, and has influenced the industrial world. There might be a meaning and a purpose to something that has happened, but if you can foresee a disaster, you can prevent it. But what has happened should not be changed, only learned from," William argued.

David nodded, understanding his perspective, but curiosity still tugged at him. "I understand, but what kind of mission did you need the dog for?"

William stared at David briefly before smiling. "The dog has been with me, walking around on different adventures. Honestly, while hiding from the Nazis, I realized my dreams, and with the dog I explored time and space and other worlds at different times. He's become my friend and companion."

"Speaking of Nazis. Why are you being chased? Why do they want to access your time machine when they have one of their own? I don't understand that," David questioned further, the Nazi connection puzzling him.

"Well, when I led a team consisting of about thirty scientists, we tried to build and develop a machine that was able to travel in time. But when we built it, a problem arose, as it was possible to travel only to the future, and traveling back was impossible. It took a lot of energy to travel backwards. We had to test it on living beings, such as dogs and monkeys, but we failed time and time again and all the experiments ended in disaster.

"One day Hitler gave us orders to test on humans, and we were given the go-ahead to use Jewish prisoners for the tests, which I was firmly against. In a personal letter from Hitler, I was ordered and threatened. It said that if I didn't test on the prisoners, my family would be the test subjects instead," he continued, nervously stroking his beard.

"Unfortunately, there were many high-ranking members of the Nazi Party who supported him in this, and we did not dare to resist. A week later, a number of prisoners were bused to the laboratory. To my surprise, I saw children among the prisoners. Four buses arrived at regular intervals. Terrified, the prisoners sat in the buses and looked at us. Some children cried for their parents," William's voice wavered, the memory clearly causing him pain. He turned his back to them, walking a few steps to a tree stump where he sat, leaning against the trunk as if trying to hide his sorrow.

"I saw Himmler in a car. He was the head of the SS. He personally supervised the entire operation very closely. I saw how he proudly looked at all the prisoners brought in. There was pleasure in his eyes. A number of times, I tried to hide the children and sneak out with them, but I didn't dare. The only thing I could do for the prisoners was to explain to them that if the experiments were successful, they would be free forever. I tried to give them hope and ease their pain."

David listened attentively as William's words painted a grim picture. "One night I was working late with a coworker, and we were alone in the lab. The prisoners were locked up in special cages and looked at us with concern in their eyes. I tried to avoid meeting their gaze and instead immersed myself in my work.

"Suddenly, I heard someone calling out to me, and when I turned around, I saw a thin child of about six or seven staring at me with sad eyes. He asked me to come closer. With no guards around, I could speak to him undisturbed. 'Do you believe in God?' he asked me. I nodded and said, 'Yes, actually I do.' I will always remember his innocent face and tears. With blood running from his nose, the little boy said, 'I know that what you are doing now is done under duress, that you are not doing it voluntarily. When I die and meet God, I will ask him to forgive you and bless you. My mother always said that hate does no good, and love will always win in the end.' I couldn't handle the pressure. Crying, I held him and apologized over and over. Secretly I gave him and the other prisoners food and water. I couldn't do more."

William fell silent. He turned away from David and Lisa, his sigh heavy with sorrow, tears welling in his eyes. He swiftly wiped his eyes with his shirt sleeve before continuing.

"Many of the prisoners were killed during the tests. Some were burned to death, and a dozen died from explosions, but with our last attempt things went a little better. We sent them back in time, but unfortunately, we didn't know whether the experiment was successful because the prisoners never came back.

"As soon as I built my own time machine, I traveled to the time period where we had sent them. I found their remains burned in the time capsule, and among the remains I found those of the child in the cage. He had been burned to death. I could see from the shape of his body that he tried in vain to get out, but alas, he had to experience a terrible death. I began to weep and cried out in profound grief. I felt responsible for his death and that of others. For a while I sat there thinking that I couldn't just leave him and the others there. I gathered the bodies in a corner and gave them a dignified burial, promising myself that one day I would find Hitler and put him to death."

David watched as William seemed to crumble under the weight of his past. He moved to sit next to him, placing a comforting hand on his shoulder. William closed his eyes, took a few deep breaths, and mustered the strength to continue his story.

"Fortunately, we sent some of the prisoners to the future, and those trips were successful. When the time capsule came back, there was no one in the capsule, so we interpreted it as the prisoners having escaped and acquired their freedom," William finished in a depressed voice.

David pondered William's words. "You mean they could travel to the future but not come back?"

William nodded. "We built the time machine in 1934. They could travel only to the future and back to the time the machine was built. That is, only to 1934, not further back. They couldn't travel to 1933 or 1854, only from 1934 forward and back to 1934 again," he clarified with a hint of pride.

David watched William closely, his interest piqued by the complexity of the time travel story. He questioned, "But what about your machine?"

"My machine is significantly better than theirs," William assured him. "I can go back to any year I want. I can travel to the birth of Jesus or to the time of Neanderthals and then come back," William replied, the corners of his mouth lifting into a gentle smile.

"Then you can travel to Hitler's childhood and influence him to make other choices later in life, or annihilate him," Lisa suggested, attempting to wrap her mind around the capabilities of the time machine.

"I could," William said, "but I don't want to. It's not my job to change the future. What's done is done, but I think that if we want to change the future, we have to learn from history, not change it. The only contribution I want to make is to stop the Nazis before they do anything drastic in the future and take power again," William explained, sighing, and looking at the dog.

David noticed a shadow of confusion in William's eyes but let the man continue his narrative.

"Hitler and his supporters have traveled to the future, to different time periods and countries. There they have created various Nazi parties, as you know. In some countries, Nazi parties have entered parliament and are trying to influence laws. I have to get to Hitler somehow, as he's in charge of the whole operation. He's the one with power over all Nazi parties throughout the world. Over the years, he has built a large network and only a dozen people are aware of his existence. If I can only manage to find Hitler, I might easily hand him over to justice, but this is not easy." William sighed heavily.

David couldn't help but express his concern, "Do you think you can get him all alone? He has built a great organization around himself – you can't fight him by yourself."

"It will be difficult, but it's not impossible," William replied, a spark of hope glinting in his eyes.

Lisa, looking thoughtful, chimed in, "Who had the idea to build a time machine from the beginning?"

"In 1933, when Hitler was appointed chancellor, he came to our university in Berlin, where I worked as a professor, along with Einstein. Hitler showed us a magazine about time travel. He looked sharply into Einstein's eyes and asked whether this is possible. Einstein cautiously glanced at me and stated, 'Technically we don't have the capacity for it, but theoretically it's not impossible.' Then Hitler smiled broadly and said we would do it. 'You can have all the resources and money needed to do this experiment. In a month's time you will gather the best possible scientists and physicists. You two will lead the experiment.' When Hitler left the university, Einstein looked at me doubtfully and sat down at the table where he muttered that Hitler was crazy. 'I have a bad feeling about this man,' he said. I nodded and asked what we were going to do. Einstein was completely silent in his chair and leaned back. He looked out the window and saw Hitler's car leaving the university. He appeared rather worried and nervously fidgeted with a pen without saying anything. A week later when I got to the university, I received a call from him. He told me that he was in the United States, and he asked me to leave Germany with my family immediately. But it was too late for me. On the day Einstein called, the military had to evacuate my entire family and me to a guarded area. Those of us who were involved in the experiment were under constant supervision and had a personal guard wherever we went. Fortunately, Einstein managed to leave the country on time," William finished, his voice heavy with the weight of his past.

"And you were put in charge of the whole experiment, right?" David asked.

William nodded and sat down. He put his arm around the dog's back and scratched it under its chin before pulling it close. He mumbled softly to the dog. "It's time for you to go home to your master now. I will miss you, sweet friend."

David frowned in surprise and looked at William. "Are you handing the dog over to us?"

"Yes, and you will give him back to Alice. I have a feeling you know where she is," William replied. "Now it's time for me to go – and you have something that belongs to me," he said, looking at David.

"What?" said David.

"The backpack and the belt," William replied and pointed.

"Oh, yes, of course! What about the machine in the room?" David asked.

"I've already removed it," William said, smiling.

Surprised, David stared at William for a moment and said, "How did you know we were using it?"

"I didn't, but when my machines noticed a large amount of magnetic activity in the house, I found out that you had activated the time machine, and after that I could see what year, the machine had sent you to. Then I could follow you to where I saw you meeting Alice and her family. The Nazis also discovered that you were traveling, but they didn't know where. Desperately, they went to your parents, sedated them, and took them somewhere in time," William said.

"You mean MY PARENTS are in Nazi captivity?" David exclaimed with worry and looked at Lisa, who held her hand to her mouth in shock.

"Calm down, not anymore. I took care of everything. As soon as I noticed that your use of the time machine became a potential risk for future existence, I decided to minimize the risk that the machine would fall into the wrong hands. Quickly, I changed your return, went to Alice's room, and destroyed the machine. I can guarantee you now that the Nazis will never bother you and your fiancée or your relatives anymore," William said, nodding happily.

Stressed, David called his mother anyway, just to make sure everything was as it should be. "Hi Mom! How are you?"

"I don't know, it's okay I guess," his mother replied in a tired voice.

"Did something happen? You sound strange," David asked anxiously, looking at Lisa.

"Today I was in the kitchen doing the dishes, and suddenly I felt dizzy and sleepy – that's all I remember. When I woke up, I was lying on the sofa in the living room with your dad, who was sitting in the armchair passed out. It took some time to wake him," David's mom said with a sigh.

"Do you have any memory of what happened?" David asked.

"I have no idea. I just remember doing the dishes in the kitchen, but after that, nothing. Somehow, I got to the couch and lay down there. I have a vague memory that people were standing around me speaking a foreign language. I felt paralyzed and couldn't open my eyes or move. Your dad had the same experience."

"I'll call you as soon as I can, but please go to the hospital for a check-up," David suggested.

"Okay, we'll do that," said David's mom, and she hung up the phone.

As the line went dead, David's grip on his phone tightened, and he was filled with a sense of overwhelming dread. His eyes, brimming with anxiety and confusion, met Lisa's. His heart ached for his mother and father who were old and fragile. Innocent victims pulled into the swirling vortex of this time-travel chaos.

A lump formed in his throat. David's fingers trembled as he placed his phone on the table. He slumped onto the sofa, a heavy weight settling over him. It was as if the air had been sucked out of the room. Lisa looked at him helplessly, her eyes reflecting his anguish.

"I can't believe this," he whispered. His mind was a whirlwind of regret, worry, and guilt. His parents had been kidnapped and forced into an unknown time, all because of a situation he had indirectly put them into.

Lisa reached out to him, her hand resting gently on his. "We'll figure this out, David," she assured him, her voice a whisper against the eerie silence that had descended upon the room.

But David barely heard her. His mind was repeatedly playing out the terrifying scenario, filling him with profound sorrow. The image of his parents, paralyzed and surrounded by foreign voices, tormented him.

"I insist," commanded David, "on knowing why my parents were kidnapped. They didn't do anything."

Chapter 24

David was caught in a whirlpool of anxiety and anger as the shadow of the previous day's revelations still loomed heavily over him. His parents had been dragged into this chaos, and for what? A machine they knew nothing about, a danger they hadn't signed up for. He could still hear Lisa's warning echoing in his mind. "Stubborn," she had called him, and perhaps she was right.

But a fresh day was breaking, promising a new beginning, and with it, David hoped, a resolution to the mysteries that had hounded him.

Across the room, William shifted in his seat in the garden, his face revealing nothing of the secrets he held. "By taking your parents, they wanted to pressure you to hand over the time machine," he started, his voice carrying a grave weight. "But I sent a message along with the destroyed time machine to a place where I knew the Nazis might be. In the message, I convinced them that you have nothing to do with the machine. You're free now.

David's blood was rushing in his ears, the anger boiling within him, but he also felt sense of relief. They were safe now, all of them. He ran a hand through his hair, frustration mingling with gratitude. He still had so many questions, but for now, there was respite.

Lisa's rebuke still hung in the air, prickling at his conscience. She was right. He had been stubborn, reckless even. Looking over at her, he saw concern etched on her face, mirroring his own feelings. A silent apology passed between them, promises of better choices to come. This was a chapter they would get through together, he reassured himself. And with that thought, he turned back to William, ready to face the next hurdle in this unimaginable journey. "Where are you going now? Or what year do you want to travel to?" David asked, taking off the backpack to hand it over to William.

David watched as William tossed the backpack away. An eerie glow surrounded it, growing in intensity until the backpack was swallowed up in an inferno. David instinctively shielded his face with his hands, pulling Lisa close.

"Wait! How will you travel now? You don't have a time machine," David shouted above the crackling fire.

With a reassuring smile, William rolled up his sleeve to reveal a sleek silver bracelet adorned with multi-colored buttons. "This," he said, pointing to the device, "is my newer time machine. In a few years, time travel will be commonplace. Time machines will come in all shapes and sizes. Some can even be implanted in the body."

David's mind was a whirlwind of questions. "You've been there? To the future?" he managed to ask, eyes still glued to the futuristic gadget on William's wrist.

"Indeed, I have," William said, his eyes distant, lost in the memory. "When I first visited the future, I was detained by their security forces. When I told them who I was and the year I had come from, they were astounded. They found pictures of me with Einstein, Tesla, and other scientists of the twentieth century. With the help of DNA comparison with my future descendants, they verified my claims."

Pausing, William collected himself before he continued. "They already knew about Hitler and his followers' escape using a time machine. They had nearly captured him at one point, but he evaded them. My wife and I are now citizens of the future. We have chips implanted in our arms." He indicated a small scar. "These chips act as GPS devices, transmitters, and electronic IDs. They can track us through time and space, even send us back if we cross the boundaries."

David frowned, "What boundaries?

"We aren't allowed to interfere with history. Step out of our boundary of our time. If we make contact during a significant event, we get send back. Influencing the future by changing the past is forbidden," William explained, his voice heavy with the wisdom of someone who had seen times beyond David's comprehension.

William's gaze softened as he ran his fingers through the dog's fur, drawing comfort from the affectionate contact. "Now, I must return to my wife and from there, we shall journey together to the future," he said, stepping back and gazing at them one last time with an inscrutable look, leaving David and Lisa to grapple with the weight of his revelations.

"Call us up when you get there!" Lisa said.

"Oh, I will be too far ahead, and you, unfortunately, will no longer be here," William replied.

"That's too bad, but good luck to you, wherever you go," David said.

"Take care of the dog. I taught him to hate the Nazis, but he loves to swim in the lake and likes dog treats. Say hello to Alice and apologize to her for me taking the dog away from her," William said sadly, looking at the dog. "I love that dog," he said and pressed the button.

Slowly he disappeared while giving a thumbs-up to Lisa and David.

David stared at Lisa. He saw she was shaken too.

"Everything is over, and all the pieces of the puzzle are in place," David said.

Suddenly the dog began to howl and pant and pulled on David's arm. David noticed the quick change in behavior, and with a deep frown, he called out to Lisa, "Something's wrong! He senses something."

The dog ran towards some bushes further away, and again and again, it looked anxiously at David and Lisa, who were trying to catch up to him. Suddenly, they heard a familiar crackling sound further away in the yard. David threw himself into the bushes and pulled Lisa down with him. They hid there with the dog. Carefully so as not to be detected, they peered through the branches. To their surprise, they saw three uniformed people out of nowhere who were now wandering around in front of them. The dog sat tensely behind David, panting down his neck. Lisa saw that one of the people was the same young guy that they had met at home.

"Look! It's the guy we saw at our house, with his wife," Lisa whispered.

The young Nazi walked up to the burnt backpack and picked it up. He grinned at the others and showed them the bag, saying something in German. Suddenly, his gaze came to Lisa and David's car parked next to them. He walked up to the car, looked through the windows, and felt the doors.

Annoyed, he kicked the car door and shouted when he realized it was locked. He scouted the area and then walked towards the bush where David and Lisa and the dog were hiding. David hushed the dog. He fell silent as soon as the young Nazi approached. David's heartbeat was so fast he could feel his entire chest vibrate. Lisa held the dog with a firm grip. The Nazi inspected the place carefully and was close to stepping on David's fingers, but he managed to remove his hand without being discovered. The young man said something again in German and turned around. He went over to the others who were examining the remains of the backpack. It was destroyed, but they took what was left of the bag and disappeared into thin air.

David looked at Lisa. She had turned pale with fear. Relieved but nervous, David patted the dog and rejoiced, "That was close. I'm glad you have a sixth sense and knew what was happening!"

They got out of the bushes and hurried to the car. David looked at it tiredly and sighed. "Most likely, it was the Nazis who wrecked the car," he told Lisa. He looked anxiously behind him to make sure they were gone.

Lisa opened the back door, and the dog jumped in and sat with her.

"The journey is over for you. Soon you will get to meet your real master," Lisa mumbled, closing the door.

As David sat in the car, his stomach suddenly growled, and the craving made him aware that he had not eaten anything in several days.

"I'm so hungry," David said, rubbing his stomach.

"Me too. We've been gone for five days, so of course we'd be hungry," Lisa concurred.

On the way home, they drove through downtown. David slowed down as the view that met them didn't look the same. Now an eye-catching sign hung over a one of the largest buildings downtown. ALICE & JAY AIRLINES, he read. "Look!" he shouted and pointed. "Look, they made it!"

"What – where?" Lisa shouted, looking at David.

"Look at the sign," David said, pointing eagerly.

"Oh, wow! I can't believe it. You're right," Lisa said, looking at the sign.

David parked next to the road, and they got out of the car to look at the big building.

When they came to a smiley receptionist, David greeted her. "We were wondering who heads this company?"

"Their names are David and Lisa Murphy," the receptionist informed them, a benign smile on her face.

David's heart skipped a beat as he turned to Lisa. "Alice must have named her children after us, just like she said she would."

The two of them grinned at each other, their joy palpable. "Can we meet them?" David asked the receptionist, who looked at him quizzically but nodded, dialing a number on her office phone.

A moment later, she hung up and looked back at them, "David Murphy will be right down."

While they waited, they found themselves drawn to a large aquarium near the entrance. The swirling colors of the fish and the amusing antics of the inhabitants distracted them until they heard a voice calling their names. They turned to see a man in a crisp black suit, his brown hair neatly combed and a kind smile on his face.

"David and Lisa?" he asked, extending a hand.

"That's us," David replied, his voice laced with a hint of nervous anticipation.

"You're much younger than I expected," the man commented, a look of confusion crossing his face. "My mom has been talking about a David Hamilton and Lisa she met in 1939. She said you saved their lives, but that doesn't add up. You look no more than forty."

David offered a sympathetic look when he mentioned his father's passing and then nodded at his question. "We did meet your parents, back in the forties. But we need to see Alice first before we can explain everything."

Murphy nodded; his eyes filled with a curious light. "She's been talking about you coming for the past few days. We've all been waiting, and now, here you are."

David asked if they could see Alice today, and Murphy agreed, a hint of excitement in his voice. He clearly had questions about how they could have met his parents in the forties and was eager to hear their explanation.

David hinted about the black dog that Alice once had. Murphy's eyes widened in surprise, but David just smiled and promised that everything would be explained when they met at Alice's home. Before they parted ways, Murphy said, "Don't be late."

David, his heart filled with anticipation, exited the building with Lisa trailing behind him. As they stepped out into the sunlight, Lisa paused and turned to gaze at the towering structure, a look of confusion on her face. "I don't remember this building," she admitted.

"It might be because of the changes we made," David replied, unlocking their car. "We gave Jay a second chance, and he used it to build a successful small planes company."

As they navigated through the busy city streets, David found his thoughts returning to their time-travelling adventures. Every face they passed, every building they drove by, had a story that stretched back into the past and forward into the future.

"Time is precious, more valuable than gold," David mused, glancing over at Lisa. "But what happens if you could actually travel back and meet your ancestors or go forward to meet your descendants? Life would lose its meaning. What's the purpose of the future if you already know what's coming?"

Lisa sighed, a troubled look on her face. "I am wondering and keep asking myself what we did was wrong. Maybe Alice and Jay's lives were supposed to end when they did."

By the time they reached their home, they were each lost in their own musings. They exited the car and let the dog out, then trudged up to their house. Lisa rushed to the kitchen to prepare some food while David murmured a comforting reassurance to their dog.

As David watched Lisa hurriedly assemble sandwiches in the kitchen, he found himself chuckling at the absurdity of it all. Once she was done, she retreated to the bedroom for a nap while David fed the dog and then wandered into the living room to turn on the radio.

The program that played was about time itself, asking questions about its nature, its purpose, and its direction. It proposed theories that time might not be a linear progression but a tidal wave, moving forward and backwards. David listened, utterly fascinated by the concept.

As the program ended, David was left with a feeling of awe. The time machine they had used was merely a tool to manipulate time, to increase its speed or slow it down, to move forward or backwards. He stared at the wall clock; his mind filled with thoughts of what could happen if such a tool fell into the wrong hands. David thought to himself, "I am happy that William is after Hitler to stop him from using the time machine." But for now, he decided to focus on the present. He glanced at the dog, who was still happily chewing on the food, and a gentle smile crossed his face. "You have to make the most of the time you have," he thought. "You should be grateful for every second."

Chapter 25

Later that night, David watched as Lisa slept, love and longing stirring within him. The rhythmic sound of her breathing lulled him into a calm Cautiously, he approached the bed and unable to resist, he knelt beside her. The soft rise and fall of her chest under his cheek and the warmth of her hand under his kiss filled him with a deep sense of contentment.

His cell phone alarm jolted them out of their shared tranquility in the morning. Lisa stirred, and as her eyes fluttered open, David couldn't help but smile. "It's time to go, love," he whispered, his gaze gentle.

Lisa sat up, her brows furrowing at the intensity of his stare. "What is it?" she asked, a faint blush creeping up her cheeks.

David caressed her cheek, his fingers trailing through her hair as he gently kissed her forehead. "I'm just grateful to have you in my life. I don't want to change anything about us. I want to spend every second I get with you," he confessed.

Lisa responded by flinging her arms around him in a heartfelt embrace. "You are the best thing in my life, David. If I could do it all over again, I'd choose to find you every time." Her words were a promise, sealed with a kiss. She changed the topic abruptly, her tone turning somber. "Are we still giving away the dog today?"

David exhaled, his smile dimming a little. "Yes, we need to," he replied.

As they exited the bedroom, their dog rushed towards Lisa, tail wagging with joyful anticipation. Lisa hugged the dog close, whispering words of reassurance as she led him outside.

Before they got into the car, Lisa asked, "We're meeting Alice at the boardwalk, number eight, right?"

David nodded, opening the car door to let the dog in. "Yes, that's right."

They set off; the journey fraught with uncertainty. Lisa gnawed nervously at her nails at the same time she is excited, voicing the question at the forefront of their minds. "What do we say when we see Alice?"

"I'm not sure. We saw her a few hours ago, but she hasn't seen us for sixty-nine years." David said, "We need to take it easy because she may be in a shock seeing us."

The mention of such time passed brought a gloomy pall over their conversation. "I wish we knew what happened to James. How did they stop him?" David mused aloud; his gaze focused on the road ahead.

"Do you think Alice will recognize us?" Lisa asked, her tone tinged with excitement.

"I'm certain of it," David replied confidently, casting Lisa a comforting glance.

As they approached their destination, Lisa gasped, staring at the grandiose building before them. "Is that the house?"

David mirrored her surprise, "It appears so," he responded, a sense of awe creeping into his voice. The building was like the White House, next to the towering columns with the stairs leading to the house, there are two big planter boxes with roses of different colors in them on each side of the columns.

David exited the car, a sense of bafflement creeping over him. "I've been down this street many times, even a week ago, and this house was never here. Our visit must have changed things here, too," he said. He approached the grand door and rang the bell. A male voice bid them to enter, and they stepped into a sprawling corridor adorned with opulent paintings and antiques.

The corridor opened onto a sunny patio overlooking a lush, manicured garden where children played with water pistols and balls. The sight of such carefree joy contrasted oddly with the dog's distress; he started whining and panting the moment they entered.

David glanced at Lisa. "Perhaps the dog smells Alice."

As they ventured further, the corridor split into two paths. "Come this way," when they heard a voice called out to them from one side, beckoning them. It was Murphy. The dog, overly eager, pulled David towards the source of the voice. The smell of coffee and freshly baked buns filled the air, paired with the gentle strains of soft music. Outside the door, a couple of rollators were parked, indicating the presence of older residents.

Seeing the dog's growing excitement, Lisa stepped in to soothe him. David, however, found himself frozen at the doorway, his heart pounding in his chest. The tension eased slightly when Murphy stepped out to greet them. "What are you waiting for?" asked Murphy. "Come inside."

David took several deep breaths and stepped inside the room.

In front of the window sat a woman clad in a patterned blue dress, surrounded by a several other women of varying ages. Murphy pointed to Alice. At Murphy's introduction, Alice turned to regard David. Recognition instantly lit up her face, and she reached out to him, tears streaming down her cheeks. "You came! I knew you were coming!" she exclaimed.

David could only stand and watch, speechless, as Lisa joined him. Alice's words of gratitude left him dumbfounded. She thanked him for saving her and Jay's life, for changing their destiny. He could only manage a humble, "Thank you for believing in us and welcoming us with open arms," in response.

Alice, still radiant with joy, invited Lisa to come closer for a hug. Lisa obliged, warmly greeting her, "It is truly lovely to meet you again."

Alice complimented Lisa saying "even though I saw you sixty-nine years ago, you are still beautiful," and mentioned her attempts at reaching out to David through calls and texts. To this, David could only apologize, "We came back today, and I saw that I had some missed calls, there were no phone numbers showing. Oh, those calls must have come from you. I didn't see your message until now."

Alice then dropped a surprise on them, "As soon as you left us, I decided to name my children after you. Meet my son, David Murphy. His sister, Lisa Murphy, is currently away on a business trip." Her words reverberated through the room, leaving David amazed by their visit's lasting impact on Alice's life.

"We would appreciate a moment alone with you, Alice. Could these ladies kindly excuse us?"

Alice nodded, telling her friends to return upon her call. Once they were alone, Murphy approached his mother, demanding answers. His words poured out in a rush, questioning her story of David and Lisa's visit in 1939, their youthful appearances now, and the seeming absurdity of time travel.

Alice merely looked to David with a gentle smile, inviting him to explain their improbable story. He recounted their experience of purchasing Alice's childhood home, the discovery of the time machine, and their decision to intervene in Alice and Jay's tragic fate. He laid bare the truth of the incident, the murder disguised as suicide, and the gardener James' role in it all. David explained their reading of James' diaries, how they learned of his murderous plans and how their warning to Alice prevented that future from taking place.

Murphy listened silently. He moved towards the window. Outside, a gardener was attempting to burn dried leaves and branches, the smoke billowing up into the air, while teenagers' laughter echoed from a nearby playground. He turned back to David, his confusion evident. "So, if you hadn't visited, Alice would be dead?" he asked to which Alice simply nodded.

"But everything changed in 1939 when you met?" asked Murphy.

David confirmed with a nod.

Murphy frowned, "And you managed to prevent the disaster by warning Alice about James' plan?"

David nodded again.

Murphy seemed doubtful. He asked for the diaries, but Alice revealed how the police had taken the diaries as evidence against James, even linking him to an airplane crash that had claimed a pilot's life.

Alice's glance at David was filled with tears. She tried to voice her feelings, but her words faltered and trembled as they emerged. Her gaze swung to Lisa. Then, she shut her eyes, drew a deep breath, and said, "I owe you for everything you've done for us."

"No, Alice. You owe us nothing," David said.

Alice's response was stubborn, her voice firm. "No, David. Without you, I wouldn't exist here. There'd be no children. The life I lead would be nonexistent. It would have been just a ghost of a possibility." Her confession poured out. Their visit had done much more than save her life, it had spurred her to seize her present, letting the future unravel on its own. Her trials of the past paved the way to a radiant future, and she acknowledged their crucial role in her journey.

Murphy's bitter words about their father's death in a plane crash stirred a melancholic note in the room. Alice, however, offset it by stating "I had spent twenty years with Jay by my side; the prospering business we had built; and the family we had grown. Jay had provided me love and security, and together, we built a legacy."

David smiled at her words, confessing his satisfaction at having altered her past despite being advised against it. The echoes of Alice's grandchildren playing outside served as a reminder of the value of their decision. Alice carried on with the narrative of her life. She revealed how she regarded her life with Jay as a bright tapestry woven from their struggles and acknowledged David and Lisa's roles as a beacon guiding them.

David found himself speechless, deeply touched by Alice's narrative. He looked at Lisa, who, too, was visibly moved by Alice's revelations. Slowly, he got up, approached Alice, and held her hands. Their warmth, undeterred by the signs of time, comforted him. Despite her aging frame, her eyes had the same vibrancy as the day before, her spirit unchanged.

Alice remarked, "It feels like you came to us only yesterday."

David replied with a chuckle, "It's been exactly five hours since we were there! Strange, isn't it?"

"After your visit and everything that unfolded, nothing seems strange to me anymore," Alice replied, followed by a cough.

As Alice delicately wiped a trace of saliva from the corner of her mouth, David's eyes wandered to Lisa. She was standing by the door, gesturing towards him, hinting if it was the right time to bring in the surprise. With a conspiratorial smile, David told Alice, "We have a surprise for you, and it's going to be a strange one."

With that, Lisa hurried out, returning with a dog who instantly made a beeline for Alice's arms. A cat, which had been lounging by the window, hissed in fear at the commotion and exited. The dog showered Alice's face with affectionate kisses. Looking at David, she exclaimed, "Is this my Max? My beloved Max?"

"Yes, it is!" David confirmed with a hearty laugh.

Murphy, if possible, looked even more startled. He stared at his mother and the dog. "Whose dog is that?"

"It's the same dog that disappeared in 1939," David replied cheerfully.

"And how did you get him?" Murphy asked.

David explained their encounter with the scientist who had initially taken the dog from Alice. The scientist, the inventor of the time machine, had intended to help Alice cope with Jay's death by travelling with her through time. But their intervention altered the course, resulting in Jay's survival and the scientist only taking the dog on his temporal adventures.

Murphy complained of a headache, his confusion evident as he tried to digest the information. He retreated to a chair by the window, hiding his face in his hands.

Meanwhile, the dog, now calm, sat on Alice's lap, staring at her. Alice groaned, clutching her chest.

Reacting quickly, Murphy checked her pulse, announced its irregularity, and dashed out to call an ambulance.

David and Lisa approached Alice with worry. They kneeled, each taking one of her hands. Alice opened her eyes, looking at them with a heavy gaze. "We were so close in the same place, yet far apart in time," she said, struggling to maintain a steady breath. She reflected on the wisdom David had imparted sixty-nine years ago to seize life's opportunities and acknowledged their role in shaping her family's future.

"Stay calm, Alice. Save your strength," David said, but Alice didn't listen.

"I... I have something for you both," Alice said, her voice weak. "It's in my will. A token... of my gratitude." She choked up, tears welling in her eyes.

Suddenly, paramedics rushed in, led by Murphy. David and Lisa stepped aside to make room. Amid the flurry of activity, a worried grandchild trailed by others approached.

"Is Grandma, okay?" the child asked.

Murphy wore a brave face. "She's in good hands."

One of the paramedics said, "She's in a serious condition due to heart problem, but we'll need to do more tests at the hospital."

As they prepared Alice for transport, Alice locked eyes with David and Lisa. She reached out, taking David's hand. "Thank you," she said, her smile both teary and grateful. Moments later, she was gone, taken away in the waiting ambulance.

Murphy, preparing to follow by running to his car, turned to David. "

"Please keep us informed about Alice.", I will leave my business card on the table.

Murphy nodded, saying a quick thanks before hopping into his car and driving off. David and Lisa watched his car merge into traffic and vanish.

A sense of guilt washed over David. Lisa turned to David, her voice full of regret. "I am wondering if there was a good reason why we interfered in Alice's life and changed her course." David replied, "Seeing the kids and grandchildren is a great reason."

The sun began to set, casting a red glow over the landscape. A voice broke the silence, startling David. He turned to find a young woman standing by the main entrance. She bore an uncanny resemblance to a younger Alice.

"Yes, she is my grandmother. Why?" the girl, Angela, responded.

David's eyes widened; his stare locked on Angela. "This... it can't be," he murmured, his disbelief loud in the quiet air.

His reaction seemed to rattle Angela, and she voiced her concern. "Why are you so surprised?"

Before David could answer, Lisa stepped in, "David, you're scaring her."

David turned to Lisa, an old picture of Alice opens on his phone. "Lisa, remember how Alice looked when she was young? Angela is the spitting image of her!"

Lisa peered at the photo then looked at Angela, her eyes widening in realization. "Oh, my... You're right, David."

Wearing a smile now, David approached Angela. "You look just like Alice, Angela."

Angela met his comment with a shy nod. "Grandpa used to say that too. But how do you know what Grandma Alice looked like when she was young?"

Lisa, ever the diplomat, replied, "We've seen old photos of Alice, Angela."

David nodded in agreement. "We promise to explain everything when the time is right, Angela. For now, we hope for Alice's safe return."

After bidding Angela farewell, David and Lisa walked hand in hand towards their car. David cast a last, lingering look at the fading sunset, sighing softly as the dying sunlight made way for the moon's gradual rise.

Once inside the car, David murmured, "We have Harry to thank for finding the house." He started the car, and they began their journey home.

Lisa broke the silence, her voice filled with concern. "David, we risked too much today. What if something happened to us? To our family?" She paused, her tone softening. "But meeting Alice's family... it did make it feel less wrong."

David sighed heavily, his grip on the steering wheel tightening. "I'm sorry, Lisa. I was reckless, putting Alice's past over our safety. I promise, no more such adventures."

Chapter 26

Early the next morning, David's phone rang. It took a while before he answered it.

"Hello?"

"It's David Murphy."

"Good morning," David replied hoarsely with his eyes closed.

"Sorry to call so early," Murphy said in a low voice.

"No, no, that's quite okay. How's Alice?" David asked without opening his eyes.

"That's what I wanted to tell you. She passed away around midnight," Murphy said. He could barely speak, his voice trembling.

Shocked, David opened his eyes and sat up on the edge of the bed. "What happened?"

"Her heart couldn't hold out anymore. After only three hours in the hospital, she insisted she wanted to come home. She complained that if she were going to die, she'd rather it be in her home, surrounded by her loved ones. I think she knew her time had come." Murphy paused, and David could hear him struggling to keep talking.

"She told me on her deathbed that everything is done and that she has been given everything in life. She said she was ready to leave her earthly life. Finally, she gave me an envelope that contained her will, and if it's okay with you, I'd like to come to your house to discuss it."

"Can you find your way here?" David asked.

"Yes, no problem. See you in an hour," Murphy said, ending the call.

"What's going on?" Lisa asked.

Subdued, David got out of bed and went to the terrace. "Alice passed away at midnight. She left behind a will that Murphy wants to talk about with us."

"It's sad that she passed away before we got to spend time with her," Lisa replied as she rubbed sleep from her eyes.

"Lisa, everything that's happened feels like a dream. That is, traveling to the forties and meeting people who are already dead was unimaginable, but the worst thing was being able to travel back to the past and being able to change the future and fate of a person. It's pretty scary that someone from the future could come to me, rewrite my story, and influence my whole life," David said.

"You mean what we did for Alice was wrong?" Lisa asked.

"I don't know. Probably not, but we played God. It felt right when I looked at her and her life with children and grandchildren. The feeling when I met her was indescribable, but at the same time, I think that maybe her fate was not supposed to be written like that, that she would live. We were the ones who changed everything and rewrote her life. If I had the same chance again, I wouldn't do it," David replied despairingly.

He got dressed and went out onto the terrace. He looked out, closed his eyes, and breathed fresh morning air into his lungs. It was nice to be out in the cool air.

David lit a cigarette. He mumbled pensively, "What is time? What is the future? Some believe that everything exists in the present and that there is no past or future. We create the future through how we contribute to and shape the present; then we build a path that, at best, can take us to our dreams and goals but, at worst, leads us to our downfall – and that's called DESTINY. Our choices in life create the future for us. In other words, all roads lead us in some way towards the future, and what the future looks like depends on what dreams and goals we have in life."

"I agree with you," Lisa said and smiled. She stood behind him, waiting with two cups of coffee and listened to what he said.

"Right? And what is time? We create time for ourselves, for our own benefit. You can't see or touch it. We can only feel the presence of time. But if we don't think, time no longer exists, and yet we constantly chase after it and believe we don't have enough of it."

Suddenly the doorbell rang. David put out the cigarette and went to open the door. He met Murphy, his eyes puffy and red. His hair was disheveled, his shirt unbuttoned, and he looked unkempt. With trembling hands, he shook David's hand.

"It was a long, hard night. Can I come in?"

Happily, the dog jumped in and began licking Lisa's hand. It ran into the house and sat down on the couch.

"Of course, come in," David said, letting Murphy in. "My condolences. I feel guilty that she died. Maybe we shouldn't have visited her at home. Maybe it was too much for her," David said sadly.

"Not at all. She'd been WAITING for you for so many years. That's what kept her alive. Twenty years ago, she survived breast cancer, and since then she'd been free from disease. Ten years ago, she survived a heart attack. It was all because of you. She wasn't done with life. She really wanted to see you, and she told me so on her deathbed last night," Murphy said. "She gave me an envelope on her deathbed that contained her will, and as I went through it, I saw that she wanted to give you a gift for what you did for her.

"She currently owns fifty percent of the company's shares. She wants to give you twenty-five percent of the shares as a gift, which is equivalent to four hundred and fifty million. She said that if you don't accept the gift, her soul will not be able to rest after death." Murphy laughed. There was warmth in his voice. "She's been waiting for this moment for so many years," he explained, the corners of his mouth pointing upwards slightly.

David looked at Lisa. He didn't know what to say, so he reached for his coffee. He swallowed it so fast that he coughed until tears started flowing down his cheeks. Lisa handed him a napkin, which he gratefully accepted.

Murphy looked at him and then glanced at Lisa. "Please, I'm hoping for your answer..."

"But this is too much! We didn't ask for anything!" Lisa replied indignantly.

"We didn't do that much. We don't deserve this gift. That's so much money. What do YOU think of this, Murphy?" David asked and coughed again.

"You certainly deserve it. Without you, none of us would exist, not even the company. The life and happiness of the whole family is because of you," Murphy said.

"Do we have a choice?" David asked with a frown.

"Probably not," Murphy replied, smiling.

"In that case, we accept the gift, but we did not expect this," David replied, feeling awkward.

Murphy gave him and Lisa some papers to sign. When everything was ready, he got up, thanked them, and spoke of what was next. "As a shareholder, I know you will be very happy with the company's performance."

"Yes! The future," David said, smiling.

"She wanted to be buried in the Church of Magdalene, north of town. I'll let you know the date and time," Murphy said. He thanked them, but before he left, he turned around and said, "And Alice wanted you to have the dog."

"Absolutely incredible. I can't believe this. We got the dog and lots of money," Lisa cheered.

"But I still don't think people should mess about with other people's lives and change things that have already happened," David said. "I don't want to talk about science or about Einstein's theory. I want to talk about the beauty of time and the future. The clock is ticking, and time is passing. The present becomes a memory for life, with all its dreams and goals included. With great efforts and work, and sometimes failures, we build our future. We think about the future of our children, and we fight for it. If one can see into the future, life loses all meaning. What is there to live for? There can be no joy when you already know what's around the corner, and it would be scary if you could plan your future in detail. You must let nature take its course and not mess about with God's plan. You shouldn't be able to sort out and get rid of the negatives and keep just the positives. Everything that happens in life is to be accepted – and in gratitude, at that, because it has a purpose. That's my philosophy." He sat down on the couch with a big sigh. He stared at the papers he and Lisa had signed.

"I'm going to call André and ask him if he can find James' diaries that the police had seized. If they're not worth anything, I can give them to Murphy as a gift," he said, and dialed André. "Hello André! It's David. How are you?"

"It's very good now that it's a little bit cooler in the air," André said, laughing. "What can I do for you?"

"You know that case that you helped me with earlier? In 1939, the police seized a dozen diaries belonging to James, the convicted man.

He worked for the Walker family. I wonder if you could find the diaries that belong to him and check with your boss as to whether I could get copies of them?" David asked.

"I don't remember helping you with any case. Are you sure you called me and asked for help?" André replied.

"What? You don't remember me calling you?" David asked, glancing at Lisa.

"No. But I recognize this case. The other day I was visited by some people with German accents. They wondered what had happened to the family and asked if there had been a plane crash in the forties. They wanted to know if perhaps there was anything in the archive. I found everything and showed them. They went through the archives, and then they returned everything. They discussed something amongst themselves in German, thanked us, and left. It was very strange," André replied.

"Did they take anything with them?" David asked.

"No, they were happy with my answer when I told them what was in the archive," André replied.

"May I have the diaries, if it's okay with your boss?" David asked.

"I'll see what I can do, then I'll call you."

"Thank you, André, you're a treasure," he replied and hung up.

David sat motionless on the couch, shaken by what had happened. He turned to Lisa. "André had no idea what I was talking about. He didn't remember anything about us previously seeking his help. Our visit with Alice has affected him too. We stopped Jay's murder and stopped William from taking Alice away. We probably never visited the police. Things that transpired a certain way before our visit NO LONGER EXIST, or at least not in the ways we recall from earlier."

Suddenly there was a call on his cell phone. "Hello?"

"It's André again! I've brought out the diaries, and you can even keep them. The case has been resolved and you can have a copy of the diaries. After sixty-nine years, everyone involved is already dead, and the convicted man who served his sentence is also dead."

"Thank you so much, André! Speaking of the convicted man, what happened to him after he served his sentence?" David asked.

"Let me see," André replied. David heard him going through all the papers. "Here it is. James Brandon. He served his prison sentence and was released. He got a job at the correctional institution. James agreed to take care of a large area where the prisoners used to go for fresh air and the opportunity to move freely. He converted it into a green area where he grew and tended to plants and flowers. He was also allowed to plant various shrubs and trees around the prison building itself. Many of the prisoners participated in the planting, and thanks to this endeavor, several of them were able to have their sentences reduced. James died in 1981 in his home.".

"Did he have any family?" David asked.

"There's nothing in here about that."

"What a story. I'm glad he did something positive with his life. Thank you! Please put the diaries aside for me, and I'll call you later," David said and thanked him again.

He had just hung up when Murphy called again. "With the help of friends and acquaintances who work with the church, we could arrange the funeral to take place in five days in the Church of Magdalene. At twelve o'clock. You and Lisa are both welcome."

"It was very kind of you to want to have us there. It's an honor for us, thank you!" David replied respectfully.

"Who was it?" Lisa asked.

"It was Murphy. Alice's funeral is in five days, and we are invited," he replied, sighing.

Lisa hugged him and gently asked, "How do you feel?"

"I don't know! Everything feels strange. I thought this surreal kind of thing happened only in movies. It feels so odd that there can be other worlds and dimensions around and beyond us that you can travel to. Dimensions and worlds were created by our fantasies and thoughts, I believed, but, most likely, evolution has come so far that we go beyond boundaries and fantasies. In the future, most likely, someone can build their future by changing and sorting out unwanted events in their past. Life will lose all meaning. There would be no motivation and dreams to which to strive because everything could be rearranged. Time will lose all value, and there won't be any shortage of time anymore," David said.

A jolt of lightning lit up the sky over the city, and at the same moment, as thunder rolled, David saw the rain fall. Within a second, the rain was beating against the window.

Lisa held David's arm tightly and mumbled, "I hope the rain passes quickly, it's so gloomy."

It didn't take long for the sun to come out again, even though the rain was still falling. A rainbow stretching from east to west appeared in the sky, creating a beautiful sight. The rain stopped, but their minds were still filled with the same thoughts. Their thoughts were like the thunderstorm, but unlike it – in that, the thoughts never ended. David went to the terrace and looked out. To his surprise, he heard a neighbor blaring music, and a song called "Back in Time" was being played.

"Coincidence?" he pondered.

Chapter 27
Epilogue?

Five days seemed to sprint by, and before David knew it, the day of the funeral was upon him. With sorrow and mixed feelings, he meticulously combed his hair and adjusted his tie. He was dressed in a dark suit and a contrasting white tie.

"Lisa, love, I recall reading somewhere that white ties are acceptable at funerals. I think it works rather well," he said. Glancing at his watch, he added, "I should give André a ring about bringing the diaries to the church."

Without wasting a moment, David dialed André's number. "Hey, friend, time is tight. Could you bring the copies of the diaries over to the Church of Magdalene, just north of town?"

"And when should I be there?" André asked.

"Would a quarter to twelve works?"

"That's my lunch break, so it fits perfectly. See you there," André responded, concluding the call.

David and Lisa promptly got into their car and set off. Along the way, they paused at a flower shop to pick up a sizable bouquet for the funeral. They arrived at the church around half-past eleven. There, they spotted André waiting, a box atop his car.

David and Lisa exited their car and greeted André. "Thanks for coming," Lisa expressed her gratitude.

"No worries. I was about to head out for lunch anyway," André replied, handing the box to David. "There are a dozen diaries in here."

"Thank you, André. You're a true friend," David responded a bright smile of gratitude on his face.

"Anything for you," André replied, a grin on his face. He hopped into his car and drove off, waving goodbye as he departed.

Meanwhile, Murphy arrived, swiftly striding towards David and.

"Glad you could make it. The rest of the guests will be arriving soon. Feel free to go inside and pick any seat in the third row," Murphy suggested.

David presented the box to Murphy. "We brought something. They're the copies of diaries you expressed interest in. They contain the journal entries of gardener James."

Murphy accepted the box, silently examined the diaries, and struggled to hold back his tears. After regaining his composure, he murmured, "I'm sorry, it's been tough. Please forgive me. This means a great deal. It might help us answer some lingering questions. I appreciate this."

Hand in hand, David and Lisa approached the church. The door was slightly ajar, allowing the soft melodies from within to spill into the outside air. David took a moment to peek inside, taking in the calm, peaceful atmosphere of the church. Together, they ventured inside and walked to the front, stopping before the coffin. David's eyes were drawn to the twinkling lights around the pulpit and the serene figure of Alice resting peacefully within her refined steel coffin, surrounded by an array of fragrant flowers.

In the soft candlelight, Alice's skin seemed to glow. She appeared as if merely sleeping, dressed in her favorite outfit—a white dress with small pink flowers on the skirt with a touch of makeup. The calming music combined with the serene environment of the church to create a comforting, memorable atmosphere. As more attendees trickled in and found their seats, Murphy entered the church, his arm tightly wrapped around a tearful woman, who David assumed was Lisa, his sister. They made a beeline for David and Lisa, where Murphy introduced his sister.

"This is my sister Lisa, and this is David and his fiancée, also Lisa."

"I'm so glad you're here! Our mom was excited and hopeful that you would come. She was right. Thank you for visiting before she passed. You gave her purpose. She got a second shot at life. Mom lived a life that everyone else dreamed of."

Standing beside his sister, Murphy seemed to battle to suppress his tears. With a lump forming in his throat, he whispered into his sister's ear, "We need to go sit down."

David watched as she approached their mother's coffin with a forced smile before breaking into a tearful outburst. Murphy acted swiftly, guiding her towards the coffin and assisting her in placing the bouquet she had brought alongside it. Afterwards, he used a paper napkin to dab at his tears before helping his sister find her seat. The sight left a heavy lump in David's throat.

The priest ascended the pulpit and warmly welcomed everyone in attendance. He offered his condolences and proceeded to recite passages from the Bible. David sat rigidly in his seat, his gaze locked on the priest, but the words seemed to bounce off him. He could not stop getting swept up in his thoughts.

"What will become of the world? I fear things might spiral out of control, and we end up misusing time travel," he thought. "Now, I understand William's caution about not meddling with the past. Our future should be built through toil and struggle, not through shortcuts offered by a time machine. What implications would this hold for future generations? What if this knowledge of time travel falls into the wrong hands and gets exploited for malicious intentions? I can only hope that humanity respects science and refrains from altering the past."

Amid his contemplation, a sob pulled David out of his thoughts. He turned to see a young man trying and failing to console a crying woman beside him. The man bore a striking resemblance to someone, a resemblance that David couldn't immediately place. Frowning in confusion, David turned back around, his gaze lingering on the priest still speaking. He took another glance over his shoulder, and recognition hit him. David, his face pale, stared at the man, turning to whisper in Lisa's ear, "That's James! But how can that be?" He glanced around the crowd, momentarily suspecting that William had brought him here. But upon closer inspection, David realized that the man was significantly younger than the James he had met at the Walker's residence.

Lisa, slightly annoyed, tugged at David's sleeve, asking, "What are you doing?"

David glanced at Lisa and whispered, "I think I just saw a face from the past, here in the church."

"Who are you talking about?" Lisa asked, her brows furrowed in confusion.

"James! The guy sitting behind us bears a striking resemblance to James, but he seems much younger," David revealed, his voice barely audible.

The ceremony concluded, and the congregation exited the church to await Alice's coffin. David circulated among the attendees, his eyes searching for the man he had spotted earlier.

"Where on earth did he go?" David murmured to himself.

Suddenly, the man materialized in the crowd, standing hand-in-hand with Angela as they waited for Alice's coffin to be carried out.

"Come," David whispered to Lisa, gently tugging at her arm. They navigated their way through the crowd, approaching the couple. David extended a greeting, "Hello."

"Hello," Angela responded, her eyes welling up with tears but a smile gracing her face.

"We extend our deepest condolences," David offered his eyes subtly studying the man standing next to Angela.

Angela, her voice shaky, expressed her gratitude. "Thank you. My father informed me yesterday about how you assisted my grandmother, and how you changed everything for her and everyone else. It's astounding. I'm still struggling to accept the truth of it all. I had to keep it a secret. Not even my boyfriend here is privy to it."

David nodded in agreement, replying, "Wise decision." Yet, his eyes drifted back to the man beside Angela, who bore such a remarkable likeness to James. Leaning forward, he offered his hand to the man, introducing himself, "My name is David Hamilton; I don't think we've had the pleasure of meeting before..."

"No, sir, we haven't. My name is Peter Brandon," the man introduced himself.

"Brandon? That name rings a bell," David said, his brows furrowed.

"Perhaps you've heard of my father who owns numerous Brandon's Gardens around the country?" Peter suggested.

"Ah, of course! It's a pleasure to meet you," David exclaimed, his gaze shifting to Lisa with a playful gleam in his eyes. "I remember reading about your grandfather being an adept gardener, working tirelessly with plants and flowers."

"That's right. Thanks to my grandfather's teachings, my father learned everything there was to know about gardening, which enabled him to become a successful businessman," Peter confirmed, a note of pride evident in his voice.

"Your grandfather was James Brandon, wasn't he?" David ventured.

"Yes, he was. But how do you know about my grandfather?" Peter asked, surprised.

"I've always been passionate about gardening, and I frequent Brandon's Gardens. That's how I came to know about your father and grandfather," David explained.

Peter nodded.

"It was nice to meet you. Hopefully, we can meet again sometime," Peter proposed warmly, extending his hand towards David for another handshake before parting ways.

"He's a decent young man," Lisa commented once Peter was out of earshot.

As the church bells began to toll, four immaculately dressed men emerged from the church, Alice's coffin in their grasp. Murphy and Lisa followed just behind them. Their heads bowed in reverence as they trailed the coffin bearers. The guests followed them one by one, their strides slow and solemn. The wind had picked up, and raindrops started to fall.

David glanced at the ominous clouds with concern. Rain began to dominate, causing the trees to shimmer with moisture, their branches swaying as they tried to shake off the droplets. Engrossed in his thoughts, he reflected, "Everything that has transpired will forever leave an impact on me."

Upon reaching the cemetery, they gathered around the Murphy family grave. A freshly dug grave was prepared for Alice, and David noticed an older, weathered grave adjacent to it. Out of curiosity, he approached it. Reading the headstone, he discovered it belonged to Jay Murphy, who had passed away in 1960.

"That's where Jay rests," David murmured to Lisa, pointing out the grave.

Lisa, tears glistening in her eyes, placed a small rose on Jay's headstone. Holding David's hand, he comfortingly draped his arm over her shoulders, offering a tender smile. "Now Alice and Jay share an unforgettable story that will be remembered by all."

His throat constricted. David watched as the rain-soaked coffin was lowered into the grave, surrounded by a colorful array of flowers. Lisa's cries echoed around the cemetery, her grief palpable, while David concealed his sorrow behind a pair of dark glasses, his jaw clenched tight. Using a tissue to dab at his eyes, he cried quietly to himself.

The crowd took a respectful step back, making way for the immediate family members – Murphy, his sister, and all the grandchildren. Hand in hand, they comforted each other in hushed whispers and mournful cries, singing a bittersweet melody around Alice's grave. To Lisa, the scene was both beautiful and heartbreaking.

David's attention was abruptly pulled away as he caught sight of a familiar figure lurking behind the trees – William. To his astonishment, young Alice stood beside him, observing the funeral with a curious gaze. Without hesitation, David took Lisa's hand and started moving towards them.

"Where are we going?" Lisa questioned in a whisper.

"Come on," David replied vaguely.

"But it would be disrespectful to leave the funeral midway," Lisa protested, glancing back at the mourners gathering around the grave.

"We're not deserting the ceremony. It will only take a moment. Everyone is preoccupied right now. They won't notice our brief absence," David assured her, his tone eager.

Upon reaching them, William greeted the pair with a warm smile. "Hello, David! I brought Alice because she wanted to see you, and I knew you'd be here."

David and Lisa stood in shocked silence; their eyes fixed on the unexpected duo. Lisa gripped David's arm tightly.

"Please tell me this is a dream," she begged, her gaze never leaving Alice. "Is that truly you?"

"Yes, it's me." Alice confirmed with a smile.

"But... but you're over there...," David stuttered, his voice faltering. He stopped abruptly, falling into a stunned silence. "What are you doing here?"

"Shortly after my wedding, I met William. He told me about who he was and his time machine. Suddenly, I had an idea. I asked if I could meet you, to tell you about what happened to me and Jay," Alice revealed.

"We're aware. We know your future," David admitted, glancing cautiously at the funeral proceedings.

"Oh? So, you're aware that I'm now married to Jay?" she inquired, a broad smile lighting up her face.

David nodded in confirmation.

"Could you tell me more about my future?" Alice requested, her gaze pleading.

"No, dear sweet Alice, we're not going to interfere in your future any longer," David responded, gently squeezing Alice's hand. "We've done enough. Continue your path and let your past shape your future. Learn from your mistakes and keep moving forward. But remember, time is fleeting. Make the most of it."

He pulled her into a heartfelt embrace.

"Will we see each other again?" Alice asked tearfully as Lisa also wrapped her in a hug.

"I can assure you of that," David responded, struggling to contain his tears.

"I look forward to that day. And I plan to name my children after both of you," Alice declared, her eyes shining joyfully. But then her gaze fell on the crowd of mourners surrounding the grave. Her smile faded, replaced by a questioning look. Turning to David, she asked, "Whose funeral is this?"

David glanced back at the congregation. Avoiding Alice's gaze, he answered, "A very close friend. Her life was never inconsequential. She profoundly influenced me and many others. She led a life that most could only dream of. And I'm going to miss her dearly."

"I, too, aspire to live the life I've always wanted and dreamed of," Alice stated, her eyes scanning the crowd curiously.

"You will, I promise," David assured her, meeting her gaze with a comforting smile.

"David, I gather you're worried about the future and contemplating the progression of time travel," William interjected.

"Yes, that's accurate," David conceded.

"I can reassure you that I've laid the groundwork for future scientists. The next generation in time travel faces a formidable task. My role is to safeguard the future. By 2047, time travel will be a commonplace phenomenon in society, and I, along with other scientists, have ensured that no one can alter the future. All travels are conducted under strict surveillance. Anyone wishing to travel must first register their journey. A transmitter and GPS operate in conjunction with the brain, allowing all travels to be closely monitored. I can guarantee that sufficient precautions have been taken to prevent any mishaps. Any individual who oversteps their boundaries and attempts to change history to manipulate the future will face severe, irreversible punishment. No excuses will be tolerated," William assured them.

"That's reassuring, but how can all the time machines be monitored simultaneously?" David asked, skepticism seeping into his voice.

"All time machines and computers are interconnected with a heavily fortified data center. Those working there operate under concealed identities. As soon as someone initiates a temporal journey, their destination is logged, and their actions at the destination are scrutinized meticulously, thanks to microchips embedded in their brains. Regardless of their temporal destination, we can monitor their thoughts, track their every move, and even observe their emotions. This enables us to prevent any mishaps," William elaborated.

"Incredible!" David thought to himself, a sigh of relief escaping his lips.

"We must depart now, Alice. It's time to return home," William indicated, placing his arm gently on her shoulder.

"Where will you be headed?" Lisa inquired.

"Firstly, I need to escort her to 1941. Jay awaits her there, after which I'll embark on new adventures," William announced cheerfully.

"So long for now. I'll miss you, but we'll meet again soon," Alice promised, taking several steps backwards alongside William.

"Indeed, until next time," David echoed, raising his hand in farewell.

Lisa waved her goodbye, tears welling in her eyes. Moments later, they vanished. Left behind, David and Lisa made their way back towards the gravesite to rejoin the others. As they walked, David found himself engrossed in his musings on the nature of time and the management of time travel.

Breaking his thoughts, Lisa asked, "Are you planning to write a book?"

"Oh, no. I've come to understand that time travel is a precarious business that could trigger a myriad of complications," David replied. "If I were to disclose all that I've learned, it could unwittingly embroil others in the time travel phenomena, which may lead to disastrous consequences."

The rain had stopped, and the weather had rapidly shifted to sunshine again. The mournful cry of the wind echoed through the cemetery. David surveyed the crowd that was gradually dispersing from the ceremony. He noticed Angela hand in hand with Peter Brandon, the grandson of James.

"Do you see that? James ended up with his Alice after all. He won her heart in the end, and there they are," David remarked, attempting to hide his sorrow as he wiped away a tear.

Lisa smiled in response, "You're right! James lives on through Peter, and with his help, he managed to win over Angela's grandfather. It's wonderful to see everything come to fruition."

David paused by the grave; his gaze sorrowful as he looked down at the coffin. He picked up a rose from the ground next to the grave, inhaling its scent before releasing a deep sigh. The steady tolling of the church bells served as a poignant reminder of the relentless passage of time. He gave the coffin one last look, tossed the rose into the grave and whispered, "See you soon!"

Taking Lisa's hand, they moved forward with determination, stepping into the uncertain future just around the corner.

Printed in Poland
by Amazon Fulfillment
Poland Sp. z o.o., Wrocław